VONNIE

For years I've been a romance junkie, ... like warm, chocolate chip cookies. Perhaps that's why I adore writing about love and passion. Passion—such a powerful word, don't you think? I'd classify myself as a late bloomer. I started college in my late forties, met the love of my life in my mid-fifties and published my first book in my early sixties. My husband and I live in Southern Virginia. We enjoy spoiling the grandchildren and traveling. My deepest desire is to write saucy, often humorous romances you'll cherish long after you've turned off the e-reader.

http://www.vonniedavis.com/

@VonnieWrites

For the Love of a Fireman

Book Two in the *Wild Heat* Series

VONNIE DAVIS

Harper*Impulse* an imprint of
HarperCollins*Publishers* Ltd
1 London Bridge Street
London SE1 9GF

www.harpercollins.co.uk

A Paperback Original 2015

First published in Great Britain in ebook format by Harper*Impulse* 2015

A catalogue record for this book is
available from the British Library

ISBN: 9780008120245

Automatically produced by Atomik ePublisher from Easypress

*To Ron and Debbie who have loaned us their condo
in Indian Rocks Beach so we could fall in love with
the small Gulf side community in Florida, where
much of this book takes place.*

CHAPTER ONE

"Quick! What aisle are the douches in? I've got three bitches at the beach cottage and they all stink to high heaven." The broad shoulders of the harried man appeared solid under his faded t-shirt, worn inside out and backward. His pale whiskered stubble was pulled tight by his clenched jaw and tensed lips. The customer practically vibrated with frustration.

"I can't let them in bed with me smelling like that." His fingertips tapped a beat of annoyance on the check-out counter. "What is it with females, anyway? Ain't got the good sense God gave them."

Behind the counter, Molly Devon's temper flared. *Oh, yeah, as if you men are the sharpest knives on humanity's chopping block.*

He brushed his neck, his fingers tangling in the worn tag of his t-shirt. He looked down, plucked at the material and muttered a curse. "Sorry, I grabbed the first top I could find and just yanked it on." He reached back with one hand and jerked it off, trying to set it to rights.

Molly's Colorado born-and-bred gaze took a skiing trip over the mountains of his hardened pecs and skied down the ridges of his abs. Along his downhill masculine slope, she noticed other things. Skin tanned dark. On his left side, a wide tribal rib tattoo ran from below his armpit to beneath his pants to who knew where. A light tan treasure trail of chest hair thinned at his navel.

1

The waistband of his raggedy jeans barely hung onto the V indent at his hipline created by well-toned internal obliques.

Sweet Lord, what a girl couldn't do with...

For Pete's sake, stop gawking! Haven't I learned my lesson? Men are bad news. Not to be believed and never to be trusted.

Firm biceps flexed as the customer slipped the faded t-shirt, advertising boogie boards, over his torso, tugging it down and shifting his wide shoulders. "Sorry, about that. But, believe me, I'd sooner be home, hammering away, than in here."

His obviously crass remark jerked her admiring attention to his overconfident square jaw.

Yeah, just give me a hammer, buddy. I'll pound some sense into your arrogant over-sexed brain.

He leaned toward her. "Well? Where are they?"

The stranger's bark startled her. With her nerves on edge from her mother's recent passing, her father's increasing signs of dementia and Wade's violent reaction after she broke off their engagement, any perceived threat—no matter how minor or brief—set her insides to trembling. Paranoia had her in its grip for she was sure she'd seen Wade's battered, dark blue SUV cruising Gulf Boulevard in Indian Rocks Beach. Both times she hid, her nerves having slipped into fear mode.

Molly tussled with her anxieties, scrambling for internal control.

"Ah…" She lifted her index finger to indicate she needed a second or two as she scanned the overhead signs, listing the items stocked in each aisle. Where had she seen the feminine products during her brief new-hire orientation two days ago? Another deep breath and calmness returned, her mind finally chugging into gear.

The customer lifted his blue ball cap with some kind of marine rescue emblem on it, forked his long fingers through straight hair—bleached nearly pale blond by the sun—and resettled the hat. "You do carry Massengill, don't you? That's the best brand, according to my research."

"Ah…" *What kind of man researches douches? A man who goes*

to bed with three women, Molly. Now concentrate.

Two broad hands clasped the edge of the counter. His index finger had a nasty red-rimmed cut on its side. An appealing mixture of sawdust, lime and ginger snagged her attention and, when the man cleared his throat, her gaze snapped upward to lock on a pair of surf green eyes flecked with blue. "Is my question too difficult for you to answer…" he glanced at her nametag, "Molly?"

Oh, this guy has a good tongue lashing coming. Molly sucked in a breath, pulled together a string of insults to hurl at him and then changed her mind. Better to smile while she enjoyed her private opinions of this man-whore, especially since she needed this job badly. She'd put a big dent in her credit card balance to substitute the laptop her dad had misplaced, along with his wallet and her carryon of her clothes. Not to mention the money she needed for groceries and her father's medication.

Finally the product's location slipped into place. "You'll find them in aisle six, on the right."

The knuckles of his fisted hand rapped once on the counter before he sauntered off.

Big-headed, demanding jerk.

Frazzled nerves got the best of her and her gaze settled on the box of chocolate bars calling her name, taunting her. Why did everything she ate have to settle on her ass? Two women strolled in the store wearing shorts that showcased slender, toned thighs and itty-bitty butts. Her thighs were toned, but thick by society's standards. Unfortunately, the only things slender on her body were her earlobes and toes. Life just wasn't fair.

Molly was shoving packs of cigarettes into racks behind the register when someone thunked items onto the check-out counter. She pasted on a smile, did a quick pivot and sighed as the grin slid off. Douche-man was back with twelve double packs of Massengill disposables.

"You only had two boxes of the mixable kind." He read the printing on the box he held, never once sparing her a glance.

He tapped the second carton resting on the counter with his cut finger. "Would you mind checking your inventory in the back? I'll need more."

"I'm not allowed to leave the register, but I'll be happy to page our stock boy."

Douche-man grunted and flipped the package around. "It's gonna take at least two boxes for Lola. She's big. Got wide hips. Skinny legs, though. Kinda like a twenty-gallon tank on toothpicks."

What an ass, talking about his girlfriend like that! Molly sneered and depressed the button on the store's intercom. "Cruz, could you check our supply of mixable douche powder? I have a man who needs three or four boxes."

"Make it five or six. And they *have* to be Massengill, don't forget. God, I don't know which girl smells the worst."

Well, quit putting your nose in their hootchies. Molly cleared her throat and rolled her eyes before depressing the button on the intercom. "Could you make that six boxes of douche powder? Massengill, please, Cruz." A few snickers floated over from aisle two.

"I can see I'm gonna have a rough night ahead. Maggie Mae hates when I give her a good scrubbing, especially if I get soap in her beady eyes or get too rough with her." He pinched the bridge of his nose between his thumb and index finger and sighed like a man greatly imposed upon. "God, I hate a whiny bitch."

Oh, I am so going to belt you.

"Caroline handles her bath pretty well. She likes it rough, especially when I hold her head under the faucet." He had the audacity to chuckle. "She tries to drink the water, but then she'll drink most anything."

She'd have to be drunk to put up with you, buster. You need some serious help.

Cruz hurried to the register, his arms full of boxes. "Here you go, Molly." He shot the customer a curious glance.

"Thanks. Would you do me one more favor, please?"

The pimply-faced teen's head bobbed. "Sure."

"Our customer needs a bottle of peroxide and Neosporin for the cut on his finger. It's showing signs of infection." Cruz nodded and hurried back to aisle four.

Douche-man glimpsed at his hand. "Thanks. I do have a first aid kit, but I've been too preoccupied with work to take care of it. Ain't nothing but an infected splinter. Can't seem to dig deep enough to get to it."

Oh, just give me a machete. I'll show you how deep a good woman can cut.

He slid his fingertips into the front pocket of his jeans, pulling them a little lower on his hips, until he finally tugged out folded bills secured with a silver fire truck money clip. "What's the damage?"

To your wallet or the self-esteem of those poor women?

After totaling his purchases, Molly handed him his change and six plastic bags. "Hope you get them cleaned up."

He grunted again. "Sure as hell hope so. Don't know if I can sleep without the girls laying all over me."

Oh, puh-lease.

He headed for the exit, high-top sneakers clunking the tile floor. Molly glared at his retreating form. *What a piece of macho jerk.*

He snapped his fingers and returned. "Where's the dog toys? They'll be expecting a treat after I scrub the skunk smell off."

"Dogs? Dogs!" Had he been talking about dogs all this time?

Douche-man nodded, his blond five o'clock shadow more an eight o'clock sexy scruff. "Yeah. An overweight Black Lab, a beady-eyed Chihuahua and a Collie mix. I'm kinda partial to my girls, but not when they chase skunks and get a good spraying."

"Skunks? Spraying?" *God, I sound like an echo.*

"Used to wash them down with tomato juice after being sprayed, but Caroline would lap at the juice and get terrible gas." He shook his head once. "Couldn't stand to be around her for days." He grinned and dimples slashed his cheeks. "So, I researched online and found out about bathing animals in Massengill after

5

encounters with skunks."

Boy, talk about a miscommunication.

He studied the bags in his hands for a beat and then raised his gaze. "I'm sorry for storming in here earlier and ranting about my dogs, calling them bitches, but they had me so damn mad." He winced. "Sorry. After a long day of tearing out decrepit kitchen cabinets and replacing them with new ones, moving walls and installing appliances, the last thing I want to do tonight is to scrub down three dogs."

His gaze flicked over her hand before his green-eyed perusal once more settled on her face. Had he just checked for a ring? "Could I interest you in a cup of coffee after work?" He peeked at his watch. "Store closes in fifteen minutes."

Not expecting his boldness, she stepped back. "Sorry, I don't meet strange men for coffee."

A wide smile spread, exposing straight white teeth with a chip broken off the corner of his left front one. Those deep dimples and chipped tooth added a boyish charm to his male persona, a charismatic contrast to the arrogant sternness he'd exhibited earlier. He set his bags in front of her on the checkout counter before tilting a hip against it and crossing his arms, obviously settling in for a chat neither she nor her boss wanted. She *was* on the clock, after all.

The door swished open and she jumped. God, she had to get beyond thinking she'd seen Wade's vehicle twice. Sure, he'd been royally pissed when she threw the engagement ring in his face, but no woman wanted to marry a man who cheated on her...and then became violent when she called him on it. But he wouldn't come all this way to find her. Would he?

The strange man's eyebrows were furrowed as if he'd been studying her and he cleared his throat. "You know, I really do owe you an apology for my ranting when I came in the store." He managed to make his grin almost unsure, as if he'd suddenly lost his confidence. How many times had he practiced this technique—and how often had a woman fallen for it? "A coffee and a piece of pie couldn't hurt, could it?"

"I repeat, I don't know you." She motioned him aside so she could ring-up another customer's purchases.

She hoped Douche-man would take the hint but, no, he patiently hovered nearby while she waited on two customers, his male aura slowly swirling around her like a testosterone fog. Turning to him, she scowled. "What part of I don't spend time with strange men don't you get?"

He extended his hand, his charming smile increased another dangerous notch. "Barclay Gray. Fireman, marine rescue diver, dog lover and pie connoisseur."

The man certainly knew how to pour on the charm, she'd give him that. But she couldn't forget that men had a potential for violence she'd never known before…

Molly shook Barclay's hand. The warmth from his calluses sending shocks of awareness through her system. When she tried pulling back, his hold tightened and a jolt of panic twisted her stomach.

As if he could read her mood, his shifted to one of reassurance. "Calm down, Molly. I don't intend to hurt you in any way. White Sands Diner is three blocks up the street and usually has good pies." His thumb slowly rubbed her knuckles and she jerked her hand away.

His gaze narrowed on her as if he were some kind of therapist, evaluating her every move. Gone, too, was his cocky smile. "What have I done to frighten you?"

"Tell me, do all the women fall for this macho lure you've got goin' on?"

One shoulder lifted in an arrogant shrug. "Yeah. Usually. Sometimes." His sea green gaze quickly swept over her face. "It's not working with you, though, is it?"

She folded her arms. "Hell, no."

He smiled again; this time as if to soothe her. "You're a

cold-hearted woman, Molly. How will you sleep tonight, knowing I'm having pie and coffee all by my lonesome?"

Molly glanced at her fingernails. "I'm sure I won't give it a second thought." Oh, but she would. Who could forget his animated eyes or those cute dimples when he smiled? Or the way his deep voice triggered a need she'd be better off denying.

"Tell you what, I'll order two cups of coffee and two slices of pie. If you don't join me, it'll be your fault I'll be up all night with a sugar-induced, caffeine high." His deep voice poured over her like honey on biscuits.

"Right. You don't even know if there are any pies left at this time of night."

Barclay whipped out his cell and thumbed a number. "Sarah, is that you? This is Barclay. Hey, you got any pie left?" His gaze locked on Molly's and the corners of his mouth twitched in a damnable overconfident way. "What kind?" He nodded, no doubt listening to Sarah rattle off flavors. "Hold on." He pressed the cell to his worn t-shirt. "They've got cherry, lemon meringue and double chocolate sin."

Was he daft? She fisted a hand at her waist. "I told you I'm not meeting you for pie. I don't care what damned flavor it is." The last thing she needed was to get involved with another guy, even if she and her dad would only be in Florida for a few more weeks.

The man had the audacity to wink at her and then lifted his cell. "Save me a slice of each. I'll be there in ten minutes. Put on a fresh pot of coffee too." He slipped the cell back into the front pocket of his jeans.

"How are you going to keep that washboard stomach, eating three pieces of pie by yourself?" She was *not* joining him.

Humor twinkled in Barclay's eyes, setting her system all wonky again. "You been looking at my abs, Sugar? Won't you give a poor guy fifteen minutes to apologize for his moodiness?" He splayed a wide hand over his heart as if he were making a grand plea.

"Why don't you do like every other man. Mumble 'sorry' and

8

then slither away?"

A flicker of something passed over his face, erasing his jovial demeanor. "Is that how you've been treated? As if you don't matter? Or that you're not damned precious?"

He was hitting too close to her past experiences with men and she didn't like it. "Look, we close soon. If you want toys for your dogs, you'd better hurry."

"True that. Quitting time waits for no man." Barclay sauntered off in the direction she'd indicated for pet products, shooting the lowest of blows over his shoulder. "Double Chocolate Sin pie, Miss Molly. How much you wanna bet it's sinfully rich?"

"I hate chocolate, bucko." *Liar.*

His laughter, rich and deep, bounced off the walls. "The name's Barclay. Don't forget it."

As much as she wanted to fire back a volley of putdowns, she didn't want to give this arrogant fireman the satisfaction of knowing he was getting to her. No doubt he flirted with every cashier and waitress he came across.

Which was why she didn't want to tell him she worked the early morning shift at White Sands as a waitress. No need to give him any encouragement. So what if he made her feminine parts sit up and beg for buttermilk, as her dad was known to say? Really, she had no right to enjoy their banter, even for one brief interlude, especially with her life so unstable. Besides, she needed to get back to the condo her dad hated and see how he was doing.

Still, how many men would come out this time of night to get something for their dogs? She sniggered and shook her head. Douches of *all* things. When she thought about it, his devotion to his pets was kind of sexy. She slapped a hand over her eyes. Enough. Men could be heartless creatures beneath the jovial, often gentle, façade.

She'd be better off praying for immunity from handsome men, like the one who charged into the drug store minutes earlier with vibrant sea green eyes, hair the color of corn silk and deep dimples when he smiled. Or wide calloused hands that could do wicked things to a woman's body while she inhaled his lime and ginger cologne. Erotic visions steamed a sensual path through her mind, and she shook her head to clear the thoughts.

After her shift was over, Molly hurried up the street toward the tiny condo in an older building on a side street across the road from the beach. Normally she and her dad stayed at Verne's Cabins on the beach side of Gulf Boulevard, but the place was closed for renovations this year. Last February, when her little family made their annual trek here, the cabin they rented had been nearly uninhabitable. Still, her mother loved those little beach bungalows. It almost seemed fitting their first trip without Mom would be to a different section of the gulf side community she so loved.

A dagger of lightning ripped through the night sky before thunder bumped the ragged edges together again. Drops of rain the size of grapes pelted her head and shoulders, and she yanked up the hood of her jacket as she started a slow jog from the small strip mall along the main drag. Three more blocks and she'd be at their temporary home.

If only she could convince her dad to sell the house in Colorado and move here to the year-round warmth. The change in weather would help his arthritis and with her job back home, a web design business, she could work anywhere. She loved this little community.

Every winter, her heart yearned to return here where she could listen to the waves and relax. Unfortunately this trip, with her dad's mental confusion coming and going, there was little relaxation to be had. She had to find quick work in order to provide for groceries, personal necessities and her dad's medicines. Buying a new computer strong enough to handle all the graphics she used in her business had slapped her credit card balance pretty hard. Luckily, restaurants and some stores were always hiring, or so it seemed.

What remained on her credit card balance, she had to keep to cover parking at the airport, gas, food and lodging for their return trip home. Only, home was the last place she wanted to go. She did not want to return to Breckenridge and the cold empty house without her mother to warm it with her laughter and love—or to Wade.

As the thought came into her head, she noticed a dark SUV, the model of her ex-fiancé's, was parked along the street, setting her heart to beat double-time. She squinted in the rain, trying to read the state on the mud-covered license plate. Although this area of the charming beach town was somewhat dark, a convenience store and the White Sands Diner illuminated the end of the street. Was Barclay there, eating his pie? Not that she planned on joining him, but there was a level of curiosity as to whether he'd really intended to spend time with her.

One more block before she made the turn to the narrow street that housed the condo building. Another clap of lightning brightened the sky. Her eyes struggled to adapt to the change in luminosity before darkness blanketed her vision.

A car door slammed and footsteps pounded the pavement behind her, and she looked over her shoulder. Dear Lord, it *was* Wade! He ran for her. Her pace picked up in time with her alarmed heart rate.

Because she was distracted, her toe caught on the uneven pavement, and she wheeled through the air. Cement smacked her face, and she bit her tongue. Stars exploded inside her head and something warm ran over her lips. Pain throbbed all over.

Suddenly, Wade jerked her arms behind her and wrapped rope around her wrists as if she were a calf in a rodeo. He kicked her twice in the side before his hands roughly snatched her to her feet. A hard jerk on the rope yanked her to his chest. "Didn't think I'd find ya, did ya, Bitch? No one walks away from me."

She stomped on his foot with the heel of her sandal. His fist made contact with her face. Pain and stars exploded once more. She collapsed onto the sidewalk again, darkness creeping over her vision like the blanket of night being pulled over her head.

"How about you get your fat ass back to Breckenridge where you belong, Molly? I told you screwing Katlynn was just one last fling before the wedding. I don't see why that got you so all fired mad."

CHAPTER TWO

Barclay smirked at the three pieces of pie gracing the table before him at a booth in the nearly deserted diner. He hoped the sweet treats would be enough incentive to draw Molly in for coffee and conversation. By now, he should be home, bathing three dogs reeking with skunk spray. Since none of his canine girls could tell time, surely he could take fifteen or twenty minutes for himself to chit-chat with Molly—and maybe ask her on a date.

He stared out the window at the end of the table, his mind snagged on the sexy-as-hell beauty spot above the corner of her mouth. What he wouldn't give to touch it with the tip of his tongue just before he captured her lips with his. Especially her desirable, full bottom lip that for some inane reason kept drawing his eye. Adding to her sensual allure was the fact she was a shade plump all over, just the way he liked his women—softness to his hardness. Her ponytail, the color of raven's wings, made his fingers itch to remove the band holding it in place and run his fingers through those silky-looking tresses. It had been a long time since a woman attracted him like Molly. Even so, desire had to take a backseat to finding answers.

Something was off about her.

For one thing, she seemed jumpy. For another, she exhibited emotional and physical signs of abuse or an attack of some kind.

Her neck bore faint traces of bruising as if she'd been choked. Her left bicep, peeking out of a red and white striped top, had yellow marks of a fading contusion.

By his estimation, she'd been beaten. Not spanked like he occasionally preferred during scene play, but a cruel pounding. She wore no ring and didn't have the tan mark of one recently removed, so he doubted she'd been married. Had she been accosted by some stranger or worked over by someone she knew? Because she definitely wore her fear like a plate of armor. Some bastard had traumatized her.

He added sweetener to his coffee and stirred. Although he'd had the presence of mind to check for a wedding band, the possibility of a live-in or other type of relationship might exist. Yet with the prickly walls she kept throwing up, he sensed a troubled soul. Something about her called to him, which was a rarity since Bella Marie.

Damn him, he'd always been a sucker for a mystery…and a frightened stray. His three canine girls were testament to that particular weakness.

If only Molly's furtive eyes hadn't pulled at him so. Barclay rubbed his fingers across his brow. Her blue-violet gaze, wary with distrust and anxiety, seemed ultra-observant as it darted toward the door every time it swept open, as if she were expecting someone to come charging in at any moment. There was no mistaking the mistrust and torment in her eyes.

From time to time, he'd seen tormented eyes resembling hers staring back at him from his own mirror in the dark, soul-searching hours of night. No doubt, she was in an emotionally persecuted place. Damn, if he didn't know the look, himself.

Molly needed help.

Not his, of course. He had enough damn problems of his own. Still, something about her worried him. She was an attractive and spirited puzzle that had surprisingly captured his curiosity. Thus the invitation for coffee and pie, which she'd shot down without a minute's hesitation. He snorted and shook his head. His typical flirtatious charm hadn't gotten him anywhere with the cashier, that was for sure. Which was a damn shame since just about everything about her attracted him.

He blew across the top of his mug before he sipped. Maybe he was losing his touch. Fighting fires and pulling dead bodies from buildings and the Gulf of Mexico were definitely taking their toll. That's why he'd decided to use three weeks of his accumulated vacation time to give himself a mental and emotional break from catastrophes. To indulge in the beauty of the beach for a while, let the sounds of the surf relax his soul. To work off some of his pent-up stress by remodeling the bungalows he planned on leasing out.

A shard of bright lightning beyond the window seized Barclay's concentration from things best forgotten. Street lights showcased Molly running through the rain toward the diner, the hood of her white hoodie pulled over her hair. His face split into a grin. She'd come after all.

His smile froze and he leaned toward the glass to get a better visual. Was someone in pursuit? His gaze bounced from the man sprinting behind her to Molly glancing over her shoulder. About thirty-feet from the diner, she fell and the man jumped her, tying a rope around her wrists before jerking her up and then knocking her down again with a punch.

Oh no! Oh, hell no!

"Be right back, Sarah." Barclay bolted out the door.

Sounds of a struggle and curses bounced between the raindrops. Molly was definitely in trouble. Some lowlife tried to drag her into a dark blue SUV. Damn, if she wasn't putting up a fight, kicking and jerking on the rope the man held. Words of their argument drifted through the air. Clearly the thug was bent on intimidating her and insulting her about her weight.

Barclay sprinted toward them. The rain increased, its cold drops stinging his arms and face and drenching the back of his t-shirt.

15

"Hey! What the fucking hell's going on?"

Molly glanced over her shoulder amid her struggle. "Barclay! Help me!" Her voice was laced with terror.

"This is a private affair, motherfucker. Stay out of it." The man dressed in cargo pants and a tan t-shirt kept yanking her toward his vehicle. It didn't take a genius to figure out she definitely didn't want to go with him. The kidnapper jerked her face inches from his. "Where's your damn car keys?" He spun toward Barclay as he got closer and pointed. "I'm warning you, butt the hell out!"

Taking orders from asshat tyrants never came easy for Barclay. He'd had enough of that shit growing up. "Duck, Molly!" She leaned and he leaped, clotheslined the potential abductor and knocked him into the street. "Roll away!" As soon as she was clear of the bastard's grasp, Barclay punched him a few times. He stood, dragging the bloody mouthed man to his feet.

A sudden protectiveness surged though Barclay for this woman with the lovely eyes and plush curves. "Get in that heap of yours, mister, and hit the road. Don't you dare come near her again." Barclay opened the driver's door and tossed her assailant inside.

"This ain't over, asshole." The stranger pointed to Molly. "That woman belongs to me. You'd best stop sniffin' around her."

Barclay grabbed the mouthy dude's t-shirt and punched his nose, breaking cartilage. Blood flew. The wild-eyed man started his SUV and sped off, slamming the door as he spun around the corner, the wheels screeching.

Barclay squatted next to Molly. "Sugar, are you all right?"

She flinched away when he reached to touch her. "Don't touch me!"

"I've never beat a woman in my life. The danger is over, Molly. Take a deep breath and repeat after me. The danger is over." Once she did as he told her, he scooted behind her to remove the ropes. "You know who I am, right? Barclay, the guy with the dogs."

"Dogs? Yes." She was slowly easing back into reality. He'd seen fire victims lose touch with the genuine world for a brief time or an extended period, depending on the level of their post-traumatic stress.

"Do you remember my dogs got sprayed by skunks?" She nodded. "Molly, I'm going to untie these ropes now and rub your wrists. I won't hurt you. Your danger is over."

Once he removed the rope and manipulated her wrists, he slipped the cell from his pocket and moved in front of her. He thumbed the flashlight app and slowly ran the beam over her battered face. Her lower lip was bleeding and a knot had risen on her cheek. One side of her face was scraped. "Did you know who that sombitch was?"

She nodded. "My...my ex-fiancé, Wade. He followed me here from Colorado." She rose on shaky legs and he steadied her. "Thanks for your help. I'll be all right now." There was a pronounced limp when she walked. "Ouch! Damn, I must have twisted my ankle when I fell. My side hurts where he kicked me."

"You need to get cleaned up and put ice on your injuries." He scooped her into his arms as if she was as light as a feather and strode to the diner. She tensed against him. "Relax. We're only going inside, out of the rain. Sarah will have towels to help us dry off."

Her muscles relaxed a fraction. "Okay. Straight to the diner. N...no-where else."

"Yes. I need to tend to your injuries and you need something warm to drink. This Wade fellow, was he the one who put those old bruises on you? What the fuck kind of man hits a woman? Holy hell, I could never figure that one out." Which was why he hadn't spoken to his dad in years.

"He's pissed because I broke off our engagement." She jerked the hood of her jacket over her head, using the edge to blot her eyes. "You see, I took offense to Wade screwing my maid of honor and he took offense when I told him I wouldn't marry him if he were the last man to walk on God's green earth." She fiddled with the string on her hoodie. "Aren't I too heavy for you? To lug around like this, I mean."

"Seems to me you're about perfect." The crass remark the woman beater had uttered about her size no doubt made her self-conscious about her weight. Hell, what did that guy know about the beauty of a woman's curves?

Barclay carried her into the diner and gently set her in his booth. "Sarah, need another cup of coffee." He glanced at Molly. "Or would you rather have something cold? Whatever you want, just tell me."

With a swipe of his forearm, he wiped rain water off his face and fought the urge to shake like his dogs when they came in from the rain.

"Ice water and blueberry herbal tea. Hot." She shakily reached for paper napkins from the chrome holder to blot at her bleeding lips. He helped her out of her wet hoodie.

Barclay changed his order and grabbed some clean rags from Sarah to dry Molly off.

"I already dialed 9-1-1." Sarah stood on her tiptoes to glance down the street. "After you charged out of here, I watched to see what had you so upset. I couldn't believe that man was trying to drag you to his SUV. Think he was some kind of human trafficker? Picking up women for the sex trade in another country?" Sarah set a fresh cup of coffee and one of tea on their table while she prattled on. "Need some more dry towels? Give me a sec, hon. Barclay, you want one?"

"No thanks, I've got another shirt in my truck." He turned to Molly and helped dry her long hair. "Stay put while I run out to my pickup to get the first aid kit and a dry shirt."

"Okay. Thanks. Sorry to be so much trouble." She cast her dejected gaze on him, sadness evident in those nearly violet eyes... and he was a goner.

"Trouble? Hell, this ain't nothing."

When he carried in a two by four foot yellow plastic container, her eyes widened. "What do you have in there? A portable operating room?"

Flipping the black closures open, he raised the lid, wiping the water off the case's exterior. "As a certified EMT, I'm qualified to help in any emergency." He shrugged, both proud of his job and embarrassed he'd bragged a little. Sarah waved a dry towel in front of him and he grabbed it to rub the rain off his face and hair. He peeled off his wet t-shirt and dried off before slipping into a t-shirt that proclaimed firemen had longer hoses.

Sarah ogled his bare chest, read his shirt and laughed as she gathered up the wet rags. "I still say Yvette was a damn fool."

"Ancient history, Sarah." He stooped and fingered through the neatly arranged emergency supplies.

"So, you really are a fireman and...what was it you said?"

"A diver with a marine rescue unit out of the best *damn* fire station in Clearwater."

Molly was starting to tremble, no doubt coming down from an adrenaline rush. He removed a blanket from his box to drape around her shoulders. "Take a piece of pie and eat. You need something to bring your glucose levels up." He glanced in Molly's eyes. Her pupils were dilated. "Look at me. Double chocolate sin pie okay with you?" She nodded and he slid the dessert in front of her. "Sarah, bring us two more slices in case she needs them."

He tore open some sanitary wet wipes to wash off her face. "Let me make sure you don't need stitches." Cleaning her banged up cheeks and lips, he tried being gentle, but every time he glanced at her eyes to gauge her pain level, a sensual pull warmed him. A faint floral scent penetrated his nose and beguiled. How long had it been since a woman caught his emotions like this and quickly tied them into knots? He wanted to protect her in the worst kind of way.

He snapped an ice pack to make it active and told her to hold it to the side of her face where the bastard had struck her.

"Who...who's Yvette?" She laid her cheek against the ice pack.

"Ex-wife for over a year. In a small community like this, even though the tourists make it seem bigger, some people know all about your life. Isn't that right, Sarah?" Few people could beat the café worker in the gossip department.

The middle-aged waitress leaned her elbows on the counter. "What we call neighborly concern, you call nosy." She sniffed and went about filling salt and pepper shakers. "It only means we care. I remember a time when you worried about everyone too. We're all waiting for the old you to come back."

"Scoot around so I can examine where he kicked you. Has the pain lessened any? Pull up your shirt so I can make sure your ribs aren't broken."

"No, I'm fine. I'm not showing any strange man my midriff."

"Now here's something novel. A woman with morals. Hon, I'll stand right here and watch his every move. He gets out of line, ol' Sarah will box his ears."

Molly slowly pulled up her blouse and he examined her side. "Any pain when I do this?" He pressed in with two fingers.

"No more than a bad bruise." Her contusions were bright red and would soon color to deep bruises. He lowered her top. "Now for your foot." After squatting in front of her, he examined with sure fingers the leg she'd hurt when she'd fallen. Her calf was muscular, but nicely rounded. The kind that would feel good wrapped around his hips, which probably wasn't the best visual to have while she was hurting. Few women got to him like that without trying. "Any pain?"

"No. So far so good."

Yeah, my freakin' thoughts exactly. Christ she had some pretty, shapely legs. Curvy. So curvy he'd probably dream about them tonight. "I'm going to remove your sandal so I can see if your ankle's broken or sprained." He carefully slipped it off.

She winced and nearly scooted backward in the booth when his fingers tested the ligaments leading to and holding her ankle joint. "Ouch! That's a tender spot."

"Sorry. I'm thinking it's a bad sprain, which will require RICE, that's rest, ice, compression and elevation." He slung an arm over his thigh. "And I'd say your big toe is broken. I can take you to the ER for x-rays or an MRI, if you like, but there's nothing they can do for a broken toe. It'll swell, bruise and hurt like hell for a week."

Tears pooled in her eyes. "Great! How am I going to work? Do you think I could wear flip-flops?"

"You'll be lucky to walk with crutches. Besides, this foot needs elevation for a couple days at least." He peeled the cellophane off a rolled ace bandage and began wrapping her foot. "You know, most people come here to relax, enjoy the white sands of our beaches and absorb the sun."

"Yeah, well." She covered her eyes with her fingertips. "Life hasn't exactly been simple lately. Not one thing has gone right since November twelfth."

"Why November twelfth?" The jut of her chin and the tears pooling in her eyes all but shouted she had no freakin' plan to answer *that* question. He activated another ice pack and taped it to her ankle and foot. "Scoot over and rest your heel on my seat to elevate it while we have our pie and drinks. He pulled out a pack of aspirin. "Need something for the pain, Sugar?"

She opened her hand for the pills while she pierced him with tear-filled eyes. "Don't call me Sugar." She palmed the aspirins into her mouth and washed them down.

"Is that what that abusive son of a bitch called you?" His stomach had cramped with temper, banked since childhood yet permanently on simmer beneath the surface to protect anyone bullied or pushed around.

She shook her head. "No, but it implies that we have a connection, which we don't."

"Has this jerk, your ex-fiancé, always been abusive?"

"No. Never. Wade's abuse back in Breckenridge—that's in Colorado—came as a complete shock. Of course, so did his cheating on me. Never in my wildest dreams did I expect him to come here, although I thought I saw his dark blue SUV cruising on Gulf Boulevard. The faded paint on the hood makes it distinctive.

That and the gun rack.

"My parents and I have come to this section of Indian Rocks Beach every February for my entire life, so Wade knew where I'd be. I just never expected him to follow me. Guess it was a good thing the little bungalows we always rented were closed, after all. At least he doesn't know where we're staying." She sighed and stirred her tea. "We have a rental car I got at the airport. Thank goodness he doesn't know what it looks like."

"Why did the goon ask for your car keys?"

"Did he? I was so scared, I don't remember." Her forehead crinkled. "Once he attacked me, I went into fright mode. Wait. I did yell for you to help me, didn't I?"

He slid his hand across the table until their fingertips touched. He'd have taken her hand in his but sensed, at this moment, she wasn't ready for that much personal contact. "Yes, you did. You must have seen me running toward you two, yelling for him to stop."

Had Wade demanded the keys to her car at home or for her rental? None of it made any sense. "If you have a vehicle, why did you walk to work?"

"To save on gas money and listen to the waves kissing the shoreline. I took ten minutes to walk out on the beach. Slipped off my shoes to bury my toes in the sand for a spell to watch the sun start to set and witness the oranges and purples. Sunsets here are phenomenal, aren't they?" There was such sadness in her voice.

"Beyond that, Molly. Way beyond that. I don't think anyone could get me to leave here."

A squad car pulled into the parking area in front of the diner, drawing his attention from their conversation. Officer George Pauley eased from behind the steering wheel and ambled toward the door. Since his wife had passed away a few years ago, the policeman had put on a lot of weight. Barclay stood so the officer could sit. "George, ol' buddy, how's life treating you?"

"Got the gout," he puffed on a wheeze. "My feet hurt like a

sumbitch." He squeezed into the booth across from Molly and tugged his notebook out of his pocket. "Sarah, darlin', get me a piece of pie and a sweet tea."

"I'll get you a salad and a glass of water."

Barclay shot Molly a smirk at Sarah's retort as he sat on his plastic first aid box. Molly rolled her eyes in response. And something inside him shifted. Not that he was looking for a relationship, but if she was only going to be here a few weeks, what could it hurt to enjoy some female companionship?

"Damn bossy woman," George mumbled in Sarah's direction and began his questioning of the incident. When he was through, he jammed his book back into his shirt pocket. "Can you come down to the station tomorrow to sign a complaint? A man grabbing a woman on our streets don't sit well with me. This is a fairly safe community."

"Since it looks like I won't be able to work, sure. I could come by in the morning."

"Sounds good. I'll see the paperwork's ready." He huffed and puffed as he maneuvered his girth from the booth. "Barclay, how soon you gonna have those cabins open for business? I saw the new sign you put up, changing the name to Grey's Cottages. Sounds classier than Verne's Cabins. Putting a new grey roof on each one was a nice touch. You gonna paint all the cabins the same color or keep the multi-colored tradition?"

Barclay's gaze slid to hers and he winced at her narrowed eyes. "I've got one just about ready to rent out. Still need to paint it, inside and out. I'll paint them a fresher version of their original colors. I'm working on renovating the second one now. I redid mine first so the dogs and I could move in. It feels good staying there again."

George clasped his shoulder. "I'm glad your uncle willed you those places. Verne knew how you loved staying there with him as a kid. Having those old style cottages keeps up the charm of the town. We've got too many condos, you ask me." He touched two

23

fingers to his cap. "See you tomorrow, Miss Devon."

"If I'm able to walk there, yes."

"I'll drive you, Molly. Remember, I told you to keep the ankle elevated and rest it?" *I bet you dollars to donuts, she's not going to listen to a damn word I'm telling her.*

"Barclay, show me the spot the attempted abduction occurred." He stood and followed the officer outside. The rain had stopped and the humidity hovered over the area like a cloud of steam. George slipped his flashlight from his belt. "How long have you known Miss Devon?"

"Just met her tonight at Walgreens. We got to talking and I asked her out for coffee."

"Damn, son, you don't waste any time."

"Well, seems my charm didn't do anything for her. She turned me down in a damn big hurry. I noticed the old bruises on her neck and arm, her jumpiness whenever someone came in the store and the way she glared at me like I was scum. Just figured she was skittish around men. I mean, I poured on the charm and she shook it off like a duck shakes off water."

The officer chuckled. "Smart girl, you old horn toad."

Barclay stopped at the rise in the sidewalk. "Here's where she tripped when she was running. Between the downpour and the dark, she couldn't see the uneven cement." He retraced her steps until he found the red rope. "Here's the rope he had tied around her wrists. So his old Blazer was parked in this spot. I pounded on him pretty good after he got behind the wheel and threatened her again. I'm pretty sure I broke his nose."

"You always were the hot head. You got a temper in you that can't be tamed, yet you also got a soft spot for stray dogs, kids in trouble and damsels in distress. See why folks label you a complex conundrum." George flashed the beam of his flashlight around the area and slipped a plastic bag from his pocket. "Roll that rope up, son, and shove it in this bag."

Evidence bag in hand, George ambled back to the squad car.

"Have you asked yourself what would make a man drive all the way from Colorado to our little town in Florida just to bring back an old girlfriend?" The officer grunted. "Hell, there's plenty other fishes in the sea. I got a feeling there's more to this story than we know. Better head back to the station. By the time I fill out the paperwork on this incident, my shift will be over." George opened the door to the squad car. "You be careful. Don't let your pecker rule your head."

The officer drove off, Barclay stepped back into the diner and stilled. Molly had pulled the rubber band from her hair and was running her fingers through the wet strands that came to her elbows. God, what would it feel like to wrap it around his wrists and hold her head in place while he kissed those soft lips?

Good thing she would only be in Indian Rocks Beach for a few weeks. With his attraction to her growing stronger by the minute, he'd be in big trouble. Since he and Yvette split up, he tended to keep his relationships short and shallow. He'd seen firsthand the damage the so-called emotion, love, could do to a person's life.

He slipped back into his seat. "I'll drive you to the police station tomorrow. I'm on vacation for another day. Some of the guys from the fire station are coming to paint the cabins. I can sneak away while they work." He smiled and reached to rub his thumb over her knuckles. Then in a self-preservation move, he pulled his hand back and wrapped it around his coffee mug. "The place you'd mentioned your family always stayed. That was my uncle Vern's five cottages, wasn't it?"

She nodded. "My parents stayed there on their honeymoon back in eighty-two and came back every February for their anniversary. I was conceived there twenty-five years ago, or so my mother claimed. It was a second marriage for both of them and I was what old wives called a change of life baby." She swiped at a falling tear. "Mom was killed in a car crash nearly three months ago on November twelfth."

An old pain of loss and devastation charged into Barclay's

body and sprinted toward his heart. His mother had died just as suddenly two years ago, although bits of her emotions had been killed with every beating his bastard father had given her. Yet his abusive parent had bawled at her funeral, blubbering over and over about how much he'd loved his Carol. *Drunk, abusive bastard.*

"I'm sorry to hear that, Molly. You have my sympathies. My mother's gone too. It leaves a big gap, especially when your siblings live in other states. Do you have any brothers or sisters?"

She shook her head and woeful eyes rose to meet his. "Life changes in an instant, doesn't it? A tractor trailer hit a patch of black ice and lost control. He rammed right into her little compact. Neither my father nor I have been the same since. Dad's grieving so badly, I don't know how much longer he'll last. I can barely get him to eat a proper meal. He's been living on junk food. He's under medication for early signs of dementia."

Damn, she had her problems.

"Somehow, from picking up our rental car at the airport, Dad lost his wallet with most of our money and credit cards, my briefcase holding my laptop and my carryon of clothes. I'm a website designer back home, so I need a computer to keep my business afloat."

"So that's why you're working instead of vacationing?"

She nodded again, the fall of her dark hair hiding part of her face. "I work the morning shift here and a few evenings at the drug store. I bought a new laptop on my credit card, but I don't want to max it out. We'll need it in case of emergencies and for our travel expenses from the airport in Denver to home in Breckenridge."

"I've got what used to be the apricot cottage just about finished inside. It needs both interior and exterior painting and furniture moved in. Would your dad be more comfortable there? It has a new deck that backs onto the beach."

A wistful expression kissed her battered face. "That's the one we always stayed in, but until I get some customers to pay their bills and the replacements for dad's credit cards, we can't afford the security deposit or the rent."

God, he wanted her to have the place for the time she had remaining here. The why of it escaped him; he just had this innate need to help, which hadn't been a part of him since he lost little Bella Marie. How the hell was she going to work with her ankle and foot all banged up? No one ever claimed he was going to make a good businessman, besides he had the income from his job at the station. "If you want the place, it's yours. No security deposit. No rent. Just clean it good before you leave."

"You can't do that. Isn't the object of fixing them up to have rental income?"

He nodded and tucked into the piece of pie in front of him. "To a degree. I'm living in the cottage next to it. The aqua one." He shook the fork at her. "You know, I'm also going to need a website under the new name. We could trade services." He grinned at her and hoped she'd take him up on his offer.

"Now that's a deal I could handle. I wasn't raised to take charity, but if I can work part of our obligation off that would be great. Dad's a retired carpenter. He might be able to help you a couple hours a day, but you'd have to keep a close eye on him. One minute, he's on track and, the next, he can't recall what he was about to do. Do you have a webpage reserved in your name?"

"It's in Grey's Cottages' name. Not much to it, Sugar, I did it myself so it's pretty lame."

"I'll get started on it tomorrow. You'll have the best website I can create. One thing though…"

His fork stilled halfway to his mouth. "What?"

"Don't call me Sugar."

CHAPTER THREE

The door to the diner flew open and a dark-haired beauty squealed as she barreled in. "Ice Man, my hero!" The woman's hands cupped Barclay's cheeks and she kissed him full on the lips.

Molly sipped at her lukewarm tea, taking note of the affectionate exchange. *One of his many conquests, no doubt.*

"Angel, you're going to make me beat his worthless ass." The tall, dark and incredibly handsome man accompanying the beauty looped his arm around her waist, pulling her away from Barclay and back to him. He kissed her neck. "You know how I get."

Barclay grinned and shook his head. "Molly, meet one of the most possessive son of a bitches to ever get married, Quinn Matisse, and his wife, Cassie." He extended an open hand to her. "This is Molly. We just met tonight and, as you can see, she's had a rough evening."

"Nice to meet you." Quinn's eyebrows dipped when he looked at her. He slid onto the seat next to Barclay, who gently wrapped his hand around her bandaged ankle and lifted it onto his thigh, evidently to make room for his friend. Once Quinn sat, their broad shoulders met, creating quite a wall of macho muscles.

Cassie sat next to her and reached for her husband's hand before turning a warm smile on Molly. "I'm happy to meet you." She peeled the ice pack away from Molly's cheek and winced. "Looks like Ice Man's been busy doing some first aid work."

"Yes. The man carries around a portable operating room."

"So does my Quinn. It comes with the job."

Sarah came over to get their orders, so conversation stopped.

The heat from Barclay's thigh warmed Molly's ankle, ice pack or no ice pack. If she slid her foot over just a couple of inches, it would touch his manhood. Her gaze rose to lock on Barclay's and a slow, sexy smile spread as if he read her thoughts. The heat of a flush spread just as slowly across her cheeks.

Quinn aimed a raised eyebrow to Barclay or, Ice Man, as the two apparent newlyweds called him. In response to Quinn's silent question, Barclay never mentioned the cause of her battered face. Quinn turned his gaze to Molly. "You're looking at a very happy man."

"Really?"

"I've started a whole new life, recently. New last name, new wife, new rancher."

"Now all we need are babies to fill it." Cassie flashed Quinn a wide grin.

Her husband shook his head. "We agreed to wait three years, Angel. Just because you held baby Andy Jace from the moment we stepped into Jace and Wendy Anne's house, don't go getting any maternal ideas. I want you to myself for a few years."

"That little kid is quite the charmer, isn't he?" Something in the tone of Barclay's voice—pain, longing, devastation—nearly tore Molly's breath away.

Cassie's hand slid across the table to touch fingertips against his rigid fist. "Ice Man," she whispered, her face sorrowful. "I know this is hard for you."

His hand moved to his lap and then rubbed Molly's bandaged leg, so both of his hands were on her—one at her instep and the other on her calf, gently and slowly massaging. Her nipples were all but crying, "Me next! Me next!" Molly crossed her arms to muffle their sensual plea.

"I took him a toy last week. Seeing him was only half as difficult as I'd expected. I actually held him for a few minutes." Barclay's voice was strained as he stared out of the diner window. "I'd put it off for months. I mean, I went to see the kid in the hospital after he was born, gave them a baby present, but I just couldn't bring myself to see him up close and personal." He shook his head. "Chicken shit, huh?"

Why would it be so hard for him to see a baby?

Quinn tapped Cassie's hand once and she pulled it back to her lap. Her husband slouched in the seat. "We just came from a family picnic and noticed your heap of a truck in the parking lot."

His friend's insult seemed to snap Barclay out of his deep thoughts. "Hey, buddy, watch it. That's a valuable antique sitting out there."

Quinn laughed. "Yeah? How many times has it been worked on this week?"

"Kiss my ass, Quinn." Barclay sipped his coffee and winked at Molly.

"Thought we'd stop by and chat a bit. How's vacation going?"

Barclay's head leaned side-to-side once, the joints in his neck popping. "Good. Haven't gotten as much work done as I'd hoped. The cabins were pretty decrepit. Plus the beach keeps calling to me. The girls and I have played a lot of Frisbee on the sand. Thank goodness some of the guys from the station have helped me on their days off."

He jerked a thumb toward his friend and spoke to Molly. "Quinn is on the same fire squad I am and he also drives the boat for our marine rescue team. Cassie is a beautician who chased him for three years until he wised up and let her catch him."

Cassie squirmed in her seat, a bundle of nervous energy, and grinned. "Men can be so dense, you know? Why, I even had to seduce him the first time." She winked at Molly, who didn't know if she should believe the sparkling woman or not. "We've been married for almost eight months." She grinned at Quinn and sighed. "It was a *very* good seduction."

Molly finished her piece of pie, her previous shakes nearly gone. "Why did you refer to Barclay as your hero?"

Cassie's eyes widened. "Ice Man? Oh, you wouldn't know the story. I was abducted by this weird guy who was working for…" she glanced at Quinn. "Well, it doesn't matter who he worked for. Not really. But my man, here, plus my brothers, Wolf and Jace, Barclay and a couple other friends formed an unsanctioned SWAT team and rescued me. Blew up the building I was held captive in. I'll never forget that night. Neither will the two guys who have to sit down to pee the rest of their lives because of what Quinn and my big brother did to them."

Quinn snickered and lifted his wife's hand to his lips. "Neither will I. She and I broke up on the way to the hospital from her rescue. Was one hell of a gawd-awful evening."

Molly's gaze ricocheted from Cassie to Quinn to Barclay. Abduction, blowing up a building, castrating men… What the hell? *I've fallen down the nutso rabbit hole.* All three of them looked normal, but what was normal anymore? "How long were you two apart after you broke up?"

Quinn held up four fingers. "Four hellacious hours. I got knocked unconscious after I got home and she took pity on me once I was found."

"Some men need a good woman more than others. Quinn just needed me. I couldn't let him go."

"Would you just listen to her brag? All full of feminine power." Quinn looked at Molly

Cassie mumbled, "Here we go. Just pay him no mind."

Quinn pointed to her engagement ring. "I had to handcuff her to the headboard to slip that diamond on her finger."

Cassie extended her ring hand and rolled her eyes. "You just *have* to tell everyone that story, don't you?" Her husband laughed softly when she stuck her tongue out at him. "And I think you might be mistaken. I'm sure we said we'd wait one year to start making a baby."

Quinn blew on his cup of coffee. "Nope. Three years." He winked at Barclay who smirked in return.

"Gee, and I was going to pole dance for you tonight."

Her husband choked and sputtered coffee on his shirt. "Dammit, Cassie!" He swiped java off his chin and t-shirt. "You never did fight fair."

Cassie laughed. "No, and you love me that way."

Over coffee, shared French fries and more pie, Molly told them about Wade.

With the ice pack against her cheek, she recanted her harrowing experience of less than an hour ago. She also shared her and her dad's bittersweet journey to Indian Rocks where they intended to spread her mother's ashes on the beach in front of the cabin they'd always stayed in.

Her gaze locked on Barclay's. "Though I'm not sure the new owner will allow that."

His gaze hadn't moved from her face since she'd started talking. The man treated her as if she were the only person in the diner. His dimpled smile—she could only describe as dangerous and damned sexy—made her toes curl, even the painful broken one. As if he could read her reaction, his fingers caressed her unbound toes. "I don't see that as being a problem."

She couldn't help herself; she smiled for the first time in months. "Thank you."

Barclay stared at her for several minutes before Quinn's elbow bumped his—twice. As if to erase some kind of mental vision, Barclay shook his blond head a few times, cleared his throat and looked at her again. "Sorry, did you say something?"

"I said thank you, Barclay. You don't know what your kindness means to us, to me. Your offer to let us stay in the little cottage we have so many great memories of and allowing us to spread Mom's ashes there." She smiled again and he looked as if he'd stopped breathing for a minute. "If Dad can spend some time at the cabin he and Mom loved, maybe it'll help calm him down. His dementia not only makes him forgetful, but he agitates easily too."

Cassie rubbed Molly's arm with sympathy. "You poor dear. One of my customers has a husband with dementia. He puts things where he can't recall. She found the TV remote in the ice maker of their freezer. He put his razor in the linen closet behind the towels. Then he tears the house apart hunting for the items he's misplaced.

"When she comes in my shop, I give her extra pampering because I know she has to be exhausted from caring for her husband. I massage her arms and fingers, her neck and shoulders. Little things, you know. It's rough to see your loved one deteriorate mentally and emotionally."

"Tell me about it. Some days, dad is coherent. Other days, he's all befuddled. He was fine on the flight down. I was so pleased with how well he did." Molly rubbed her forehead and sighed. "Then there was a bit of a mix-up with our car reservations. He got flustered and impatient. Started pacing and mumbling. Then he swore we left Mom on the plane and went into a panic that she'd been flown to Iraq or Afghanistan." She shook her head and sighed. "Two places you don't want to be yelling in an airport. Calming him down took a lot of effort. When I told him she was dead, his eyes went wild and he started crying and screaming." She twisted her napkin in her hands. "Security came running and told me I'd have to get him out of there. Like that wasn't what I'd been trying to do all along."

Quinn pounded on the bottom of a ketchup bottle. "Give a man a badge and his common sense shrivels."

Molly nodded in agreement. "We always got a sedan and this trip we ended up with a compact. Dad started whining as soon as he saw it. Claimed his long legs would never fit in it." She shot a glance at Cassie. "He's only five-eight and to hear him talk, you'd think five feet of him are legs.

"Anyway, somehow, between the emotional fiasco at the car

33

rental desk and our arrival at the condo, his wallet, my briefcase and carry-on had disappeared. My fault, I guess. When I asked Dad where everything was, he narrowed his eyes and jutted his chin, claiming he had it all and to stop treating him like a child. I was just too frazzled to push the issue and check behind him."

Barclay's pressure as he massaged her toes and calf increased. She nearly purred, even if it was just an act of pity on his part. What else could it be?

"I called the police, the Tampa International Airport and the car rental agency but, so far, no one's seen a thing. So now I'm working at two jobs, trying to keep us financially flush. Dad's medicine is pretty expensive. He's lost it twice since we've been here. I found the bottle inside his pillow case the first time, but could never locate it the second time he misplaced it. So I had to call his doctor back in Breckenridge to send a prescription to the Walgreens here where I work."

Tears pooled and she blinked to clear them. The stress of living in a continual scavenger hunt with her dad was getting to her. Then to have Wade show up and knock her around. "It's...ah... been a little rough." Two traitorous tears overflowed.

Cassie's arms instantly went around her. "Oh, honey. I know some of what you're going through. I lost both of my parents in a fire. You just cry when you need to. Get it out." She kept patting Molly's back. "Besides, you've got friends here now. There's no one sweeter than Ice Man. I've known him since I was a teenager. Course he was known to everyone as Barclay back then. He and my brother Jace were good buddies. Let him help you. My own personal hero and I are here for you too." She pulled out of the embrace and slipped a business card from her tiny purse. "Here's my cell number." She jotted a number on the back and handed it to Molly. "Just wait until you meet the whole gang. Firemen, their wives and girlfriends. You're not alone anymore." Cassie cast her gaze on Barclay. "Is she, Ice Man?"

"No. I'll keep an eye on her and her dad. Which bedroom did

34

he and your mom use? I'll see most of the same furniture goes back in there so he feels a sense of familiarity. I've ordered new mattresses and living room furniture for each unit, though."

"Oh, Barclay, that's so kind of you. Or would you rather I call you Ice Man?" He was such a caring individual, what had prompted such a nickname?

"Barclay's fine."

"They had the room that overlooked the beach. It was always painted blue and there were oars crisscrossed over the headboard, fish net wrapped around the oar handles with star fish and pretty shells tucked in the net. When I was a kid, I thought that arrangement was the neatest thing. I had the bedroom toward the driveway in front." He nodded, no doubt making a mental note. "Cassie and Quinn, it's been great meeting you, but I have to get home to Dad. He'll be wondering what's happened to me." Her gaze swept to Barclay. "Thanks for chasing off Wade and tending to my sprained ankle and bruised face. Good luck bathing your dogs tonight."

She went to slide her heel off his thigh and his hold on her tightened. "I'll drive you to your condo. You're in no condition to walk anywhere. Besides your foot's probably swollen so bad you won't be able to get your sandal back on. Stay where you're at. I'll come for you as soon as I carry my first aid kit out to the truck." Quinn stood and Barclay slid out, grabbing his case and lugging it outside.

Well, really, she could walk. She didn't need to listen to him. "Would you let me out, please, Cassie?"

"And have Ice Man give me the stink eye? No way. A smart woman knows when to listen to her man."

Her man? Cassie must be delusional. "Barclay is most definitely not my man. He's not even my type."

"Type? If he was any more your type, he'd have you sitting on his lap. I sense a definite attraction. You've never been around a group of men like the ones at Fire Station Thirty-two." Cassie snorted. "If you try to go off on your own, he'll just catch up with you, toss you over his shoulder in a fireman's carry and—if you're lucky—smack your behind." The woman actually winked at her.

He smacks my behind and I'll pop him in the eye. Although the more she thought about it, the more appealing the idea seemed—having a man take control. She could use a break from all the problems and pressures.

Barclay sauntered back into the diner and Cassie obediently slid out of the seat. He reached in, slipped his hands under Molly and lifted her as if she weighed no more than the role of Ace bandage he'd wrapped around her foot earlier.

Quinn stood and extended his hand for Cassie. "I'll be at the cabins to help paint tomorrow, Ice Man. You'll be back on the job the day after, right?"

"Yeah, can't say I've missed those forty-eight hour shifts. By the time you get rested during your days off and do a few things, it's time to start another round."

Quinn wrapped his arm around Cassie's waist, drawing her close. "See you in the morning. Just not *real* early. I do believe my wife promised me a pole dance tonight." He leaned in and planted a kiss on her neck.

Oh, yeah, I've dropped into some strange kinky lifestyle hole. Women handcuffed to beds and dancing on poles—seemingly on command. With a gentle strength, Barclay pressed Molly to the firmness of his pecs and carried her from the diner. She clutched her wet hoodie to her side.

"You seem upset. You okay, Sugar?"

"Didn't I tell you not to call me Sugar?"

He tilted his head to the side and, for a few seconds, she could have sworn his jaw clenched. Would he hit her too? Choke her? Knock her around?

Oh, he'd call her Sugar, all right. And before he was through with her, she'd damn well know how a man should treat a woman, because he bet she'd never been shown tenderness and protectiveness before. He gave a mental shrug. Okay, maybe from her father, but certainly not from any guy she'd dated. She had no clue she was about to start school—Seduction 101 and maybe, if she was into it, light BDSM 102.

He'd left the passenger door open on his reconditioned antique truck when he returned to the diner to get her. With great care, he placed her on the wide bench seat, pushing his bags of shopping products over. Slipping his hand beneath the silky fall of her long hair, he cupped the back of her neck to hold her head in place. With slow, deliberate movements, he leaned in and, using the barest of touches, dragged his lips across her cheek until they scarcely made contact with the corner of her mouth. Good God, he couldn't help himself, couldn't resist that beauty spot of hers and, against his better judgment, he swept the tip of his tongue over it—ever so lightly.

Her breathing hitched and his all but seized in his lungs for the want of her, the taste of her, the feel of her under his hands. His lips whispered against the curve of hers, where her cheek ended and her very sexy mouth began. "Then what shall I call you?"

She swallowed and the sound echoing in his old Chevrolet was something he'd never forget. He couldn't recall anything so damn enticing. "My...my name is Molly. You know that."

He tilted his head toward her a fraction as he reached for the seatbelt and stretched it across her stomach that quivered at his brief touch. "No nicknames?" His eyes focused on hers in the dim interior lighting. Beautiful, magnetizing were the only terms he could think of to describe them. He'd been resisting their pull from the first time he'd seen her.

She cleared her throat. "N...no." She jutted her chin. "Well, one, but I refuse to divulge it." Her gaze centered on the windshield and she wiped her palms on her capris. Was she nervous over his closeness or turned on?

Either way, she obviously had his attention. Fuckin'A. Both his and his cock's.

"Then, with you being so sweet, I'd say Sugar fits. At least between you and me. And I can tell you I have never abused a woman. Argued with, yes. Hit or called names, no. Never. A real man provides and protects." His lips lightly brushed hers as their breaths mingled and his words stroked her mouth. "Do you know you have the most beautiful smile I've ever seen? It makes your indigo eyes go almost violet. A man could virtually fall into them and never want to climb back out."

She jerked back as if he'd struck her. "Your normal seduction techniques won't work with me. I'm not that easy." Her eyes narrowed. "How long has it been since you've been with a woman?"

His fingers slipped into her midnight silky tresses, rubbing their rich softness. "That's one of those trick questions you women like to ask, isn't it? If I tell you I had a date last night, then you'll classify me as a player. If I say I haven't gone out in two or three months, then you'll just call me a horny bastard. Either answer puts me in a bad light when all I'm trying to do is be honest."

There, let her stew on that.

He closed the door and rounded the front of the brown pick-up, a picture of an aqua-colored cabin by the sea and Gray's Cottages painted in an arch over the dwelling. A website address was below it. He settled behind the steering wheel, clicked his seatbelt and aimed a smile her way. "Now that we've got that settled, where to, *Sugar*?"

CHAPTER FOUR

Molly crossed her arms and gave him the directions, although the way her jaw clenched it was a wonder she could force out one syllable much less a complete sentence. She was so damn pissed she could spit fireballs. This man, this stranger, this hunk of muscle with his sexy-as-hell smile had practically kissed her.

They'd met mere hours ago and this rascal was coming on to her. He must have mistakenly thought she was desperate for a man, any man. Still, he had saved her from Wade and taken care of her injuries. But even those kindnesses didn't warrant his frisky nature.

Ice Man, his friends had called him. She'd give him a different nickname, like Sex on a Stick or Horny Toad.

What ticked her off, if she were honest, was her body's reaction to his very male appearance and his gentle, yet almost assertive touch. Thank goodness her mind still contained some wits. For although her body had all but melted into a pile of feminine goo over his toying, her brain and all the common sense it contained resented his subtle flirting, if she could classify it as subtle.

The blond man with more muscles than those hunks in movies was mounting an offensive as if he were a war general. She shifted her shoulders in annoyance. Okay, so maybe *mounting* was the wrong terminology here. Her gaze drifted over his t-shirt stretched taut across hardened pecs and the clichéd washboard abs. *Just what would it feel like to have him mount…oh hell, I must have a concussion to even think about him like this.*

What kind of woman did he think she was? Just because she carried more than a few extra pounds than other girls, did he think she was desperate for a man's attention, especially when society only saw beauty in being thin? No doubt, he was playing her because he thought she'd be someone who'd spread her legs for a compliment and a smile. She rolled her eyes. Sugar, he wanted to call her. *Huh, I'd like to sugar his balls and plant his manly parts in an anthill.*

When he eased his ancient pickup in front of the old motel converted into condominiums, he jumped out and came around to lift her from the vehicle. "I was thinking I'd talk to your dad a bit. Tell him about the changes I'm making at the cottages so he won't be upset things aren't the same as he remembers."

She was surprised at his proposed consideration toward her father. Why should this Romeo care about an old man with early dementia? Or care enough about her to carry her to the door of the condo? He set her down and placed his hands at her waist to hold her up as she teetered on one foot while unlocking the door. Although his body wasn't blatantly touching hers, the heat from him all but singed the back of her shirt. His nearness flustered her so badly, she could barely hit the lock with the key.

After several failed tries, his warm hand engulfed hers and inserted the key. Damn, if it didn't feel so good, she almost turned the lock again so he'd have to help her one more time. What in the world was wrong with her? Her hormonal reactions were all over the place. One time, he'd touch her and she'd prickle with annoyance and the next she'd get all hot and bothered. It had to be the head injury. Wade's punch must have left some lasting effects.

She opened the door. "Dad, are you still awake?" Barclay lifted her and carried her inside.

Her dad sat on an old rocker, a bag of Cheetos on his lap and the TV blaring. "Sure am. Been waiting on you. What time does that store close anyway?" His paternal gaze zeroed in on her face and slid to her bandaged foot. He bolted from his chair, a few orange curls falling out of the bag when it hit the floor. "What in the hell happened? Why can't you walk?" His fingers curled into fists as he narrowed his eyes on Barclay. "You hurt my little girl?"

"No sir." Barclay carried her to the plastic covered sofa and laid her so her head was on the armrest. He shifted and extended his hand. "I'm Barclay Gray, sir."

Her dad shook his hand, a quizzical expression played across his features as his scrutiny slipped from Barclay to her. "Name's Sam Devon." He jerked his head toward the empty end of the sofa. "Suppose you have a seat while my daughter explains why she's all battered and bruised again." He reached for the remote and turned off the television.

Barclay lifted her feet and sat so they were elevated on his thick thighs while she shifted to her side to face her dad and told him what happened.

He ran his wide palm over his mouth, his whiskered stubble rasping in the silence of the room. "Wade followed us here?" His voice was incredulous as if he couldn't grasp the reality of the situation. "The bastard tried to tie you up and take you away from me?" He glanced around the living area, his gaze turning wild. "Tammy, come here and listen to this! You won't believe what's happened to our little girl."

His confusion was back. "Daddy, Momma's not here." It was no use to tell him she was dead; he'd only start crying again.

"Did she go to the store for milk and bread? I hope she remembers the ice cream."

"Sam?" Barclay leaned forward, his forearms over his spread thighs, sliding her feet against his firm abdomen. "Do you recall a place called Verne's Cabins?"

A smile broke through her dad's muddled mind. "Yup, sure do. Me and Tammy spent our honeymoon there and every February since. Twas always a slow month for carpentry work, so I'd bring the wife and daughter here. Place is closed up now. That's how we ended up in this dump." He scowled as if he'd tasted Aunt Willa's prune cake. "Walls are paper thin. Hell, you can hear couples screwing, moanin' and a groanin.'"

"Well, sir, Verne was my uncle."

Her dad settled back in the rocking chair. "You don't say?"

"A massive heart attack took him a year ago. He willed the property to me and I'm trying to remodel the place. You wouldn't feel up to swinging a hammer a couple hours a day, would you? I could use the help and some advice from an experienced man like you. There're lots of things about carpentry I just don't know. I could use an advisor."

Molly stared at Barclay. His invitation for her dad to be both a helper and a carpentry mentor was totally unexpected. The man's personality had many facets. She wasn't sure what her opinion of him was, but there was no doubting she appreciated his kindness toward her father.

Her dad's chest puffed out. "Hell's bells, ain't been a hammer made that didn't fit this old hand." He waved his arthritic right arm.

"Your daughter was telling me what a fine worker you were." Her dad smiled in response to Barclay's compliment. "Sam, if you think the two of you can stay here another night, I'll help move you into the apricot unit I'm almost through fixing up. Still needs painting and furniture moved in. You could work off your rent by helping me a few hours in the morning before it gets so hot."

He glanced at her and then her dad. "I've installed a security gate. I think you'll be pretty safe there. Wade would need the code to get in."

"I'm worried about her, son. This is the second time the sombitch put marks on her. She's a good girl. Spirited, like her momma, but never been in any trouble. She's got a heart of gold under all the attitude she's had of late."

Barclay stared at her for a minute, his gaze sweeping over her face almost like a warm caress. What was up with that?

"I won't let him hurt her again. Not as long as the two of you are here in Indian Rocks Beach." He placed her feet on the sofa before he stood and bent to the floor to pick up the spilled snack and return the bag to her dad. The Cheetos he'd plucked from the carpet, he tossed into the wastepaper can by her dad's chair.

He clasped his hand on her dad's shoulder, stopping his rocking. "Meanwhile, Sam, I think you're gonna have a pretty hard job on your hands. Molly needs to rest and keep her ankle elevated. That means no more working for her while you're on vacation, except for her website design business. She can prop her ankle up while she does whatever she does on her computer."

Barclay placed a throw pillow where he'd been sitting earlier and shifted her down so her feet lay on it. Raising her head, he sat, placing it on his lap and sifting his fingers through her hair, making her relax all over. "Getting her to listen might be a job in itself. She hasn't complained, but both her head and her ankle have to hurt like hell. Bastard kicked her in the side, too, but I don't think he broke any ribs. Still, she's going to be in a world of hurt for a day or two."

Her dad narrowed his eyes on her. "Don't you worry about a thing, Barclay. I'll keep her in line."

"Bastard," she muttered under her breath.

"Sugar." Barclay's deep and sensual whisper made her female parts stand up and do the hula.

"I owe you a debt of gratitude for rescuing her from Wade and fixing her up the way you did. Strangers helping strangers just don't happen like it used to. I thank you, Barclay."

"You're welcome, sir." He shifted and slipped his cell from his pocket. "Molly, how about you give me your cell phone number so I can call tomorrow before I come over to pack up your stuff and move you out? Don't give me that mule-headed glare. You know you're going to need some help. Besides we need to stop at the police station so you can sign the complaint."

He thumbed in her number when she rattled it off and showed

43

it to her, asking if he'd gotten it correct. She noted in place of her name, he'd put Sugar. If it wouldn't have hurt her sprained ankle so much she'd have kicked his fine ass to the door.

Her dad grinned and rubbed his hands together. "We'll be in our little beach cottage tomorrow night, Molly, with the sounds of the waves lulling us to sleep. You won't have to work at two jobs. I won't have to be alone so much, plus I'll have a part-time job. Things are looking up." He turned to Barclay. "You promise you'll protect her from Wade?"

"Or die trying."

Her dad stared at him for several minutes. "You a married man?"

She bolted to a sitting position. "Dad!"

His bald head barely turned in her direction. "It's an honest question." He rocked slowly. "I'm widowed, myself."

"I'm divorced."

"Another woman?" Her dad stopped rocking, his chair leaning forward.

Barclay stared at him for a few seconds. "My wife and I lost a baby to sudden infant death and we could never get beyond it. We both grieved in our own way, growing further and further apart instead of closer in our mourning. So, we ended up with a double loss. Sweet little Bella Marie and our marriage." Mournful eyes hinged on her dad's and it was as if invisible links launched between them. Bonds of loss, agony and soul-deep pain.

Tears blurred her vision. She understood and felt those emotions herself, just in a different manner.

"Well, now. I think we understand each other." Her dad started rocking again. "I thank you again for taking care of my daughter. She's all I've got left."

"I'm a fireman and marine rescue diver. It's my job to take care of others. Besides, there's something special about Molly." He lifted her onto his lap. "Do you want me to carry you into bed and tuck you in?" Barclay smiled with that shy, yet sexy smile he seemed able to call forth on command. Her dad laughed as if the two had been best buds for years. She was none too happy with either of them, treating her as if she were a child and a helpless one at that.

"No. Thank you, I'll be fine on my own." She was damned tired of his constant charm. No man could be this appealing all the time—dimples or no dimples—and she was sick of it. Her head gonged like St. John's church bells on Sunday morning, her side hurt when she breathed and her leg throbbed. Her face and knees were scrapped raw. Was it any wonder she was cranky? *God, I ache all over.*

Two of his fingers tucked under her chin, raising her head so they gazed into each other's eyes. "You're in a lot of pain, aren't you? Where's your aspirins?"

How did he know? "The medicine cabinet in the bathroom. Top shelf."

He cupped her unbruised cheek. "Be right back." His voice had softened and, for just an instant, she wanted to lean into him for support, but cursed her weakness instead. If Wade had taught her one thing, it was men were never what they seemed. She sat up while Barclay went for the medicine. Her dad kept rocking… both of them…no, wait, there were three dads in a trio of rocking chairs. She blinked to bring her father into focus.

Barclay held a tiny paper cup with the pills in it and another filled with water. She had to make two tries to wrap her fingers around the one with the pills and who knew how many to grasp the cup of water to wash them down.

"That's it. I don't give a damn how mad you get." Barclay lifted her off the sofa. "Sam, would you mind showing me to her bedroom. She's in no fit condition to walk or stay up any longer. I want her to sleep. Christ, she's been battered to hell and back."

Her dad, who'd always been her hero, stood and waddled to her room. "He messed her up pretty bad, didn't he?"

"Yes. A man has no business hurting a woman. Bet you were the type of husband to protect your wife, weren't you?"

"Did the best by Tammy I could, son."

Barclay sat Molly on the edge of the bed, kneeled in front of her and removed the remaining sandal she still wore. "Sam, I'm going to pull these muddy capris off her so she'll rest better. You're not going to tar and feather me for it, are you?"

Her dad chuffed a laugh. "I'm not the scrapper you need to worry about."

Darn if Mr. I'm-Going-To-Charm-Your-Dad didn't lean in, lime and ginger filling her nose, his lips against her ear and ask if she was wearing underwear under her red capris. The nerve! She hurt from her hair to her toenails and he wanted to be damn ballsy? Her hand fisted and rose.

His fingers coiled around her wrist, breath feathered her hair and his cheek touched hers. "I'm sorry, Sugar. That was out of line. You're not up to my teasing, are you, baby? I'm sorry. I was only checking. I guess it's we guys who are more prone to go commando."

"Do you?" *Crap, this is the last question I need to be asking him.* "Often, yes."

Oh God, I do not need that visual.

His eyes locked on hers as he unbuttoned and unzipped the capris before sliding them off her hips and legs. Pulling the sheet and blanket up to her shoulders, he pressed a gentle kiss to her forehead. "See you tomorrow. Sleep well. Use aspirins as you need them. I'll come by in the morning to rewrap your ankle after you shower. Will eight o'clock be fine? I'll bring donuts."

"I don't want any of your damn donuts. Not even the ones with chocolate icing and sprinkles." Her eyelids were already getting heavy. "Dad likes the glazed kind." She yawned.

"I'll bring half a dozen glazed for your dad and half a dozen with chocolate icing and sprinkles for me then. Guess you'll just have to watch us eat them. I'll bring you a bagel. How's that?" The corners of his mouth spread enough the creases of his dimples deepened.

"You eat the damn bagel and leave my chocolate donuts alone."

46

Easy, deep male laughter floated over her and somehow comforted. "I'll get you whatever you want, Sugar. Dream good dreams tonight. No nightmares." He traced the backs of his fingers down her face. "Do you know poets for centuries have written poetry about skin as fair and soft as yours? Alabaster skin, like pearls." He stood, walked out of her bedroom behind her dad and turned out the light.

Her eyes drifted shut. *What the hell was all his kindness about?*

CHAPTER FIVE

Barclay jammed the key into the truck's ignition and leaned his forehead on the steering wheel. How could one man's life get turned upside down in a few hours? All he'd wanted was some damn freakin' douche powder and what did he get? A pair of indigo eyes, a smile that practically numbed his mind and a body that sent his cock on high alert.

Oh, and her gutsy attitude, he couldn't forget that. He'd never been one for women who were pushovers, not that he wanted a life of verbal sparring and arguing. God, he'd had enough of that growing up…at least from his dad. His mother? She'd caved every time to "keep peace" and save herself from another beating. There were times when even that tactic didn't work. The old man just wanted, needed, to hit something and it was either her or Barclay.

Still, he held no ill-feelings for Mom. She did her best to fill the house with love. Her goal was always to bring happiness to a house covered by the dark pall of abusive sickness from his dad. If only she'd left him, but she swore she loved the man. Why, Barclay could never figure out.

He'd always protected his younger sisters so Dad couldn't get to them. Until the night he played in an away high school football game. The old man had put bruises on Jasmine, the youngest, because she'd been fussy with a sore throat. When Kayla, the middle child, had stood up for her younger sister, their father had whipped her across her back with his belt. The next day, Barclay had marched into the coach's office and, with a heavy heart, quit the team.

Protecting his sisters was his responsibility. One he took damn seriously.

Now, there was another woman being battered, and he wasn't going to allow her abuse either. Why did life have to be one fucking problem after another? Why did he have to meet Molly? Hell, she wasn't interested in him. That much was damned obvious.

But I sure as hell am interested in her. Damned interested.

He inhaled a deep breath and exhaled slowly. Life was catching up to him; that was all. He'd been alone too long. The occasional visit to the club wasn't enough anymore. Maybe he needed someone more regular in his life. Not someone to love. Hell, love always brought loss. Just a woman he could rely on seeing once or twice a week.

Maybe he needed to spend more time at Dark Desires, even though the club scene was never his thing. Not really. A friend from another fire station had taken him there after he and Yvette separated. A night out to blow off steam and watch the sights of the BDSM lifestyle. What play turned him on the most—spanking and sex toys—were what scared him more than anything, given how he'd grown up.

Thank goodness an intuitive Dom invited him to the bar for a drink and a long talk. Barclay was so shocked and ashamed by what had aroused him, he could barely get the glass from the bar to his lips. How could he feel arousal for what he'd grown to hate all of his life? The silver-haired Dom listened while Barclay told this stranger about his family and his abusive father.

"My friend, there is a great difference between the open hand of a controlled slap or spank and the closed fist of abuse." He clasped Barclay's shoulder. "A huge difference. In our lifestyle, it is a power exchange. Some people need or enjoy a spanking to become highly aroused. They give the Dom the power to provide that stimulus, which heightens our sexual pleasure. A good Dominant wants to please and protect their sub. Never hurt. Never downgrade or belittle."

He extended his hand. "My name is Aaron Karl. I'm one of the training Doms here, if you care to be considered for the proper teaching of our lifestyle. You'll have to go through background checks and a vetting process, of course, but it might help you work through some issues of your own."

Barclay took another sip and chuckled. "What? Kink counseling?"

The training encompassed some of his lonely free time and helped him come to grips with the reasons behind his dark desires. He never regretted all he learned; he just never had the urge to use it all in his playtime. He was a Dom with simple tastes. In fact, Aaron had told him he doubted he'd make a true Dom, but was a man turned on by kink. Barclay had insisted he was wrong.

Mainly, he was a private man who disliked sharing or having other men seeing what was his. Would a friend with benefits be so bad? One he didn't have to love, just respect and take care of. Love was just too soul-shattering.

Losing little Bella Marie in the space between two fragile heart-beats had dragged him through an emotional hell the likes of which he never thought possible. Yvette mourned her deep loss by drinking and getting high. Barclay had done his fair share of drinking, too, but never went the drug route or did the party scene the way she had. Then his heart-adopted father Uncle Verne's sudden heart attack, followed by another in the hospital, became another unbearable loss. Barclay distanced himself from emotion. A good time, sure. Caring, no problem. Love, never again.

Knowing Yvette was going through men and drugs like water through a drain didn't ease his soul any. Although the love was gone between them, a part of him would always care. And therein lay his biggest liability—he cared too much for people. Wasn't that why he went into the occupation he had? *Christ, what a sap*

I can be at times.

He shuddered another sigh and lifted his gaze to the lights in the old condo. Now he had two more people to worry about. When would he ever learn? He straightened and turned the key. The old truck growled to life and he headed for home. Thank goodness he had three dogs to bathe, because it would be a few hours before his libido calmed down enough so he could sleep. A traffic light turned red and he braked.

Getting Molly out of his mind was going to be an all-night chore. Her hair was like black satin a man dreamed of having draped over his chest. Her full breasts made his hands ache to hold. He banged his head once on the steering wheel before the light changed and he peeled onto Gulf Boulevard. What man didn't want to wrap his hands around those perfect fruits and kiss their pink tips? Man, shifting gears with a raging hard-on could be a bitch.

Wade, the woman beater, came to mind and Barclay ground his back molars. If he caught the sonofabitch coming near her, he'd strangle him with his bare hands.

Anger and possession—two emotions he had no business feeling where she was concerned—surfaced and anchored in his soul. He had to get home to his dogs and all the work ahead of him… anything to occupy his mind for he was fuckin' losing it over a woman he'd just met. Two weeks, three tops and she'd be gone. He'd help her all he could, but he wouldn't allow himself to get emotionally involved. He needed to hold back more, to care less and make *his* solitary life a priority for a change instead of thinking he could fix everyone else's problems.

Armed with a strong dose of determination to keep his emotional distance, Barclay knocked at Molly's at eight-fifteen the next morning. Her dad's face brightened when he opened the door. "Did you bring the donuts?"

He held out a box. "Half a dozen glazed and half a dozen chocolate covered with sprinkles. Sorry I'm late. I stopped at

51

Home Depot for paint. How's the patient doing this morning?"

Sam glanced over his shoulder toward her bedroom door and then back. "Grumpy as a woman who needs a good dose of lovin'." He winked. "My Tammy used to get like that and I'd just love the mood right out of her. Know what I mean?" He elbowed Barclay as laughter rumbled and shook his pot belly. "Hell's bells, sometimes I thought she got sassy on me right on purpose." He elbowed Barclay again. "Are you catching my drift, son?"

Christ a mighty! What has the old man horned up this morning?

"Yes, I think I might. I brought along crutches and a boot. Thought they would make getting around easier for Molly."

Sam motioned him inside. "She's had her shower and is waiting for you to bandage her ankle. Looks like hell, so she does. Damn that worthless Wade. I never took him for a woman beater or I'd have talked her out of dating him. Did notice him getting moody of late. Jumpy. Always looking over his shoulder like he thought someone was watching him."

Barclay didn't know if he should believe the old man or not. "Wade won't touch her again, Sam. I can guarantee you that. Got a coffee pot here you can make us some fresh java while I wrap her ankle and adjust the crutches to her height?" He tapped the box the old man set on the counter. "There better be some damn donuts left when I'm done." The bald old man snorted and called him a bossy rascal. "You got a ballcap to wear while we work outside?"

"Got one in my suitcase. What jobs you got lined up for today? Wouldn't have an extra tool belt, would ya?" Sam acted like a kid on Christmas morning. Poor old coot appeared super eager to return to work, even if only for a day or two. Being with the guys would do him good.

"Do you know how to hold a paint brush and a roller?"

Sam's face split into a grin. "Do I know…well, hell's bells, there ain't been a paint brush made that don't fit this hand." He made painting motions as he talked. "Nor a paint roller, neither."

Shit, why did the old fart have to be so likable? Damn shame about his dementia. Bet Sam didn't even remember the inappropriate remark a father just made about his daughter needing a good loving. Barclay would think about it all day but, from what he knew about the disease and all the different ways it manifested itself, he doubted Sam even knew what he'd said.

His heart went out to Sam. How was he to keep his emotional distance with ol' Hell's Bells following him around like a pup needing affection?

Barclay knocked on Molly's bedroom door before entering. Half of her face was badly bruised and framed by long, wet hair she kept dragging a comb through. She wore a navy t-shirt, faded denim capris and an I'm-pissed-at-the-world scowl. He bit back a smile. The man who ended up with her would have a jewel if he treated her right.

Her ankle was most definitely swollen; in fact, nearly twice its normal size. "I'm not using crutches." She pointed to them with her comb and her lower lip pooched out like it needed him to suck on it then kiss the tingle away. Man, what he wouldn't give for one taste of her mouth. He imagined kissing her would be like savoring the sweetest edge of heaven.

He closed the door and leaned against it as he willed his breathing to settle into its normal pattern, and his erection to stop straining against his zipper. What the hell happened to his promise not to get emotionally close to these two? First, Hell's Bells and now that sexy plump bottom lip on this pistol of a woman. No female since Yvette had affected him the way Molly did. And damn if that didn't rattle him deep down where he'd shoved all the pain of the past few years.

"Two or three days walking with them won't kill you, Sugar. How's the pain today on a scale of one to ten?"

"Pain?" She tilted her head and pursed those lips that fascinated him so. "You want a freakin' number? Well, let me see." She shifted her legs so the soles of her feet touched. "My foot thumped in agony all night. My face was too tender to lay on my side and give my throbbing ankle some relief. My other side was sore where Wade kicked me so I couldn't lay on it. I crawled to the bathroom twice to pee and once to take my shower, stubbed my broken toe getting out of the tub and hobbled back to my bed through a cascade of pain-filled stars to get dressed. I'm hungry and grumpy. And if you call me Sugar again, so help me God, I'll rip your balls off."

"I'll take that as a twelve."

He sat on the bed and unwrapped a new Ace bandage. "If you're through complaining for the day, straighten your leg." Cranky, he could handle. If they were in a relationship, he'd smack her firm bottom until it turned a pretty pink. If that didn't take care of her crankiness, he'd use a clit massager and make her come over and over until his control was all she could think of.

A sob burst from her and his head snapped up. Indigo eyes rimmed with diamond-like tears stared at him. Trembling hands quickly rose to cover moist cheeks and her lips. She took huge gulps of air as if trying to regain control.

"Are you in pain?" He gently wrapped his hands around her forearms. "What's wrong, Sugar? Tell me. I can't help you if you're not honest." Lord, how he wanted to protect her.

"I...I'm being so freaking nasty to you."

"True, but I just took you for the snappish sort when you're hurting." He swept his hand over her damp hair, resisting the urge to kiss away her tears.

She pointed to her chest. "This is not the normal me. Listen to how grumpy I am. You've been nothing but kind...and I've been a total bitch. I'm sorry." The backs of her hands swiped her cheeks. "Lately I can't seem to say a kind word...or think a caring thought. All...all I do is complain. It's been so long since I've laughed or enjoyed a single moment until our time with Cassie and Quinn last night."

"They're some pair, aren't they? Those two have loved each other for ages. Long before Quinn was willing to admit it. If you liked being with them, then maybe you're starting your path of healing."

She shook her head. "I doubt it. Life seems such a damn chore since Mom died. I hate it that I've become this whiny, self-centered person. I don't even recognize myself anymore." Her face dropped into her opened hands and her shoulders shook.

If anyone could identify with how she felt, he could. So, what was it to be? Ignore her crying and take care of her ankle? Or envelope her in his arms and offer comfort?

Well, fuck it all to hell.

He pulled her close. "You cry, Sugar. Cry all you want. I got you." He rubbed her back in soothing circles a couple times before he realized what he was doing and stopped in a big hurry. While she sobbed, he embraced both her and her despair, trying hard not to concentrate on how good it was to hold her close. Her softness to his firmness was a heady combination.

Talk, fool, before you start touching.

"This crying is more than the sprained ankle. You're still grieving the loss of your mother, you know. It's only been a few months. Mourning takes time, Molly. And we all do it at our own rate, in our own way. No two people grieve on the same preconceived schedule." Hell, when did he start rubbing her back again?

"Grieving takes a lot out of you, Sugar. I lost four people I loved in the span of sixteen months. I got so I couldn't feel anything. Went to a really dark place. I've worked hard to dig myself out of that black hole." He exhaled a bark of laughter. "Hell, I'm still not back to the old me. Maybe I'll never reach that point. If I don't, who will I be?"

Her violet-blue eyes bore into his. "A man caring enough to help two strangers. A man with a heart big enough to hold a woman while she has a crying jag."

"In addition to the emotional trauma of losing your mother, you're watching your father die, mentally, day by day."

She nodded. "That part is harder, I think. Sometimes he says the most inappropriate things at the worst times. Things he wouldn't have said a year ago." She pulled out of his embrace, reached for some tissues from the box on her nightstand, and blew her nose. "He'll be fine and then forget something he's sure he should know. So he becomes argumentative. And these are only the early stages."

"No doubt your mother's sudden death has increased his decline. You know, it might help him to be more social. Let him hang around with some of the guys from the station on their days off. Hell, someone's always up to something. Remodeling. Fishing."

She nodded and reached for more tissues. "I know he hates being retired. We get on each other's nerves sometimes. Yet, you should have heard him cry the night Wade beat me." She shrugged and twisted the Kleenex in her hands. "Who knows, maybe I pushed Wade into Lacie's arms by being so disconsolate, so distant after Mom's accident."

"Now you know that makes no sense. Wade made a verbal commitment to you. If he truly had feelings for your maid of honor, he should have broken things off with you first. Done things the right way."

"You feel very strongly about how a man should treat a woman. Yet, you're divorced." She winced. "Oh God, that was insensitive." She raised her hands and let them drop. "See what I mean? I'm treating people as if their feelings don't matter."

He shrugged and started to unroll the bandage. "Goes with the territory. Now, lay back and I'll rewrap your lower thigh and foot." A yawn escaped as he set to work. "Sorry, late night bathing the dogs, but they do smell better."

"So the Massengill worked?"

"Like a charm. They weren't overly wild about me using the blow dryer on them, but I didn't want three wet dogs in my bed. Then Wolf and Jace were pounding on my door at six, coffee in hand and a cooler of beer, raring to go to work."

"Jace is the one with the baby boy?"

He nodded, trying to keep his eyes and fingers off her soft skin, which was damn near impossible. Better to just keep talking and wrap her foot like a madman.

"Wolf is the eldest brother and then Jace, followed by four sisters. Cassie is the youngest of the brood." He extended his hand. "Sit on the edge of the bed and I'll put this support boot on you. Between the boot and the crutches, you'll be able to get around a lot better. Might even reduce the level of your pain." He talked as he worked, concentrating like hell to keep his thoughts off how good she smelled and looked. "I brought donuts."

He fiddled with the straps on the boot. "Wolf and Jace are painting the inside of your bungalow so it'll be dry to move the furniture in later today." His gaze drifted over to the sexy red toenails on her other foot. His cock rose to take a peek too. "I brought donuts."

God, he felt like a moron. "I was also thinking you and your dad could spend the day at the bungalows. Bring your laptop and sit on the deck. I've got wooden chairs and a chaise lounge out there. You could stretch out on it, work a little and watch the seagulls. Get some sun. My girls will keep you company. Your dad will be surrounded by a gang of firemen who will have him laughing all day while we work. I'll make sure he sits and rests with Milt, another senior citizen we've kind of adopted. They're both about the same age. Milt's got a bit of a gas problem, but he's a decent sort. Comical as hell."

He inhaled a deep breath. Hell, he hadn't talked this much since, well forever. God, she smelled so good. "It's supposed to be in the low eighties today and sunny." He adjusted one of the Velcro straps a little tighter. "Winds will be coming from the southwest. And I brought donuts."

"Are you always this talkative in the morning?"

He helped her stand, supporting her with his hands at her waist. "Did you pack sunscreen?"

"Yes and you brought donuts." Her voice held a strong tinge of humor.

God, he couldn't look at her eyes. The floral fragrance on her hair and skin knit a spell of need around him so badly, he could barely think. If he looked into those eyes of hers or at that beauty spot he'd dipped his tongue over last night, he'd never be able to keep his distance. His fingertips had somehow slipped under her shirt, opening and closing on the softest skin he'd ever been lucky enough to touch.

"Why won't you look at me? Is my face that badly bruised?"

He kept staring at her feet, the Dom in him, fighting for control. His voice lowered and he hoped he didn't scare the crap out of her. Christ, she'd just been beaten last night.

Slowly he raised his gaze. "If I look at you, I won't be able to retain control. I want to kiss you where my fingertips are." She did a quick intake of breath. "And I want to kiss your lips until I memorize the feel of them." He fisted his hand in her hair and pulled her head back until her shocked eyes locked on his. "I've been trying not to look at you because, if I do, even the hounds of hell couldn't stop me from tasting you, and not one quick sip either. I'd make a feast of your mouth because damn if I didn't think about you all last night."

Her pupils were dilated and the pulse at the base of her neck had picked up speed. Was she submissive? Hell, he couldn't be that lucky. He rubbed his cheek against hers. "Baby, you've been through too much at the hands of a man. I promise I won't let anyone else hurt you while you're here."

"I...ah...I don't know what to say." Her voice was breathy and all but whispered submissive. "I'm not ready for another relationship."

"No. You're not, especially not with a man like me." He snatched the crutches and loosened the wing nuts to adjust their height to fit her body. "After the way you were treated by Wade, you need someone to cherish and adore you. You deserve no less, Sugar."

CHAPTER SIX

The firemen, who'd shown up to paint or tease each other to hell and back, were making quite the ruckus inside. It didn't take long for her dad to join in the laughter. Molly smiled as she turned her face toward the sun. Today would be good for him.

She exited out of her email programs. Both her personal and business email addresses had messages from Wade. All were sent since last night. The first couple were sweet…well, as sweet as Wade knew how to be. He'd asked her to call his cell so they could talk. Then they turned nastier to the point of threatening. How could she have missed this part of his personality? Was she that blind or just plain desperate to have someone in her life?

What about Barclay? Was she seeing him for the person he truly was? Or was her opinion of him also as skewed?

She didn't know how wise it would be for her to spend all day so close to him. He had a way of talking to her as if her pain mattered, as if it were okay for her to hurt and cry from the emotional agony of losing Mom. Was he being serious when he talked about wanting to kiss her? To hear him talk, he referred to some serious smooching. Her tummy fluttered. She might even enjoy that. She'd been shocked at what a turn-on it had been when he'd used a deeper, more commanding voice and pulled her hair.

I must be losing my mind. Dreamy eyes, a sexy-as-hell-grin and a kind heart, and I'm ready to fall into his arms. After Wade, I need to get a grip.

Maggie Mae, the black and tan Chihuahua who had snuggled between Molly's breasts for a nap, raised her head and licked Molly's chin several times as if the dog could read her mind and sympathize.

"You're as big a kisser as your master, you know that?" Caroline, the mixed collie, whined from her place next to the lounge chair, stood on her hind legs and pawed Molly's arm. "Yeah, I can see you've got his pawing down flat too."

Between her dad and Barclay, they'd had their luggage packed and the kitchen cleaned when they left this morning. Barclay went along with her to the manager's office and explained their situation. When the manager saw Molly's injury, she took pity on her and refunded a large chunk of her rent and security deposit to her credit card.

Of course, it didn't hurt that Barclay knew Zelda, the manager, and teased her terribly about her ten grandkids during the check-out process. Molly turned to exit the office, lost her balance, fiddling with the crutches, and fell, or would have if Barclay's quick reflexes hadn't stopped her mid-tumble. His deep whisper of "I've got you," had her hormones all a twitter, as her mother would have said.

He'd been there to take care of her, just like he'd been from the moment he came to her rescue during the rain storm when Wade had his grimy paws on her. Assertive, strong and protective. In many ways, he was very thoughtful. He helped her into the police station to sign the paperwork, finding her a chair and bringing the papers and pen to her so she could stay off her ankle.

"How's my patient doing?"

Barclay's quiet stride across the wooden deck startled her and she jumped. How did he sneak up on her like that? Tanned, muscled calves drew her attention as did his army green cargo shorts that bore a wide smear of lavender-blue paint across his crotch as if someone had taken a paint roller to him. He held a container of aspirin and an icy bottle of water. "I figured you were about due for some pain killers."

She pointed and struggled not to giggle. "First, you need to explain the lavender paint."

A faint blush spread across his cheeks. "Oh, that." He shrugged. "Damn Quinn and his sick sense of humor. I told the guys the biggest bedroom would get the blue paint like it was when your folks stayed here before. I bought pale yellow for the kitchen and living room and navy for the bathroom. I made the mistake of mentioning the smaller bedroom, the one you'll be staying in, would get a special color. Quinn got this smirk and claimed he knew the shade."

"How could he know that?" What had Barclay chosen?

"Quinn suspected I picked the color of your eyes." Barclay gazed at her, warmth oozing from his sea green orbs. "Asshole was right, of course. Quinn snatched the can and carried it into the smaller bedroom, pried off the lid and poured some into the roller pan. The smartass called me over and…" He motioned to the crotch of his shorts.

"Now, take your meds. In about an hour, we should be done inside. Then we're gonna move to the outside to start painting. I was thinking about removing your boot and carrying your lounge chair out to the beach. Give you a chance to soak in the sun and sand while we paint this side of the cabin."

"I don't want Dad out in the sun too long."

"I agree. I was thinking fifteen minutes or so and then we'll send him and Milt, the other senior citizen I told you about, to get some lunch for everyone. Milt still drives. He's aware of your dad's condition. He'll take good care of him."

"You're sure?" Taking her dad anywhere required keeping a close eye on him at all times. He would wander off and get lost. Though Milt seemed alert, like one of those nosy neighbors who never missed a trick. He was certainly friendly enough. Skinny, hollow chested and stoop shouldered with a thin fringe of gray hair around a bald crown to which about eight hairs were plastered with mousse or hair gel, one could easily tell he was a lonely man who adored these firemen. By their teasing, they adored Milt in return.

"Remember the team Cassie spoke of that rescued her?"

Molly nodded as she swallowed her aspirins and drank her water.

"Milt was one of our drivers. He'll keep a close eye on Hell's Bells. Don't worry."

She choked and sputtered on the liquid. "What did you call my dad?"

Barclay squatted next to her and scratched behind Caroline's ears as she inched across his thighs. His arm automatically went around the mixed collie and he leaned to kiss her furry head. "We all have nicknames on the squad. Some nice. Some not so nice." His smile spread and his dimples deepened. "Okay, few of them are nice. We call Milt 'Gas Ass' because he's got this flatulence problem. I think it's all the pork rinds he eats. After the fourth time your dad used the expression hell's bells, the guys snatched onto that and have baptized him with the moniker. Dan Wolford is simply 'Wolf' from his SEAL days. His younger brother Jace is 'Lil Wolf', and God how he hates it. We call Quinn the 'Comic.' We refer to Boyd as 'Tiny' cause he's so freakishly big with muscles. Noah, our captain, is 'Straight Up' because that's how he drinks his scotch.

"Although we've got four female EMT's in the ambulance division, we finally have a woman on our fire squad. Hell of a good fireman, or fireperson. We call Ivy Jo 'No Balls.' None of us were sure how she'd fit in, but Ivy Jo's great. Super nice person. Damn hard worker."

She did her best to ignore the pang of jealousy that jolted her heart. Was he seeing this woman? "And you're Ice Man."

"Now, yeah. Before my life went to shit, everyone called me 'Ghost' because of how quiet I can get in and out of places. It was a nickname left over from the Rangers."

"You were in the Army?" My God, Rangers were special ops and endured some rough training to earn the scroll they wore with honor. "My mom's eldest brother was a Ranger in Vietnam."

"Oh yeah? Wow, that was a rough time. A lot of us at the station were in one branch of the service or the other. It's not something we brag about because we know inside what we were, how hard we had to work to earn the title. We don't have a need to boast about any of it." The fingers of his hand not scratching behind Caroline's ears trailed across Molly's knuckles, creating sensual sensations. Now was the time to speak up.

"Back at the condo, you mentioned kissing me. Dad and I are only going to be here a little over two more weeks. Then we'll be gone. I don't do temporary flings, even though I am attracted to you. Heck, I imagine most women are."

He glanced overhead at some seagulls cawing and then aimed his gaze on her again. "Here's the thing, Sugar. I don't want this attraction any more than you do. Why open my heart to someone who can barely stand me?"

"I never said that." Oh dear, her snappishness had hurt his feelings. She never intended for that to happen.

Ice Man made an appearance. He shrugged, his sea green eyes now a blustery jade. "Hey, it is what it is." He stood and stretched his arms over his head, leaning first right and then left. His tight abs peeked out of the bottom of his faded red Crabby Bill's Seafood House t-shirt. "Too bad the heart has no common sense, huh? Because wonder of wonders, you've become the crack in mine."

"Crack? What do you mean?" The man was talking in riddles.

"The crack that lets in the sunshine. My heart really has been iced up for a long time." He stepped to the edge of the deck and whistled. All three dogs ran toward him. Lola, who really did resemble a twenty-gallon drum with legs, carried a sand-covered sneaker in her mouth and dropped it at his feet as if it were a precious gift. He tossed it back onto the beach before shoving his hand in his cargo shorts side pocket and pulling out some treats.

On command of the snap of his fingers, all three of his girls sat and waited, their behinds wiggling along with their tails.

To Molly's surprise and amusement, he sang a few lines of a song that contained each canine's name—"Sweet Caroline", "Whatever Lola Wants" and Rod Steward's "Maggie Mae." Each dog pranced in circles on her hind legs during *her* song and then came to him for a kiss, some petting and a treat. After all three were taken care of, he quietly stalked inside, never sparing Molly a glance.

As soon as he went inside, Lola ran down the steps and retrieved the sneaker she'd given him earlier. She brought it over and laid it next to Molly, who patted her head and told her she was a good girl. How did one treat a dog who was determined to gift someone, anyone, with this sandy shoe? She didn't want to hurt her feelings. Lola licked Molly's hand in gratitude.

The dogs sprawled out and chewed on their snacks, delivered with musical accompaniment. Molly had to admit, Barclay had a great singing voice. Truth be told, he seemed to do everything well—too well, she feared. No matter what she said, deep down inside, she was drawn to him.

Barclay grabbed his plastic bowl of paint and brush to coat the woodwork around the windows. Molly was right, of course. He had no business mentioning kissing her this morning, memorizing the feel of her lips. Hell, she was probably half-afraid of guys after Wade. Yet, Barclay was very interested in her. Her spunkiness mingled with her vulnerability was like his private siren's song, especially when he saw signs of a submissive in her.

Between losing her mother in an auto accident, watching her dad's mental capacity diminish and being stalked and beaten by an abusive bastard, was it any wonder she had her protective walls up? But this morning, as she'd cried in his arms, she was his. All his. And what a damn heady feeling that was. She'd cracked his heart open and allowed the warmth of the sun to seep in.

The experience told him one thing; he needed a woman. Not

just a one-night stand woman like he'd been using. No, he needed one of his own, someone to care for on a deeper level like he could do so easily for Molly. Something about her beckoned him, drew him in so tight he didn't want to let her go. He knew all the negatives of starting anything with her. She'd be leaving for Colorado soon and, if he allowed himself to get as close to her as he wanted, he'd have a rough time surviving her leaving. He couldn't endure another loss.

He grabbed a cloth to wipe the navy wall where he'd smeared white paint from the window sill. For just a minute, he stared off into space as the image of Molly's beautiful face floated through his mind. Those eyes. That smile.

After all this time, I finally find a woman who warms that cold spot deep inside and she'll be leaving in a couple weeks. Just my damn freakin' luck.

The teasing between the guys had settled down now that all the walls were rolled. They were painting the floorboards and the wood trim around the windows and doors. The more tedious work required closer concentration. Gas Ass and Hell's Bells had removed all the doors and taken them out front to lay over saw horses to coat with white. The two old coots were becoming thick as thieves, telling jokes and laughing. The more Gas Ass farted, the more Hell's Bells laughed, stomping his foot and adding a few toots of his own. It was a match made in senior ass heaven.

As soon as the window trim was dry, Barclay would hang white wooden blinds. Considering how rough this cottage had been when he'd started on it a couple months ago, he was pleased with the improvement.

The lime green cabin that sat at the entrance to the property, just inside the wrought iron gates, had always been the office with a separate outside entrance to a registration area. He'd already offered Milt the manager's position and the little green cottage that came rent-free with the job. So when the guys called him Gas Ass, Milt would quip, "That's Manager Gas Ass to you."

Barclay had already laid claim to the aqua cabin next to Molly's. He'd remodeled it first, putting more effort into it since he'd be there year-round, sipping coffee from his kitchen counter while he watched the waves roll in from the Gulf. He had a gas fireplace installed in the living room for cool Florida nights to augment the furnace. His girls loved curling around it, soaking up the heat.

He'd already started remodeling the fuchsia unit on the other side of Molly's, hoping to get the most of it done before he had to return to work, but it wasn't happening. Milt was moving in next week, so he'd be around to help a little. That would leave the yellow unit to fix-up, the three bedroom house where he'd been storing all the furniture from the cabins plus his building materials and tools.

Molly was sleeping when Wolf and Jace brought their equipment out to start painting the back wall of the unit. They told Barclay they'd work out front instead. Quinn and Boyd Calloway, one of the newer men on their team, carried the bedroom furniture from the yellow cottage into the apricot cabin. They set up the beds and wiped off the chest of drawers. Barclay placed the dishes and utensils in the dishwasher.

Recalling what Molly had said about the oars and fish netting over the master bed, Barclay rummaged around until he found them. The netting was too dirty to use, so while everyone else was busy doing trim work, he made a run to a little souvenir boutique up the road for fresh netting, star fish, shells and some pictures.

On impulse, he bought a hummingbird Tiffany-style lamp and a large picture of a hummingbird fluttering near bell flowers to hang over Molly's bed. There was also a pair of sunset over the gulf pictures he thought would look well on either side of the window in the living room. He made a quick stop at a department store for bed linens, blankets, bedspreads and new pillows.

By the time he got back to Gray's Cottages, the furniture delivery truck was pulling onto the property. Gray leather furniture and a gray and yellow floral print rug brightened the living room. White wooden table and chairs sat in front of the kitchen window that overlooked the driveway and fountain, if Barclay ever found the time to get it working. New mattresses and box springs sat on each of the beds.

So, while everyone chowed down on lunch out on the deck, after Gas Ass and Hell's Bells returned from their food run, Barclay laundered the sheets and hung the wooden blinds before positioning the oars, netting, colorful shells and a couple of big starfish over the bed in the blue room. He placed a sea picture over the chest of drawers and a light on the nightstand.

How could he convince the two of them to stay longer than a couple weeks? Time to give them a chance to see if he and Molly could develop a relationship. He quickly shook off that idea.

Why the hell should I care when they leave? Caring only brings along its best friend—Pain.

CHAPTER SEVEN

Once the guys were through eating, Quinn came over to Molly. "Ice Man said since we already knew each other you might feel more comfortable if I carried you down to the beach."

How so like Barclay to worry about her reaction to a strange man picking her up and carrying her around.

"Would I be in Wolf and Jace's way if I stayed here? The battery on my laptop's low and I'm charging it with the outlet beside the sliding glass doors."

"No, don't think so. Once they get the protective canvas spread out, I'll set your chair on the edge of it, as far as your cord will reach. Ice Man warned Wolf and Jace against getting any apricot splatters on his new deck. He's damn particular." He lifted her and swung her seat around so she could watch the guys work and be out of their way.

Quinn squatted next to her lounge chair, his arm draped over his one raised knee. "Cassie was really impressed with you. She was super excited you and the Ice Man met. My angel claimed she could sense you were melting his heart. We've all been concerned with the changes in him and, although we tried, could never reach him deep enough to bring him back to what he once was. Then you came along and Cassie claimed she could see small parts of her old friend again."

"How could that be when we'd only met a couple hours before? Your angel is quite the romantic." Molly hated to tell Quinn his wife was in love with love—and half loopy in the bargain.

"Yeah." He bore a rather sheepish expression. "The guys," he jerked his chin toward Wolf and Jace, "voted me to be the one to talk to you about Ice Man."

"What about him?" Did Barclay already have a girlfriend? If so, what difference would it make? She had no designs on him, although she did have a great fondness for how he'd treated her and her dad.

Quinn forked his fingers through his hair, cleared his throat and glanced at her. "I'm not happy to be the one to talk to you about this. I sometimes word things wrong."

"Ooo-kay." *Just come out with it, buster.*

He looked at the decrepit, paint-covered Nikes he wore and snorted. "Do you know my angel thinks I've thrown these perfectly good sneakers away? I've had them for years and, in her opinion, they should be burned. Hell, once I had to dig them out of the dumpster. The woman had the *nerve* to throw these classic shoes away." He glanced at Molly with a sheepish expression. "Bear with me. I'll get to the reason for my ramble soon. See, I've been hiding these sneakers in an empty plastic container of cat litter ever since."

Molly's gaze leaped from his raggedy Nikes to his self-satisfied smirk. Both of his big toes peeked out and, at one point, the worn rubber sole had separated from the nylon upper.

"Men have secrets, Molly. Some little like a raunchy pair of sneakers. Others have them so damn painfully huge, they hardly know how to talk about them. So, the man with no ability to deal with the agony of loss after loss after loss sometimes changes. Hell, it's harder for a man to communicate than it is for a woman. He internalizes everything and becomes someone totally different. Instead of being warm and caring, like the old Barclay we'd known for years, overnight he became the Ice Man." His eyes locked with hers.

"Do you think you ought to be telling me all this? Should a friend talk about another's secrets to an almost total stranger?"

She was really uncomfortable with Quinn's revelations.

In fact, she was ready to protect Barclay's privacy. His business was his. Did she want everyone to know her ex-fiancé had sex with her maid of honor? No, she did not. So, maybe there were things Barclay wanted kept private too.

"Wolf, Jace and I talked about this while Tiny was on the phone with his lawyer. We've been worried about Ice Man and his grieving. So, like I said, I was chosen to speak to you about helping him. You know, pay him some extra feminine attention. We can tell by the way he watches you, he's interested." He shrugged. "Just perk his spirits up. Help him feel again."

"Exactly what are you suggesting?" Her temper ignited like a pilot light.

"Come on to him."

"Come on to him?" Embarrassment boiled with anger. Had he just asked her to screw Barclay? Not that the idea was revolting, but she'd rather it be her idea, not one fabricated by a group of firemen.

"Well, yeah. Some hugging and kissing and touching." Quinn's eyebrows rose. "You know. Help him remember what it's like to feel like a man again."

She bolted from her reclined position and swung her feet onto the deck. "You all work with him. Maybe the best thing you guys can do is stop calling him Ice Man. All that does is remind him of all he's lost. Pull him back to who he once was by using his old nickname or his real name. You do him no favors by using that terrible moniker." She was so pissed, if she'd had on a long sleeve top, she'd have shoved up the sleeves, ready to do battle.

Why the hell were they coming to her with this? She had no right to nose into Barclay's life, pry into his private pain. And she'd not be a whore for any man, no matter how enticed she was by him.

Quinn's eyes widened...as did his smile. "Well, now, I do

believe my angel was right. She claimed Ice...ah...Barclay has met someone who, for whatever crazy reason, has cracked open the stone cold casing of his heart. I think maybe he's had an effect on you too."

"You have no idea what you're talking about." Barclay had been kind to her and her dad. That's all. It wasn't as if she was developing emotions for the man.

"Deny it all you want. Been there. Done that. You're going to worry the piss out of him. He'll fight you, but you could help bring back the old Ghost."

"Dad and I are only going to be here a couple more weeks." Besides, it wasn't her job to rescue some lost soul. She all but groaned. There she was, being nasty again. Barclay never hesitated to help her last night when Wade was dragging her to his SUV, *or* with all the other caring gestures he'd made.

"Your father's retired. Right?"

"Yes, with his dementia, he can't hold down a job." Her stomach started churning. She could tell where this conversation was heading. Some men were so transparent.

"And didn't you tell us last night you ran a web-design business? Couldn't that be done anywhere? Would staying on a few more weeks be such a hardship?"

Quinn's cell rang and he glanced at his watch. "That would be the wife. I left a note on her birth control pills this morning. Tied it onto the pack with a ribbon so she wouldn't miss it when she pulled them out of her purse after lunch." His smile was nearly ear to ear when he answered. "Hey, Angel, whatzup?"

He held the phone away from his ear and laughed as squealing and excited talk blared through the speaker. "Yes, Angel, finish out this month's pack and then stop." He glanced at Molly and winked. "Unless you'd rather wait. I mean, if you think another year would be better..." A loud, enthusiastic reply blasted back. "I love you too, sunshine." He ended the call. "God, I adore that woman."

For a minute, Molly nearly forgot how angry she was and

struggled not to laugh. "So the pole dance did it?"

"No, just her huge, caring heart. How can anyone resist?" He stood and stared off at the waves. "I was hiding from some emotionally bad shit, just like Barclay, when I met Cassie. It was love at first sight for both of us, but it took her three years to wear me down."

"I don't believe in love at first sight. I'm not even sure I believe in love. Not after Wade."

"Bastard did a real number on you, didn't he?" Quinn glanced at her over his shoulder. "Cassie taught me all people aren't alike."

He stooped beside her chair again. "Some of us go through emotionally rough times. Barclay used to put everyone's needs before his own. He was warm, funny and quick to help others. Then he lost four people he loved in about fourteen months and he just shut down." Quinn shook his head. "Man didn't give a damn anymore. I mean, he does his job same as he always did. Top notch. No errors. He's just cold toward most everyone. When Barclay talks to his co-workers, he sits off to the side—alone."

A wrench of pain squeezed her heart. She'd lost one person and could barely hold it together, yet he'd lost four and still managed to reach out to others. "That's not the man I met last night. Or the man who held me this morning while I cried. I'm a little confused by your description of him."

Quinn read a text that dinged into his cell. "That's because something about you touches the wounded part of him. He doesn't know it yet, but he'll soon crave it, just like I craved Cassie. Hell, I guess I always will. Good talking to you. I need to get back to work."

"Wait. Help me stand. I have a few opinions of my own to share with Wolf and Jace." Their ideas of her getting close to Barclay had her damned mad.

Evidently he could tell by the set of her chin, she was pissed. "Oh, we don't order the Wolf around."

She grabbed the crutches. "We is *not* me." She teetered on her crutches as she made her way across the canvas covering. "Wolf,

Jace, may I talk to the two of you a couple minutes?"

The two stopped painting and waited as if she were a pain in the ass they had to endure. Oh, if they only knew how much of a pain she could be when provoked—and she was mightily provoked right about now.

She shook a finger at Wolf and one crutch fell. "Friends don't talk about each other behind their backs. Nor do they butt in on their lives." She hobbled a couple steps closer on one crutch, her finger still waving in his face, all but batting his nose. "If you want the old Ghost back, then stop calling him the Ice Man. What a dumbass nickname to give a friend and then piss and moan because he's not healing from all he's been through. Where's your freakin' common sense?" Her voice rose with her question, almost to the point of shrieking.

"What in *the hell* is going on?" The Ghost—aka Ice Man—snuck behind her. By the harshness of his voice, it would probably be best not to look at him. He sounded a mite pissed himself.

"This is between me and the guys."

He stepped in front of her, his face red with anger or embarrassment. A muscle ticked in his jaw. In one swift movement, he scooped her into a fireman's carry. "No. I think this is between you and me. You don't talk about me to the men I work with?" With a yank of his wrist he opened the sliding glass doors and carried her inside.

"Ghost?" Wolf's commanding voice halted Barclay. "She was only being truthful."

"And protective," Jace chimed in.

Barclay whirled toward the guys and she got dizzy from the sudden movement. "Do I look like I need fuckin' protection? No one takes care of me, but me."

"You can't carry me around like this!" She pounded on his back.

"Well, Molly, looks to me like I am. Those men are my co-workers, my brothers. When we enter a dangerous situation, we have each other's backs. You show them and me some damned

73

respect." He carried her into the bathroom, locked the door and plopped her bottom on the vanity. He stepped between her thighs. "Now what the hell was that about?"

Fear banded around her head and terror quaked through her muscles. She tensed. "Don't hit me." Memories of Wade's beating flooded back because Barclay was so much stronger than Wade. He could really hurt her.

He exhaled an audible sigh. "Sugar." His hands cupped her face and his forehead touched hers. "Baby, I would never hit you." His cheek rubbed against hers. "Never. I promise you." Her fingers had curled into his t-shirt and he removed them, rubbing his thumbs over her knuckles. "You don't need to fear me. Even when I'm mad as hell. Now what was going on out there?"

"I told them to stop calling you Ice Man." She intertwined her fingers on her lap to keep from touching him, which she really wanted to do. "I told them you couldn't heal if you were reminded of your loss every day because they used that nickname. I told them they should go back to calling you Ghost or even Barclay."

Barclay leaned down so he could glare directly into her eyes. "Seems to me you were doing a lot of telling for someone who just came into our lives."

He couldn't have hurt her anymore if he'd have stuck her with a knife. From the moment he stormed into the drug store, he'd been ordering her about in one way or another. But that was okay was it because he was a man and men could issue orders. Women, who did, were referred to as bitches. Her earlier fear morphed into anger.

She pressed her *bitch* hand to his chest. "Step back, please, so I can get down."

"I'll help you." He reached for her waist and she raised a fist to his chin.

"Step. A. Way."

He raised his hands in a stop gesture and stepped back. She slid off the vanity and hobbled over to the door, unlocked it and headed for the deck. Her ankle hurt, but she was so mad, she didn't give a damn. All she wanted was some time alone to work through her resentment—like maybe two or three hours.

She limped past the sliding doors and across the deck. Wolf called her name and she shot him a go-to-hell scowl. Three painful steps down and she walked through the bent sea grass growing between the cottages and the sand before she headed up the beach—and damn the person who tried to stop her. She'd had her fill of testosterone for the month, maybe even the year. She was tired of sitting around and damn fed-up with macho orders.

It didn't take long for sand to gather in her boot, but what was a little discomfort along with the pain and seething anger? Quinn had almost asked her to become Barclay's red-hot lover to help ease his pain. But, hell, what did one expect from a guy who hid dilapidated sneakers in an empty cat litter tub?

Harsh words floated her way from somewhere, but she was too wrapped up in her own anger to glance over her shoulder. She just wanted time alone to think, put things in perspective and calm down.

"Molly! Molly, stop. You'll mess up your ankle."

Oh, doesn't Mr. You're-too-new-to-tell-us-what-to-do sound full of concern now that he's through insulting me? She did something she hadn't done since the tenth grade when Johnny Miles called her bubble butt—she extended an offensive finger over her head.

These sugary white beaches had always been her favorite spot in the whole world. Not home. Here, where the surf gently rolling in and out in an endless soothing sound. She loved the blues of the water and meandered toward its edge.

Barclay, the Ghost, to her surprise, lifted her off the sand and sat with her on his lap. How could he sneak up on her all the time?

His hand slid down her arm. "You feel warm. Are you using your sun screen?"

"Gee, have we known each other long enough for you to be concerned about my skin?"

"Don't get smart with me."

Two teen boys worked their way toward them, throwing a Frisbee. One pass came dangerously close to Molly's head and Barclay's hand snaked out to snatch it. In the process, he'd pressed his other hand against her head, bringing it to his chest for protection. The boys moved farther up the beach as he suggested, which was a good thing because one of them clearly needed to use a bit more deodorant. Surprisingly, the odor lingered after they left.

Barclay held her head against him and wrapped his other around her hips. "Why didn't you speak up for yourself earlier? Why didn't you tell me what those three knot heads had cooked up?" He pinned her with his sea green eyes, and she sensed by his refusal to drop her gaze he'd accept nothing but the truth.

"Because the conversation was between them and me." She jutted her chin and looked across the waves rolling in, their foamy edges like bubbly fingers trying to grasp the sand as if clutching for a permanent place to stay.

"There's more." There was sternness in his quiet voice.

"No."

"No? Then Quinn is going home with a jacked jaw for nothing, because damn if I didn't belt him when he told me what he'd suggested you do. Now why didn't you defend yourself with the truth…all of it?"

She glanced at him out of the corner of her eye. He'd think she was stupid, but he'd have no rest until she confessed it all. "I wanted to protect you from their thinking they had to fix you up with a woman, as if you aren't handsome enough to have any one you set your eyes on. Dammit, they pissed me off."

With his arms still around her, he lay on the sand and shifted her around so she was on top of him. "Molly, Molly, Molly, what am I going to do with you? Don't you know no one's ever taken care of me? My brothers in the Rangers and the firemen at the station, sure. But personally…I've always been alone, even when I'm taking care of everyone else. You worry me. You're worming your way right into the middle of my heart."

His lips covered hers, taking sips, each one growing longer and firmer. He grabbed her hair and pulled her head back. "There's something about you I find damned irresistible and I think it's the whole package. The silky hair, those stunning eyes, that sexy beauty spot and your soft lips and skin. And, yes, even all that attitude you're trying so hard to drag around on your shoulders. I'm not even going to mention all your incredible curves because I want to slowly drag my fingertips over every delectable inch."

She picked at a spot of dried paint on his shirt. "I can't believe I'm going to admit this." Her gaze bore into his. "Part of me wants that too, but Dad and I are leaving in a few weeks. I've never been one for quick flings."

"Good to know." He brought her face to his again. "You are so beautiful and appealing, I can't think straight." His lips were a breath away from hers. "Tell me to stop, Sugar, or I'm going to start a firestorm of emotion neither one of us will know how to handle."

She smiled. "I've always loved storms."

He jerked her face closer and her heart rate kicked up. "Then it's time you were introduced to a Florida hurricane." His tongue traced the outline of her lips. He kissed her, each one harder and needier than the one previous. As soon as his mouth covered hers and took control, her arms wrapped around his shoulders and she leaned into him, her breasts against his pecs.

Oh. My. God. Who knew a man could kiss like this? But what is that horrible smell?

Distracted by a waft of foul odor, she eased out of his embrace and rose on her hands. About twenty feet away, in the sea grass, lay a man with a bullet hole to his head. Dear God, from her position, it looked like Wade.

CHAPTER EIGHT

Molly went stiff in Barclay's arms. The color drained from her face as her eyes nearly popped out of her head. Puffs of air gusted from her mouth as if she were trying to say something but couldn't.

"What is it?" He craned his neck to look behind him at whatever had her attention. "Holy hell! Stay here!" He pushed her off, setting her on the sand. "Do you hear me? Stay here. The less footprints, the better."

Finally, her puffs formed a word. "Wade."

Barclay had never seen the man in the daylight, but the cargo pants were the same. Only now, Wade wore a black t-shirt. He slipped his cell from its scabbard and dialed 9-1-1 to report the murder.

"Wade's been shot. Are you calling for an ambulance?" She struggled to stand.

He pointed a finger at her. "I told you to stay there." As an ex-Ranger, he'd seen plenty of dead bodies. Wade was beyond needing an ambulance. As he gave the dispatcher the information, he stepped behind Molly and wrapped one arm around her shoulders in comfort. She'd known this man, loved him and, at one time, planned on marrying him. Plus, chances were she'd never seen a person with a bullet hole to his head and his heart. This incident had the hallmarks of a professional hit.

He ended the call, whistled and made some hand signals he knew Wolf, an ex-SEAL, would recognize. Wolf and Jace ran toward them.

"What did you find?" Wolf and Barclay walked to within eight or ten feet of the body while Jace held Molly in place.

"Two bullet wounds. Close range, I'd say. It's Molly's fiancé... well ex-fiancé."

Wolf stared at him for a beat. "What the fuckin' hell is going on, Ghost? He blows into town, beats her up and tries to drag her back to Colorado. Now, here he is, a victim of what looks like a gangland hit job." He glanced over his shoulder at Molly and lowered his voice. "He must have been one annoying sombitch to make enemies in Indian Rock Springs that quickly."

The wail of police cars and an ambulance grew louder.

"Wolf, call Boyd and have him bring Sam and Milt down here. Tell him to warn them first there's a dead body, but not to tell them who. Molly's dad is liable to not take this too well with his dementia." He clasped Wolf's shoulder and realized it had been ages since he'd done that. Why now in the presence of death?

"Ghost? Our plan of having Quinn talk to Molly was probably an asshole of an idea. For sure, the way he bungled it was a clusterfuck. But it feels damn good to have the old you coming back."

This was not a conversation he was ready to have; besides, Molly needed him. He dipped his head in acknowledgment and returned to the raven-haired woman who'd felt so good in his arms earlier.

Barclay slid his hand across her back and she turned from Jace's arms to his. Was it Barclay's imagination that she burrowed into his embrace unlike she had Jace's?

"I just can't wrap my mind around the fact that Wade's dead. He changed the last few months I knew him, but he was still a human being, you know?" She pulled back and tears pooled in her blue-violet eyes.

"Come here, Sugar." He pulled her closer. "I got you." She was a gentle-hearted soul for all she'd been through. Oh, she could be a spitfire; no doubt about that. But she still had enough kindness in her to cry over the death of the man who had beaten her twice.

Officer George Pauley hobbled down the walkway between two condos. His assistant, Darius Tomlin, followed carrying a CSI kit. Two medics pushed a stretcher and the town's longtime coroner, who appeared older than Zeus, brought up the rear, toting a leather bag.

George ordered his deputy to cordon off the crime scene area before he limped to where they stood. "Barclay, dispatch says you called this in. Want to tell me how you discovered the body?"

Molly hobbled forward. "I saw it...him first."

The officer pulled a pen from his pocket protector and his notebook from his other pocket. "Go on. Tell me everything."

"I smelled something foul. When we walked in this direction, it was faint, yet distinctive. But when we laid over here," she pointed to where they'd been kissing, "the odor was stronger. I rose to see where it was coming from and saw Wade's body." A couple tears raced down her cheeks and she brushed them away. "He...he looked like he had a bullet hole in his face."

"Wade?" George flipped through the pages of his tablet. "Is this the same man who attacked you last night? Wade Bender?"

"Yes, sir. Do you think he was staying in one of these condos? He sent me a lot of emails last night, but he never mentioned where he was staying."

The officer's eyes narrowed. "Did you erase the emails? Would they be on your phone?"

"No. I still have them." She tugged the cell from her denim capris. "I thought if I needed evidence to get a restraining order when I got back home, they might help." She thumbed through a few screens and handed her phone to George. "As you can see, they start out sweet enough. Then they turn threatening."

Barclay shifted a few steps so he could read over the police-man's shoulder. She'd never mentioned the messages to him. Not once. And damn, it galled. Wade's emails went from apologetic to demanding to insulting to maniacal to threatening. "Holy hell."

"Is this the first time you've seen these, Barclay?" George glared over his shoulder at him.

"Yeah. She never so much as mentioned them to me."

"Uh-huh." George glanced at Molly. "I'm going to need this as evidence. The time of his last email was two-ten this morning, so we know the murder occurred after that." He pulled a plastic bag from his pocket and labeled it. "Do you have a firearm, Ms. Devon?"

"Me? No. Dad has a couple rifles and shotguns at home. But we flew here, so he couldn't have brought one along. Wait," she glanced from George to Barclay, "you don't think I killed him, do you? I might have belted him a shot." She winced. "Maybe the word 'shot' was a bad choice.

"I've fired Dad's .22 rifle a few times at snakes, but I was jumping and hopping and squealing too much to ever hit one. I blew apart Mom's flower pot the first time I tried." She waved her hands. "Petunias and dirt everywhere. I once put a hole in our mailbox, blew apart Dad's "Popular Woodworking" magazine and the phone bill that the mailman had just delivered. But the day I shot Dad's truck in the radiator, he forbad me from touching any of his rifles ever again."

George and Barclay made eye contact before they burst out laughing. Wolf and Jace doubled over with laughter. One thing you could say about Molly, in her own way, she was a piece of work.

"Boss?" Darius was through taking pictures of the body and the surrounding area. "Looks like a gang killing. One shot to the head and two to the heart." He shook his dreadlocks back.

The coroner had somehow gotten on his aged knees. "High caliber bullets. Won't be able to tell for sure until I do the autopsy, but I'm guessing .357 or 9mm. Close range."

George glanced around the area. "Why here? This is a low-crime area. Was he running from someone or just mistaken for another person?"

Darius pointed with his gloved finger. "I can't figure out the meaning of the one shoe."

The coroner leaned over to get a closer look. "Dog. See its footprints?"

"Lola! Remember the sneaker she brought you earlier today?" Molly's mournful eyes settled on Barclay's. "After you threw it out in the sand, she ran after it and brought it to me. It's probably still on the deck."

"She's right. My dog, Lola, brought me a black leather sneaker I figured she found on one of her beach scavenger hunts. What is Wade's other shoe?"

Darius grabbed Wade's shoed foot and moved it around. "Black leather. Gucci. Top of the line. Man had expensive tastes in footwear."

Barclay nodded. "It was probably a match then. I didn't look at the brand name, I just tossed it back on the sand. You'd be surprised what Lola brings me...bracelets, shampoo, bikini tops, used rubbers."

"Eww!" Molly wiped her mouth. "Lola kissed me. How long ago did she find that used rubber?"

He couldn't help himself. He tried his best to look innocent. "Which one?"

She planted her hands on her hips. "Are you freaking kidding me?" She spat repeatedly on the sand, rubbing her lips so hard, it was a wonder they didn't wear off.

George palmed a snigger. "Darius, you wanna check the deck behind the apricot cottage? See if you can locate the deceased's other shoe. Don't know that we need it, but I like to keep everything together. Does your dog chew shoes on a normal basis?"

"No, but that would be the foot Wade kicked Molly with. Maybe Lola got a whiff of her from it. Labs have a great sense of smell and Lola's pretty smart."

Molly touched the officer's forearm. "If you think you can make it to the apricot cottage, I'll make you some lemonade. You can sit and question any of us." She spun toward Barclay. "Is that okay with you? It's easy to see his gout is bothering him."

"Sure." Her ankle would need to be rewrapped and the sand washed from her leg and foot. "Only if you let me help."

"That's mighty kind of you, Molly. There'll be another homicide detective here shortly. We'll be an hour or more before we haul the body away." George glanced around at the spectators gathering. "The vultures are circling." He shot the curious people a glare. "Stay on your side of the crime scene tape, folks."

Wolf was on the phone, pacing as he talked. He was no doubt filling in his wife Becca, a newspaper reporter in Clearwater, on what had happened. Knowing her, she'd come zooming into Barclay's cabin complex as quickly as she could.

Christ, the quiet neighborhood would soon be pandemonium.

Boyd, Milt and her dad joined the group. Molly stepped in front of her dad and slung her arms over his shoulders, whispering in his ear. His hand covered his mouth and his eyes went wild. Barclay joined the two in case she needed his assistance in dealing with the old man's confusion, evidenced by his clenched jaw and the way his fearful eyes darted around.

"It was your momma. Hell's bells, I knew she was up to something. I can't find her anywhere." His hand movements were jerky and nonsensical.

"Daddy, Momma's dead."

"You think I don't know that? Weren't we going to spread her ashes here on the beach? But I can't find them. Your momma up and left. I'm thinking Tammy got so pissed over Wade hitting you again, her spirit got loose and shot the bastard." His hand covered his mouth and a few sobs escaped. "Will they put her ashes in jail if they can find them?"

"Dad, are you telling me you've lost Mom's ashes?" She beheld Barclay's gaze for a few seconds as if she wanted to lean on him in the neediest sort of way. He wrapped his arm around her shoulders and drew her to him. Damn, she'd been through enough for any one person in a day's time.

"I...I didn't lose my Tammy's ashes. I just don't know where they are. They escaped from the box and formed a demon that shot Wade."

Officer George Pauley's jaw dropped.

Molly grabbed her father's forearms and gently shook them. "Think, Dad. Mom would never harm another soul. Walk over to Wade's body with me and tell me you believe the sweet, gentle woman we loved could do such a horrible thing."

The two stood side by side and stared at the corpse. The older policeman stood next to them, his watchful gaze obviously assessing them both. Molly slipped her arm in the crook of her father's. "Dad, if she were alive, she might have slapped Wade or cussed him out, but shoot him? Never. Reason it through. Remember all the years you lived with her. Did she ever display this kind of violence?"

Her dad stood there for quite a while and Barclay marveled at how she made the old man think things through. Finally, the confused man shuddered a sigh. "No. No, she never would. Alive or dead, my Tammy didn't have that kind of evil in her. I just get so confused sometimes."

Molly kissed her dad's cheek. "So do I. When I first saw Wade's body, I thought I was asleep, having a nightmare. Thank goodness Barclay was with me. He held me together." She faced the policeman. "My father has early dementia. I may have mentioned it to you last night. Talk to him about things that happened several years ago and he's fine. The last two years are fuzzy. The last few months, murkier still."

George nodded and held out his hand so the men could shake a greeting. "Sam Devon, my name is George Pauley. Did you ever teach your daughter to shoot a gun?"

Sam's face split into a grin. "Hell's bells, I tried. Lord knows I did." He shook his head a time or two. "See, we live near the mountains and snakes are a problem. I tried showing her how to fire at a serpent, but between the fear of shooting her own foot and being attacked by the dang snake, she couldn't stand still long enough to hit one.

"The day she blasted a hole in my Dodge Ram pick-up, I took all gun privileges from her. Word got around, and next thing we knew, there was a cartoon made to look like a wanted poster in the local paper. It had my truck lying on its back with its wheels in the air, smoke rolling out from under the hood." He laughed and slapped his leg. "Beneath the cartoon was 'Wanted. Truck Killer. If armed with a .22, do not approach or drive your vehicle near the suspect.' Folks is still laughing about it. They called her 'Truck Killer' for nigh onto a year."

"George, if you have investigative procedures to do for a while, I'm going to take Molly to the cottage and clean the sand off her bad foot and rewrap it. Come when you're ready to talk." He glanced around at all the guys. "Each of us will be there until you clear us to leave." He wrapped her hand in his. "Come on, Truck Killer."

"As soon as I take a shower, I'm going through Dad's things to look for Mom's ashes. They were in a heart-shaped walnut box. We put the container in his suitcase together and talked about how she used to sit on the beach and say, 'When I die, cremate me and spread my ashes here at this place I love so much. Do it at sunset. I love the sunsets here.' So we were sure we were doing the right thing. Now he's talking about losing her ashes."

"Maybe he was just confused, Molly. Seeing Wade dead had to be a shock to him. It probably took him back to when he lost your mom. We've kept him too busy to misplace anything."

"God, I hope you're right. I don't need this on top of everything else." They slowly headed for the peach cabin. "Why, Barclay? Why would anyone want to kill Wade? He was an ass at times, but aren't we all?"

"We don't all beat women."

She stopped dead in her tracks. "Barclay, you...you didn't...I mean, you didn't kill him, did you?"

"Hell no, I didn't shoot him. If I didn't kill my old man for all he did to my mother, I sure as hell wouldn't have ambushed a guy I didn't know, no matter what I feel for the woman he beat up."

She nodded as if she agreed. "I'm sorry. I'm in shock, my ankle hurts and I'm worried about Mom's ashes."

"Why didn't you say something?" He scooped her into his arms and strode toward the cottage. "First order of business, when we get back to your place is aspirin. Then, Sugar, what I'd like you to do is take a hot shower and put on clean clothes. After that I'll rub lotion on your bad ankle and foot and rewrap it. I only hope your walk on the beach didn't undo all the resting today did to help it heal."

She tugged on his hair. "I'll have you know I'm no weakling."

He grinned and kissed her forehead. "No, it takes a strong woman to kill a truck."

CHAPTER NINE

Wade was dead. Molly's mind was awhirl with it all. On one hand, she'd never have to fear his stalking or beating her again but, on the other, he was a human being she'd once loved. She'd given him her virginity. The memories of the man he used to be warred with the person he'd evolved into this past year. What had caused him to change? Why was he murdered and by whom?

More importantly, had her dad misplaced her mother's ashes? He hadn't mentally declined to where he couldn't choose his own clothes for the day. Therefore, she'd had no reason to get into his suitcase, the last place she'd seen the pretty heart-shaped box they'd chosen at the crematorium.

Barclay carried her through the living room toward her bedroom. She glanced around at the gray leather furniture, the floral rug, the blinds and pictures. "Wow. This is the first I've seen the rooms furnished. The place looks great. I can't believe how much you all got done."

"Your room is ready for you. Sit on the edge of the bed while I get you some water and aspirin."

Her little bedroom was beautiful and feminine. "Oh, Barclay, this is wonderful. I love the paint color and the white eyelet coverlet." She gave a small gasp when she noticed the humming-bird picture above the bed and the matching glass Tiffany style lamp on her nightstand. "How did you know hummingbirds were my favorite?"

"You had one on your keychain. Where's your aspirin?"

"In my purse on the closet shelf." He'd taken notice of what she had on her keychain? Most men weren't that observant.

He pulled both her purse and her suitcase down. "Dig out some clean clothes for tonight. Something warm. Sweats, if you brought them. I'll get you some water."

Once she took her meds, he plopped her clean clothes on her lap and carried her into the bathroom and sat her on the commode lid. "Throw the bandage away once you get it off. I have plenty of new ones I picked up at the drug store when I was out earlier. Are you sure you'll be okay in the shower? There are safety bars to hold onto."

"Yes, I'll be fine, once you leave so I can get undressed." She was still so aroused by their earlier time on the beach, if he touched her, she wasn't sure she'd have the willpower to say stop. More than likely, she'd start pulling his clothes off too. What would it be like to have sex in the shower?

"If you're sure. I'm going over to my place to check on the girls and take a quick shower too. Then I'm going to buy you a cell phone to replace the one George took. We need to be able to reach each other. Once I get back I'll wrap your ankle again and we'll make lemonade together. I'll call an order in to Crabby Bill's for supper. We can eat while we talk all this out. Sound like a plan?"

She placed her hand on his face and he propped his whiskered cheek against it, almost as if he needed tenderness from someone. "Sounds fine to me, Barclay. Thank you for all your kindnesses, big and small. You're very special."

His eyes darkened with desire and his head leaned toward hers. "I know I should have sympathy for a man who died, but if it means you'll be safe that's all I care about." His lips made contact with hers, and heat and shivers sprinted through her system. She had no clue which reached her toes first...but, *oh*, what a race it was.

Molly was rubbing lotion on her neck and arms when the front door opened. "Sugar, are you decent?"

"Give me a sec!" She grabbed her sweatshirt and tugged it over her head before reaching for her comb to fix the mess she'd made of her hair. "You can come in now, I'm on the bed."

"Now, those are words a man lives to hear." Barclay's broad shoulders almost filled the doorway and nearly took her breath away. He was the only man who could make a pink sweatshirt with the words "There's strength in Pink" written in black look sexy. The long sleeves were pushed nearly to his elbows, showing off his veined, muscular forearms.

His sweatpants were black with wide, pink, side stripes. He had on black flip-flops adorned with a pink ribbon. What kind of man would wear an outfit like that? He turned to tell his dogs, who'd followed him in, to lay down. Written across the back of the shirt was "Fire & Marine Rescue Station 32 supports Breast Cancer Research."

He sauntered into her bedroom, his wide shoulders shifting back and forth slowly as he moved. Oh yeah, pure sex in pink and black sweats. The material bunched and stretched over his muscles as he sat on the edge of her bed. "Feel better after your shower, Sugar?"

His fingers were pushing buttons on a purple phone. "Now, I'm number one in speed dial. My land line is number two. Milt is number three. I'm also programing in all the wives of the crew so you can keep in touch and your dad's new doctor." He laid it on the night stand. "There, you're all set. Now, lay down." He wrapped his hand around her bottle of lotion and he read the label. "Roses and lilacs bouquet. It suits you and drives me freakin' out of my mind every time I smell it."

Lola jumped on the bed and sniffed Molly's side where Wade had kicked her. The black lab licked the area a few times, whined and laid her head across the bruise. Lola cast sorrowful black eyes on Molly.

Molly reached to pet her. "She knows. Did you see that? She went right to where I'd been kicked and kissed it almost in healing. She must have smelled me on the toes of Wade's shoe and worked it off his body to bring to you." Lola crept farther up the bed and licked Molly's chin. "What a good girl you are." She kissed the top of Lola's head.

"Just my luck to have a dog who gets more of your lovin' than I do. How am I ever going to make any progress where you're concerned with intuitive Lola around, showing you affection?" The corners of his mouth turned upward slightly as if he were fighting a smile. "Pull your sweatpants up so I can rub this lotion in and wrap a new bandage around your ankle."

"I can put the lotion on myself."

He stared at her with one eyebrow arched and the muscle in his jaw bunching displaying his determination. "I *will* put the lotion on you. Wouldn't you take care of a friend who was hurt?"

"Yes, of course, but you don't kiss me like a friend."

He squeezed a quarter-sized glob onto his palm and rubbed them together. "Well, with all the commotion you were making over Lola's kisses, I wasn't so sure I'd been kissing you properly." With gentle kneading movements, he rubbed in the cream and she wanted to purr. He tilted his head to the side. "I mean when a dog gets more complements than a guy, it downright hurts his ego."

The man had a way of making her laugh. "It's the texture of the dog's tongue. It gives me the warm and tinglys."

He entwined his fingers in hers. Passion darkened his eyes as he pushed their joined hands into the pillow on either side of her head. He leaned in so his lips nearly caressed hers as he spoke. "You might be comparing apples and oranges, Sugar. Maybe you should see what magical hot tinglys my tongue could give you. How many times I can make you climax and have you screaming my name every time you do."

She squeezed her thighs together where desire pooled. *Dear God, he's talking about oral sex.*

Lola squeezed her nose between their faces and licked Barclay's freshly shaven cheek before she licked Molly's chin.

"Don't you lick my mouth, dog. I know where your lips have been, you old condom chaser."

Barclay's chuckles grew to giggles and, after he rolled onto his back, they bloomed to full-out deep laughter. He hooked his arm around Molly's head and brought it to his shoulder. "Oh, Sugar, is there any way I can talk you and your dad into staying here for a longer period of time? I haven't enjoyed being with anyone as much as you for a long time, if ever. Between you and Hell's Bells, I feel like…well, hell…I just feel again."

Oh, if only they could stay. Maybe she could talk her dad into another month. She wanted more time with this man…much more. "Has the Ice Man died?"

"Fuckin' A, especially with you shaking your finger in everyone's face and threatening them if they used it. Woman, you can be fierce, at times. I bet that poor truck trembled on its tires when you aimed that .22 at it."

She straddled him and placed her hands on his cheeks. "Deal. I don't call you Ice Man and you don't call me Truck Killer. Sugar is fine, but only from you."

He wrapped his arms around her and rolled over, nuzzled her neck and sucked on her earlobe. "That's a deal I can agree with, and you are so right. I catch any man calling you Sugar," he smacked her bottom once, "…and I'll come after him so fast and hard, he won't know whether to shit or go blind." He kissed her again, ran his tongue over her lips and, as she opened her mouth, he swept in and took control. His hands fisted in her hair and he rubbed his erection against her.

Sweet Lord, the sensations.

Caroline jumped on the bed, too, and Maggie Mae whined from her short-legged position in the world. Barclay extended an arm and scooped her up.

"The night I make love to you—and I *will* make love to you—the girls are getting locked out of the room. Come on, let me wrap your ankle so we can get the lemonade made before everyone gets back and wonders what we've been up to." He gave Molly a quick kiss. "Wear your hair down for me, Sugar. I don't think I've ever seen a woman with prettier hair than you."

After he got her foot wrapped, he took her boot outside to pound out the sand while she combed her hair and applied some lip gloss. He stepped into her room and stilled. "Oh, now that was a bad move."

"What?"

"Putting that shiny stuff on your lips to make them stand out. As if they don't draw my eyes all the time, anyway, unless you're walking away from me. Then it's your fine behind and the fall of your hair that makes me want to go wild. Let me get this boot on you before you start walking around again." He adjusted the Velcro straps. "On a scale of one to ten, what is the pain level of your ankle after your walk on the beach?"

"My ankle? A five, maybe." *My female parts crying out for your attention? One hellacious strong fifteen.*

"What are you thinking?" Barclay tilted his head and smiled. "A pretty blush just crept from your neck to your cheeks."

"Don't you give me that smile." The last thing she could tell him was how wet he'd gotten her panties or how hard her nipples were.

"What smile, Sugar?" He slid her pants leg to her knee.

"The one that says 'if I turn on the masculine charm I can get whatever I want.' Besides, my thoughts were private."

His lips curved into another masculine "I got you, babe" smile and he leaned his face against her skin, pressing kisses from her ankle to her knee. Her toes curled tightly in response and her nipples hardened to painful points. "What were you thinking, sweetheart?" He nipped the flesh at her knee and she yelped. Even so, she found she loved every way he touched her—tender or rough, which was hard to understand after Wade's abuse.

Lola barked and licked Molly's knee where Barclay had gently bit her.

He jerked the leg of her sweatpants down. "Lola's never attached herself to someone this quickly, not even me. She'd growl, yet give me a pitiful-eyed stare that snared me when I found her wondering the street, hungry and scared." The edges of his lips curled upward and his eyes sparkled. "Hell, you could see her ribs."

Something in the tone of his voice made her lean across the bed in hysterics. "How...I mean...does...does she even have ribs now?"

Barclay wrapped his hands around her calves and leaned his head against her unhurt leg again as he laughed. "Sure...twenty... twenty gallon drums...ha...have ribs."

The more they laughed, the funnier it all seemed. The dogs jumped, spun and barked in canine joyful abandon. Molly wiped tears from her eyes. "I haven't laughed like this since I was a kid." She sat and stared at Barclay who gazed up at her with those sea green eyes. She fought the urge to sigh. *God, he is so handsome.* "Why did you let her get so big?"

"She needed the security of knowing she'll always have food. Just like you need the security of knowing not every man will hurt you. We aren't all like Wade, Sugar."

Slowly Barclay was teaching and showing her that. At first, she'd been afraid to believe his kind behavior. Now, she was beginning to trust it and to depend on his virtuous innate nature.

He stood and reached for her crutches. "Are you ready to go to the kitchen?" He wrapped his arms around her waist. "You make me happy, care again and be just plain silly." His large hand cupped the back of her head. "What in the hell will I do when you leave?"

"We've only known each other a short time but, in a way, it's like we've always been a part of each other's lives. Senseless, isn't it?"

"You're a permanent type of woman, Molly. I'm going to be honest and tell you I'm struggling with that. I keep reminding myself you'll soon be leaving. It's my body that doesn't want to listen. Believe me, if I could talk you into staying, I would. I like both you and your dad. I'd love having the two of you in my life."

93

He grimaced. "And, yes, I know I just contradicted myself.

"Crazy, isn't it, Sugar? But the pair of you touch a part of me that hasn't been affected in years."

CHAPTER TEN

Reading Molly wasn't hard. Her mind was on her mother's ashes. Even as she quietly washed, squeezed and sliced four lemons to add to the powdered mix of two pitchers of lemonade before Barclay took them from her and set them in the refrigerator.

"If you sit on your dad's bed beside his luggage, I'll put his clothes in the drawers for you."

"Thanks, I need to start looking for mom's ashes. I won't rest tonight if I don't know where they are."

While Molly handed him piles of underwear, socks, pants and shirts, desolation filled her eyes. "We'd put the wooden heart urn in the right corner of this suitcase. Where would he have moved it?" She even went through his shaving kit even as she kept saying, "I know it would never fit in here."

Meanwhile Barclay lay on the floor with a flashlight and looked under the bed, behind the headboard, in every nook and cranny of the closet and behind and beneath every piece of furniture. "Sugar, I'd say this room's clean. I hear the guys talking. Their onsite investigation must be over. Do you want to pour the lemonade while I stick your dad's suitcase in the closet? We'll look more later."

Christ, where could the old man put the ashes and what will it do to Molly if they never found them?

Barclay took one look at her dejected demeanor—her slumped

shoulders and thinned lips—and both his heart and his arms opened to embrace her. "Come here, Sugar." He kissed her hair, her cheek and then her neck. "I got you. I won't give up looking until I find her." Damned if he didn't mean it. This woman's peace of mind, her happiness, her well-being were suddenly all-important to him. He hugged her tighter and rested his face in the crook of her neck, inhaling her essence, never wanting to let her go. Because for the first time in too long to recall, he needed someone…and that someone was her.

Christ, in less than twenty-four hours I've fallen in love.

Well, hell, if that didn't make a fella's balls draw up. No. No, this can't be. She was only passing through his life and he was lonely and horny is all. He always did care too much for others.

One thing about being the Ice Man was the emotional isolation it provided. Perhaps he needed to close himself off again.

He pulled out of the embrace. She placed both of her hands on his cheeks and stared deep into his eyes with hers that, at this moment were more lavender than blue. "You are one of the kindest men I think I've ever met."

Prickles of unease jittered up his spine and skipped over his skin like a bad hip-hop rash. Oh fuck, he was in some deep passionate shit, because he wanted her. Craved her like he'd never desired anyone else.

Barclay called Crabby Bills for a large take-out order while Molly made sure everyone had something to drink, including the dogs. The only law enforcement officers on the deck were George and Darius. Wolf's wife Becca had joined the group earlier to report on the story. She was a stunning redhead and it was obvious Wolf adored her the way he kept kissing her hand and whispering things that made her blush. Their love for each other was so solid, one could almost reach out and touch it.

Everyone was quiet as they watched the sunset, almost as if they were all talked out or lost in their thoughts of Wade's dead body.

The colors of the sunset were gorgeous and vibrant. All the adults had their chairs positioned so they could enjoy the reds, purples and oranges as the giant ginger ball slowly slipped beneath the cover of water's edge for its nighttime rest, or so it seemed. Barclay had lit several tiki torches to chase away the impending darkness.

Once the food order arrived, everyone circled the table. George had talked to Jace, Boyd and Milt at the crime scene and told them they were free to leave. Jace and Boyd headed for home, but Milt was too nosy or lonely to miss any of the conversation and stayed. Wolf and Becca lingered so she could work the story. But it was plain to see, the main people the police wanted to talk to were Barclay, Molly's dad and her.

To her surprise, Barclay slid his chair amid everyone else's, grabbed her hips and set her on his lap. No one reacted except for her dad who fought a grin and winked at her.

Becca, who was on Wolf's lap in the next chair, smiled and whispered, "Get used to it. Firemen have a knack for getting who they're going after...whether it's someone in a burning building or a woman they want for themselves."

"Dad and I are only staying a couple weeks."

Becca held her sandwich partway to her mouth. "I'll bet you a new pair of shoes Barclay changes your mind." She leaned toward Molly. "I know this fabulous shoe store."

Wolf squeezed his wife. "Did I hear you mention the 'S' word?"

Becca pursed her lips for a second or two. "I've only just met Molly. I wouldn't be talking to her just yet about sex."

Wolf leaned his head back and laughed. "Oh, wife of mine, don't think I can be so easily led astray. You were talking shoes. Your voice had that new-leather breathy quality to it."

"I was thinking about the leather blindfold I bought today but if you want me to return it, I will." She pursed her lips and trailed her finger up his chest. "They'll probably charge me a restocking fee, though."

Wolf glanced around Becca toward George. "Officer, are you

through with me? My wife and I would like to go home now."

Becca took the first bite of her sandwich. "Wolf, I haven't eaten yet. It would be rude to leave without enjoying the food Barclay provided." She winked at Molly and grinned.

Wolf set Becca on her feet and stood. "Ghost, thanks for the grub, but we've gotta run. See you at the station in the morning." He smacked Becca's bottom. "You just have to tease me like that don't you? Eat your damn sandwich in the car." They wrapped their arms around each other's waist and said their goodbyes before they hurried off.

Geesh, what is it with these firemen and their kink?

Quinn admitted to handcuffing Cassie to the headboard when he proposed. Cassie pole danced for him. Wolf and Becca got all hot and bothered over a new leather blindfold...and just which one it was for, she didn't even want to know. She glanced at Barclay out of the corner of her eye. Was he into kink too? If so, what? And maybe what she thought of as kink was part of normal sexual activity and she was too inexperienced to know it. Wade was a hop on-hop off kind of lover. Sometimes he rolled over and went to sleep. At other times, he'd tell her to get dressed and leave since he had an early meeting in the morning. She doubted one could compare Wade to Barclay.

The soft shell crab sandwiches were the best Molly had ever eaten. Evidently the girls thought so, too, since Barclay had gotten them each one. And the baked beans, cole slaw and two gallons of sweet tea he'd also ordered were fabulous.

George crumpled his sandwich wrapper and slipped his notebook and pen from his pocket. "Where did you meet Wade, Molly?"

"At the University of Denver. He was studying computer systems management and safety, how to spot hackers, that kind of thing. I was studying web design. Even though I was a year ahead of him, we had a few classes together. He seemed on the fast track to nowhere."

George jotted a few notes on his pad. "Why do you say that?"

98

"He never worked at one place longer than six months, sometimes only a month."

Her dad leaned in George's direction. "The kid was one of them mouthy know-it-alls. He could walk through your police station a couple times and tell you how everything ought to be rearranged, organized and run. Yet, he wouldn't know shit about police work. Ever meet the type? Kid had no respect for experience."

Molly jumped into the conversation before her dad drew more attention to himself as a suspect. "Wade started his own computer repair business, cleaning out viruses and male ware. He also installed customized bookkeeping programs for small businesses and showed them how to keep their books up to date."

"Did he set up your book system for you?" Darius poured more sweet tea into his cup.

"No, I'd taken a couple classes in accounting. I did my own bookwork. I like to know where every penny is at all times."

"My girl's too smart to let the likes of Wade Bender near her finances. He was a likable fella at first. Gentle, respectful, interesting to talk to, but eight, ten months ago, he started to change his ways."

George stopped writing. "How so, Sam?"

Molly held her breath and Barclay rubbed his hand up and down her back. "It'll be okay. No matter what he says." His lips moved against her ear. His reassurance eased her somewhat frazzled nerves. One just never knew what would tumble out of her father's mouth next.

"He started talking big dreams, expensive plans. Yet when we went anywhere, he was tense and always looking around as if he thought he was being followed. Wanted to sit against the wall in a restaurant so he could watch all the comings and goings. Tammy said he reminded her of a wannabe gangster. She wasn't crazy about our girl marrying him." Her dad shook his head. "She said she was going to talk to our sweet Molly about putting off the wedding for a while, hoping he'd get tired of waiting and move on."

George shifted in his wooden deck chair, wheezing with the effort. "Did you notice a change in Wade, Molly?"

"Yes, but in different ways than my parents. He became more demanding about me losing weight. Insulted me more. Played mind games with me, telling me if he threw me aside no one else would want me. I was foolish enough to believe him."

Darius smiled. "There's nothing wrong with the way you look. Most men like a woman with soft curves."

A low growl emanated from Barclay's throat and his hold on her tightened. Goodness, was he jealous over what the deputy said? The end of February, when they planned to return home, looked less and less appealing. Could she and Barclay develop a romantic relationship?

Lola leaned against Molly's sore leg and licked her wrapped ankle, then she rested her chin on the edge of Barclay's thigh and turned those woebegone eyes on Molly. Her hand automatically went out to pet the black lab. Maggie Mae, the Chihuahua, had somehow found her way onto her dad's lap and he petted the dog.

"Who did Wade hang out with? Any new friends?" George looked up from the notes he took as they talked.

Just my Maid of Honor.

"What friends he had were all from college. No one new that I knew of."

Barclay entwined his fingers in hers. "What about that remark he made about wanting your car keys?"

"Now, see, I don't remember that. I was so scared with his tying me up and hitting me, I don't remember what he said to me. My mind just kind of went blank."

George pierced Barclay with a scowl. "I recall you mentioning that when we walked down the street to where he attacked her. Refresh my memory."

"Wade told her he wanted her damn car keys."

She looked at the officer and turned her palms upward before letting them fall. "But we'd rented a car. Why would he want the

100

keys to our rental?"

George reached for the last sandwich. "Maybe he meant your car back in Colorado. You'd have those keys, right? Did you drive to the airport or did he take you?"

"I drove. By then, we'd broken up."

"Why was that?" Darius wiped his mouth with his napkin.

She did not want to share this embarrassing bit of personal information. "He and my maid of honor were having an affair. The keys are in my handbag." She went to stand, but strong hands caught her waist. "Stay here, Sugar. I'll go in and get your purse." Barclay kissed her head and sat her back on the chair. Within minutes he returned with her bag and sat it on her lap. While she searched for her keys, he gathered up the wrappers and napkins from the table, shoving all the supper trash into a bag.

She wrapped her fingers around the keys and pulled them out. "Here they are." She handed them to George.

He hefted the key ring in his beefy hand. "Lot of keys here. Can you identify them all?"

Molly leaned over and touched each key as she named them off. This smaller ring on my hummingbird holds the ones for this cottage and the rental car. The sturdier one holds my SUV key, the front door key for the house, back door key, this is for the filing cabinet in my home office, the one for the garage, dad's truck key..." she pointed to the last one and stopped. "May I look at those keys closer? I don't recognize that one."

George dumped them in her outstretched hand and she studied the last key. What was it for? She went over each key on her ring another time, hoping repeating their use would help spark her memory. Nothing. "Dad, could you come here and look at these? I've got one here I don't know what it's for."

He ambled over, Maggie Mae tucked in the crook of his arm. Molly named off each one and then pointed to the unknown key. "Do you know what this is for, Dad?"

"Reminds me of my lock-box key at the bank. You know where

101

I keep it, right girl? Taped to the bottom of my top desk drawer. You might need it someday. Your name's on the lockbox, the same as Tammy's, so you'll have no trouble accessing its contents. This ain't the key to her little car, is it?" His confusion was coming back. "No, her key had an 'H' on it. Remember? Maybe we should ask her." He looked around as if searching for his deceased wife.

Milt stood and hooked his hand at her dad's elbow. "Hell's Bells, we put in a long day working. I don't know about you, but I'm beat. A shower and I'm crawling between the sheets. Maybe it's time you did the same thing. Let these young pups sit out here and talk." He tweaked some gas and Darius's head whipped around to shoot him a glare.

"Sounds like a good idea to me, Gas Ass. You coming over tomorrow?"

"I'll be here about nine. I need to take Killer for his walk first."

Molly stood and reached for her crutches. "Dad, Barclay helped me unpack your suitcase. Let me show you where all your stuff is and where the clean towels are in the bathroom. It's been a long time since you worked as hard as you did today."

"True." Her dad nodded. "But hell's bells it was fun. Damn, it was good to be useful again."

"Molly, would it be okay if Darius came by tomorrow for the key you can't identify? Maybe we can do some research. See where it belongs. I'm ready to head for home, too, this damn gout is killing me. Say, you wouldn't know where Wade did his banking?"

"At the Wells Fargo in Breckinridge."

Barclay took her hand. "Sugar, why not give Darius the key now and save him a trip out here?"

"Sure. That makes sense." She slipped the key from her key ring and laid it in Darius's outstretched hand that immediately closed over her fingers. Damn, he was bold.

He extended his business card with his other hand and pressed it in her empty one. "In case you need to reach me for anything, Molly. Sometimes you recall things later. You know, little details."

"Unless you want your fingers broken, you damn well better let go of hers." Barclay's warning was low and menacing.

Darius had the audacity to smirk. "Are you threatening a law enforcement officer?"

"George, do all your officers make it a habit of touching women any way they please? Don't make me have to teach this slimy bastard some manners. She sat on my lap all evening with my arms around her. Any man with a lick of common sense would see she was off limits."

"I haven't heard her side of things yet." Darius laughed.

She jerked back. "You touch me again, officer, and I'm filing a complaint."

George stepped between the three of them. "Darius, get in the squad car and bring it up here so I don't have to walk back down the beach." After the deputy stalked off, George shook his head. "I haven't a clue what all that was about. I've never known him to act that way.

"Molly, I apologize. And thank you for your openness in answering our questions. If there are any more things I need to inquire about, I'll make sure I'm the one to ask." He glanced off in the direction Darius had walked. "Good night." He lumbered off the deck and between the cabins toward the street.

Molly swiveled in Barclay's arms. "I never took you for a jealous man." Possessiveness didn't begin to describe how he had practically vibrated with anger as he stood behind her, threatening a policeman.

"I never did either until I met you. So, unless you say no, for as long as you're here, you're mine and I learned tonight I can be one possessive son of a bitch."

CHAPTER ELEVEN

The shower was running when Molly, Barclay and the canine girls came inside for the night. He locked the sliding glass doors and placed an old broom handle in the track for added security. The water turned off and so did her dad's off-key singing. Barclay carried her to the sofa and slipped off her boot.

"Want anything to drink?" His one hand rubbed up the back of her thigh and over her butt. He dipped his head and nuzzled her neck, making her tummy do its twitchy thing. "Your wish is my command, Sugar."

Oh, she had a wish, all right. It involved a lot of kissing, touching and as much raw sex as he could deliver.

The bathroom door opened and bare feet padded on the floor. "Is Barclay still here?" Her dad entered the sitting room wearing his worn red flannel pajamas and settled on the recliner. "Got a question for you, son." Her dad squinted one eye the way he did when he was on an information hunt.

"Sure. I'll answer if I can." By now Barclay had moved his hands and was holding her feet on his lap, innocent looking as a choir boy. His expressions could change as quickly as the wind.

Dad leaned toward him. "Gas Ass told me a story. I don't know whether to believe him or not. Fellas get to talking and a lot of bragging goes on, you know?"

Barclay's thigh muscles tensed under her feet. "Yes, I know exactly what you mean. What did he say?"

Her dad proceeded to tell this convoluted tale of how a group of ex-military personnel rescued Cassie. It sounded bizarre, yet Cassie had mentioned part of it at the diner last night, but not all of this.

"We prefer to keep those details quiet. Gas Ass needs reminding to be careful of whom he tells the story to. I mean, you're fine, but he might be spreading it around a little too much."

Molly stared at Barclay. "This sounds like a cheap movie plot. Why would you all put yourselves at risk like this? Why not simply call the police?"

He looked at her for a few beats. "We're alphas. Alphas take care of their women, no matter what danger we have to wade through. We protect what's ours. I don't have anyone officially," he squeezed her good foot, "but when my friends need me to help them, I'm there."

"You work with some good men, son." Her dad stood and stretched. "You young whipper-snappers keep on talking. I'm beat."

"Sam?" Her dad stopped at Barclay's mentioning his name. "Thanks for your help today. No man worked harder than you and I appreciate it. Tomorrow will be an easier day. We'll be back at the station. It'll be just you and Gas Ass. He has a list of things I want done. Sir, would you give some thought to staying on for another month? Same arrangement. You help me around here a few hours a day and the rent is free."

A wide grin spread. "Well now, I had the time of my life today. I surely did. Molly and I will talk about staying longer over breakfast tomorrow." Her dad yawned and glanced at Maggie Mae. "You coming, girl?" The dog yawned and stretched as she stood and followed him inside the bedroom.

Molly glanced at Barclay. "Is it okay if she stays?" He nodded. "Maybe we should get a dog when we go back home. How can you tell an alpha dog from a non-alpha?"

"You have to train the pup or dog that you're the alpha. Dogs are pack animals. They need an alpha. Just like some women need an alpha male." He scooted her on her side and lay on his side beside her, his one leg draped over hers. "Lift your head, Sugar, so I can slide my arm under your neck."

In a matter of seconds with a few minor moves, they were entwined on the sofa. Being cocooned in his body was an almost natural position. He was a flexible wall of warm muscle and lying so close, a breath of air couldn't pass between them, brought a relaxing security. She rubbed one hand up and down the hardened muscles of his back. "This is nice." She kissed his neck and inhaled his lime and ginger cologne.

A deep exhale from his chest caused his muscles to relax as if he enjoyed the closeness too. His hand drifted from her hip, beneath her sweatshirt to her breast. "Yeah." He kissed her long and slow while he unhooked her bra. A deep male groan crawled from his throat as his palm covered her breast. "Sugar," he moaned as his thumb and index finger plucked at her nipple, sending sweet sensations straight to her core.

"I wish I could hold you like this all night, but I go back to work in the morning. We work forty-eight hour shifts. Text me or call. I left my numbers on the refrigerator. If I don't respond right away, I'm out on a call."

"Okay." *Just keep doing that thing to my nipple.*

"Now where was I?" He pushed her sweatshirt up. "Sweet Jesus. His palm swept over her breasts. I've never seen anyone as beautiful as you." He drew her nipple into his mouth and rubbed his erection against her.

She was pretty sure her eyes rolled back in her head before reality pulled her sexual heaven down to earth. "We can't. Not with Dad in the next room."

"I know. I want our first time to be slow, not rushed on a sofa like a couple of teenagers, but I have to tell you, I want you so damn bad right now." He slipped her sweatshirt down to cover her breasts. "Talk to me about something else. Get my mind off of sinking into your sweet body."

Talk? With his hard-on against the juncture of her thighs? And her hormones chanting, *Come to me, hunky man. Rock my world.* But she did have a few questions. "Earlier, you mentioned alphas. I get the concept in the animal world, but I don't in the human. To me, it's just an excuse for a man to be bossy."

"Not bossy. Protective, for damn sure. Indulgent, joyfully so. Yet, an alpha is a man, who expects to be first in a woman's life, but understanding when other family members need her. There's a lot of respect the two share. It's a power exchange." He tensed and brought a strand of her hair to his nose and inhaled its fragrance. "Actually, there are two kinds of alphas. Because I want to be honest with you, I'm going to risk everything here."

"What do you mean?"

"There are normal alphas like Wolf and Quinn, who like to run the show, yet would give their wives anything. Then there are alphas in the BDSM community. A few of those alpha men want control all the time, even to the point of choosing what their submissive will wear for the day. Some have protocols they perform in public that only the two of them understand. Most simply demand control in the privacy of their bedroom."

"Are...are they mean to their submissives?" A creepy feeling shuddered through her system. "How...Barclay, how do you know so much about this...this...?"

"Lifestyle?" His eyebrow arched and she knew.

Somehow she sensed he was a part of it and her heart folded in on itself. She'd fallen for another abusive man. "In many ways, I'm naïve sexually. Wade was my only partner. We never used handcuffs or blindfolds. I don't pole dance. There was no kink between us, so when you use the word 'lifestyle,' I'm not sure exactly what you mean. I just know it makes me very uneasy. Are all firemen into this...this lifestyle?" She waved an open hand and stared at him to gauge his reaction.

Barclay rubbed his hand along her side as if he were stalling to compose the right answer. "The handcuffs and blindfolds are just a little kink, some harmless sex play between couples that both enjoy. The expression 'lifestyle' involves something more involved; emotionally and physically deeper. Those who are into it, don't talk about it to just anyone. Confidentiality is important. We like and, in some cases, need, the concealment and safety of privacy."

"We."

He exhaled an audible sigh. "Yes, before this goes any further between us, I need to tell you I'm a trained Dominant. I don't frequent the clubs very often. I prefer the privacy of my home. There are a lot of things I don't relish doing, like inflicting pain even if the submissive needs it. I enjoy other ways of arousal."

She tried to push him off the sofa, away from her. "You'll beat me, won't you? Use whips and chains on me. Good God, why am I always drawn to the abusers? I need counseling."

"Calm down, Sugar. Allow me to explain." He tightened his hold on her and viced his legs around hers. "I won't ever do anything to you that you don't want. Like right now, I'd like to carry you into your bed and kiss you all over. I want to show you how a man can go from gentle to adoring to heavy-duty strong without one second of abuse. Have you ever been loved so sweetly, so tenderly by a man with dominant tendencies? At times, I'll be a little rough, but you'll be so hazed with passion, you'll like it."

Well, when he put it like that…

He reached into his back pocket and pulled out a condom, holding it between them. "It's up to you, Sugar. It's always up to you, but once we enter the bedroom, I'll be in charge. You'll follow my orders. You'll call me Master. And I promise I won't hurt you. Let me introduce you to the lifestyle I prefer, one step at a time."

She trembled, recalling the beatings from Wade. "Okay," she whispered.

He returned the foil packet to his pocket. "No. You're quaking shows me you're not ready for this. Maybe you never will be." He held her close and kissed her neck several times. "This involves a large level of trust. Your reaction just now proves you don't trust me enough. You need time to heal from Wade before you're ready for an intimate relationship with any man, much less a man like me. I do ask you keep my sexual preferences to yourself. I'd rather not be fodder for gossip."

He stood and extended his hand. "Come, walk me to the door and say goodnight. I'll see you in a little over two days after I get some sleep from my shift. I put a key to my place here in case you need it." He pointed to a wooden fish-shaped key holder next to the front door. "Milt is supposed to look after the dogs, but they like an earlier walk to water the grass. Plus, they're used to being together during the day."

"Of course." She'd scared him away with her fears. Maybe for good. She glanced up at him and noticed sadness in his eyes. "I'm sorry, Barclay. Some of what you talked to me about, I just don't understand. And, yes, if I'm to be truthful, I'm afraid of being hurt again."

"We must always be truthful with each other, no matter how much it hurts." He trailed his fingers down her cheek. "Don't you know? I'd sooner cut off my hands than beat you. Earlier this evening, I smacked your bottom once. You didn't freak then, nor did I mark you. I adore you. That's me being truthful." He pressed his lips to hers for a brief kiss. "Sleep well, beautiful. Sweet dreams." He smiled briefly. "Come on, girls. Let's go home."

Lola whined and leaned against Molly's leg. She was evidently spending the night too.

"Caroline, are you coming?" The Collie mix licked his hand and followed him to the door. "Lock up behind me, Sugar."

Molly flipped the lock and hooked the chain. "Well, I certainly flubbed that up. I could be having some hot sex right now, but noooo, I have to be the chicken. You ever sleep with a chicken, Lola?" The dog whined. "Yeah, that's what I thought. Let me brush my teeth and go to the bathroom before I crawl into bed."

The bedside clock read four-forty when Lola started whining and prancing from the bed to the door. "Maybe we won't get a dog when we get home. Couldn't your bladder wait a little longer?" By the time she'd finished mumbling, Molly had her slippers on. Once she opened her bedroom door, Lola made a beeline for the front door. No sooner had Molly opened it and the barrel on skinny legs shot out and ran around a palm tree a couple times before she squatted and relieved herself. Caroline was out front watering the grass too. The two dogs barked and sniffed each other's butts as if they hadn't seen each other in a month.

Barclay stepped out onto his front porch. Coffee mug in hand, he was bare chested and wearing blue plaid pajama bottoms. "Sorry, I forgot to tell you about the early morning pee run. You look like you haven't slept well. Did you have doggie paws in your back all night?"

She rubbed her back. "Yeah. You forgot to warn me about that too."

"I'll take them both now. Go on back to bed. Get some peaceful sleep. I'll be heading out in about thirty, forty minutes, so if you hear a Harley, it's only me." He looked at the gray sky, streaked with pink. "Looks like a great morning for a ride."

"What if it rains and you get wet?"

"Molly, I'm a diver. Sometimes I spend hours underwater, hunting for bodies." He gulped some more coffee.

His curt attitude ticked her off. "What has you so grumpy this morning?" She hobbled the few steps from her porch to his.

"Sorry, I didn't sleep well. I think I lost someone very precious last night." He stared into his mug. "I don't handle loss well."

"Maybe this someone just needed time to think things through a little. To ask herself some hard questions." She'd tossed and turned all night. Why was she so afraid of Barclay; he'd been nothing but kind. The man certainly turned her on. More than Wade ever had. What if she was allowing her fears to block her from having some awesome, feel-good moments? Just being held in his arms was a pleasure like nothing she'd ever experienced.

She laid her hand on his bare chest. "Sometimes, it takes a while to accept new things."

His gaze rose and locked on hers. He tossed the mug onto the gravel driveway. One hand fisted the back of her hair and drew her to him. "Get the *hell* inside." He cupped her ass and lifted her, toting her a few quick steps to a wall and balancing her against it. She wrapped her legs around his hips.

"I'm not playing with you. Either accept me as I am, for the man I am, in every area of my life, just as I'll accept you for the wonderful woman you are, or this all ends now. I've been through too much, Molly, too damn much to let you or anyone flay open my heart again."

His stormy green eyes bore into hers and something about his demeanor—his total honesty, perhaps—displayed his deep-seated vulnerability. In that moment, she knew. "Yes, Master."

All his control seemed to snap.

His fingers forked into her hair so he could hold her head in place while he bit her lower lip, soothed it with his tongue and sucked on it. A whimper rose from her throat and her fingers tightened in his hair. He rubbed his pajama-clad erection against her and her mouth opened with an aroused gasp. His tongue swept in, teasing, touching, tasting her every place it could reach.

God Lord, the sensations he could create.

He pulled back enough to moan what was evidently racing through his brain. "God, Sugar, you're so fuckin' sweet. Something… an intuition….a desire so damn deep…I don't give a fuck what it was. I just knew from the first moment I saw you." His lips covered hers again and he feasted on her mouth.

Rocking against her a couple times had her so ready to take him, she was losing rational thought. He pulled back far enough to slip his hand between them and stroke her pussy with his fingers. "You're wet for me, Sugar. Let me make you soar. I want to hear you scream my name when you come." He stroked her some more and she made enticing sounds she'd never made before, moans and pleas that couldn't possibly be coming from her. He set her feet on the floor so he could slip his hand beneath the elastic waist of her pajama bottoms. His thumb found her clit and circled it while she fought for air. "Come for me." He inserted one finger, then another.

She shook her head. "No, I can't." Even as she uttered the lie, her abdominal muscles coiled into mass of sexual energy, ready to explode. She shuddered with it.

His laughter was low. "But you will. I won't give up until I can make you come on command. My command. No one's, but mine." He pressed his thumb on her engorged button and bit her earlobe. "Come, Sugar." And she shattered and trembled in his arms as she screamed his name.

"Sweet Jesus, you're like heaven in my arms." He kissed her neck and held her to him until her vibrations stopped. With one arm wrapped around her waist, he opened the screen door to whistle for the dogs, who charged in and barreled for their filled bowls.

He scooped her in his arms and carried her to his bedroom. "I wanted our first time to be long with multiple orgasms for you, but I need you so damn bad." He closed the door and shucked out of his pajama bottoms before he sat on the edge of his bed. "Take your pajamas off." His voice had lowered and she found that interesting. She hesitated. "Who's the boss in this room?"

"You are." She tugged off her top, but dilly-dallied on pulling off the bottoms. What if he thought her ass too big?

"Sub, the proper address in this room is Master. You may use it anywhere we're alone, but never in front of others. Now, I've ordered you to take off your pajamas and that includes your bottoms."

She stuck her thumbs in the elastic and sighed. "Yes, Master."

She stood in front of him naked, in all her glory for him to see and examine and judge. She covered her pussy with her hands and wished she had two more for her breasts. Why didn't he say something?

"Move your hands. Your body is for me to see and enjoy."

"Oh, darn you. Give me some privacy. I'm embarrassed. I'm naked for the first time in front of you and—." Tears pooled in her eyes and she looked at the wooden floor so he wouldn't see them. They plopped nonetheless.

"There's no need for tears, my beauty," he whispered as he stood and slowly walked around her, trailing his fingertips over her skin and planting kisses here and there. "I love your pearly smooth skin." Behind her, he ran his palm down her back and grabbed her hips, pulling her back to his erection. "I adore your firm, plump ass." He inclined his head and bit her shoulder as his hands lifted her breasts. "I could die right now and be a happy man, except for two things."

"Wh...what?"

"You fail to properly address me and you downgrade your body that will, in a few minutes, belong to me. I don't like junk, Sugar. I don't require a lot of stuff in my life, but what I do have is quality." He stepped in front of her and held her chin in his hand. "And you, my sweet sub, are pure quality. Who's in charge in this room?"

The level of his voice and his words spun a spell of yearning over her. "You are, Master."

"Who has the prettiest, sexiest body in my eyes?"

She couldn't say it.

He fisted his hand in her hair and jerked back her head. "Answer me, sub, or leave."

Dear God, he meant it. "I...I do, Master."

"Those are the answers I will require from you every time we are about to make love. Now, sit on my bed." He reached for a condom laying on his nightstand and handed it to her. "Put this on me."

"Yes, Master." She opened the packet and looked at the thing. "You'll think I'm totally dumb. I've never held one before."

"Slip the ridge on first and roll it over my shaft."

She bit her lower lip and followed his directions. "Will this little thing fit over that big thing, Master?"

His soft laughter embarrassed her. "It will. It's a maximum."

The heat of a blush rose on her cheeks. Geesh, she was worse than a virgin.

He rested his hand against her cheek. "Good girl, my pet. Which do you prefer I call you in the bedroom? Sub, subbie, pet? A warning. When you're bad, it'll be brat."

She chuckled. "I'll probably get called that a lot, but pet is kind of nice."

"Spread your legs, pet, until I crawl between them, then place your knees over my shoulders." She did what he told her and he leaned down to rasp his tongue over her nipples. Between what he was doing to her breasts and his whispered words of praise, currents of desire swept through her. But her undoing was when he drew a nipple into his mouth and sucked. She nearly came off the bed when he shoved two fingers inside her with her abdominal muscles coiling again. Surely she couldn't be having a second orgasm. She never came twice.

"Whose pretty body is this with all this wetness?"

"Yours, Master."

He positioned himself and entered her with one long stroke. "Oh, pet, my sweet, sweet pet," he moaned with every stroke. You're so tight and wet." He pulled her hair again as he delved into her with more force. "Say my name!"

"Master." She curled her fingers into his hair. "My Master."

Her thighs quivered and her breathing slowed so she could sense every feeling, every stroke and every pulse of him inside her.

"You're going to come again, aren't you? Who's climax is this? Tell me, pet. Who do all your climaxes belong to?" He kept pounding away, his face reddened from the exertion of holding back his own release.

"Yours, Master!" And she screamed his Dominant title over and over and she came in the longest climax of her life. This wasn't just a little ripple, this was a tidal wave of sexual reaction to all he'd done to her

He reared his head back and called her Sugar as he poured into his rubber. Finally, he collapsed on top of her, panting and, with sweet gentleness, slid her legs off his shoulders before he rolled on his side, taking her with him.

After a few minutes, he rubbed her back and bottom. "Did you enjoy your first private lesson in a few of the parts of BDSM I enjoy?"

She nodded and yawned. "I had two climaxes. I've never had more than one before. In fact, I'm not sure what I was having were truly climaxes. The ones you gave me had a trace of violence to them. They were so violent, they took my breath away." They kind of scared her, too, for she reacted so strongly to him.

"Sugar, next time I promise you more. Maybe we'll try for three. I'll give you oral until you come at least twice. Now, love, I have to take a quick shower or I'll be late for work.

"Will you text me when you get there, so I know you made it safely?" His footsteps stopped. Shit, she'd forgotten, already. "Master."

"If it pleases you, I'll be happy to. A Dom also lives to make his sub, his pet happy, both in and out of the bedroom. As I may have said, it's a power exchange." He pulled clean clothes from his drawers. "Now, get dressed and crawl back in your bed. Sleep a few more hours, my sweet one." He sauntered into the bathroom.

Molly was settling into a deep sleep when her cell phone dinged on her nightstand. *Am here. Had a g8 early visitor. Will think of her all day. B.*

After reading his text three times, she replied. *Will smile as I think of it. Stay safe. Yours.*

The cell chimed before she'd laid it back on the stand. *Fuckin' A...Mine!*

CHAPTER TWELVE

Wolf eased his Harley in the parking area beside Barclay's and took off his helmet. "Welcome back, Ghost. I'm glad to have my diving partner back. Jace did a good job, but he's not as intuitive as you." They ambled toward Station Thirty-Two, their helmets under their arms. "So, did that young policeman get off your property unscathed last night?"

Barclay glanced at Wolf. "What do you mean?"

Wolf swiped his keycard and opened the door to the equipment room. "You know what the hell I mean. I saw him eyeballing Molly. Hell, he was half-flirting with her."

"The fucker's lucky he didn't go home with his dreadlocks shoved up his ass. She'd been on my lap all night. Any man in his right mind would take that as a 'hand's off' signal." He slipped out his cell. "Hold on. Need to text Molly." He snickered when her reply chimed in and he sent a reply. "Woman thinks she can get ahead of me."

Before the squad could start their morning wipe-down and polishing of equipment and rigging, the Captain's voice sounded over the intercom. "Need all diving personnel in my office ASAP." When Noah Steele used that tone of voice, everyone hustled.

Wolf, Commander of the Marine Rescue Unit, Quinn, watercraft driver and the divers, Barclay, Jace and Armando, filled Noah's

116

office. As head of the unit, Wolf asked what was up.

Noah's face was especially grim. "We have ourselves a potential cluster-fuck. First off, two boats collided offshore about an hour ago, he pointed to the spot on the map. One went down. It was armed with explosives, a bomb bound for some rich dude's estate farther up the coastline. Drug cartel revenge looks like to me.

"The driver started singing like a canary when the Marine Rescue Squad from the last shift pulled him out of the water. Guess the dumbass was so grateful he wasn't going to drown, after all." Noah glanced at Wolf. "That squad doesn't have the caliber of men yours does. So I'm sending yours out to finish the job. Hell, I don't even know if the boat still afloat has survivors, or not.

"Headquarters needs to replace some men on that team; makes us look bad. Coast Guard is on the way, but we've been asked to do preliminary location dives."

"We'll take the Rescue One Connector Boat and should be in the water in five, six minutes." Wolf glanced around the room at his crew. They'd trained hard for things like this. "Barclay, you were a demolitions expert in the Rangers. I'll need you in the water with me."

"You got it."

"Jace, you've got damn good eyes and medic training. Armando, you're thorough as hell. I want you two on the boat still afloat. Search for bodies and any fires." Both men nodded.

Quinn flipped the dial on his diving watch. "Give me the exact coordinates of the wreckage site and I'll key it in." The rest of the squad rushed out of the office. Each had a specific job to do. No further orders were necessary as they headed for their equipment room to change into their dry suits. Jace called ahead to their marina to make sure the boat was fueled and ready to go.

Once they were in the van hauling ass for the marina, Wolf pulled out his cell. "Call your women. You've got one minute talk time."

Wolf's directive to call home was a signal the boss thought

things might not go well. It wasn't like they called their wives or women before responding to every fire. They were going into some dangerous shit on this mission, especially him and Wolf, diving for the explosives.

Barclay hadn't done this in ages, but he had something he had to tell Molly. Thank God, she answered on the first ring. "Sugar, listen." He kept his voice low since others on his team were making their calls too. "There's been an accident with two boats. One was equipped with a bomb and has sunk. Coast Guard is on the way, but we'll be first responders. I want you to know I love you. Do you hear me? I love you. I have to go, Sugar." He ended the call, barely giving her a chance to talk.

It was time now to focus on the job and all the scenarios that could go wrong.

The van skidded to a stop at their destination—a wide bottomed yellow boat with black painted wide stripes at the front and back. The craft had a non-skid flat floor to prevent slipping and provide extra balance as they skimmed over the waves. Its hundreds of cubic inches of foam made the vessel extra buoyant and virtually unsinkable.

The team scrambled aboard with their equipment and Quinn took over the boat's controls, speeding away while everyone else stored what they'd brought in compartments. In a matter of minutes, they were organized and sat to take a moment's breath.

Noah contacted them on his iPad with the latest intel he'd gotten on both the wreck and the bomb. Wolf sat on the floor of the vessel and the rest of the divers leaned in to watch and listen to the Captain. "We have no clue as to the size, shape or composition of the explosive device. So, be on the lookout for anything strange or normal, but out of place."

"Well, hell, that gives the two of you a lot of information to go on," Armando growled.

"It's more than we had in Iraq." Barclay closed his eyes to block out some old, grotesque memories.

Wolf moved up front and showed the Captain's message to Quinn and he nodded as he focused on the vast bay ahead. Wolf took his seat and nudged his brother with his fin. "Jace, I'll need you to check for three small children, ages ten, seven and four. Armando, do a quick run-through for fires. Hell, we don't know how damaged the boat is at this point so it's hard for me to give specific orders. But you two are smart enough to work on your own. Use your common sense, your gut feelings."

Quinn soon yelled and pointed. A mangled cabin cruiser was floating off to the right. No active fire was apparent, which was a good thing. Wolf tossed Barclay a handheld sonar device. Barclay examined his to make sure it was completely operational. Meanwhile Wolf checked the real-time sonar screen until he saw something and motioned Barclay over.

Wolf pointed. "Looks like our boat. One side is completely crashed in. No wonder it sunk, must have taken on water pretty damn fast."

"How far away are we from it?" The adrenaline started flowing through Barclay's system. Diving and demolitions, one hellofa heady combination. God, he loved his job. Only now he had a reason to excel at it even more—to get back to Molly.

"Looks to be about fifty yards. Let's get ready to dive." Both took their positions opposite of each other on the craft, their sonar devices in hand. They inserted their mouth pieces for their oxygen tanks, Wolf gave a thumbs-up signal to Barclay and they both flipped backwards into the water.

Since they wore full facemasks with underwater communication systems and transceivers designed for the demanding needs of search and rescue teams, they were able to keep in touch as they searched for the sunken boat.

"I'm thinking the device will be in a box of some sort a guy could easily carry to the house." Barclay had been thinking on this on their boat ride out. "It would be concealed somehow."

"Give me a clue, Ghost."

"A tool box, maybe. Battery for a car. A repair item for a house. If it was a gift, all wrapped up in paper and a bow, that disguise will be waterlogged to hell and back."

"My sonar reader says we're coming up on it. Are you getting the same reading?"

"Sure am, Wolf. I can see it from my position."

"Wait. We'll go in together. Send up a location balloon."

Barclay waited for his commander to enter the craft first. "I have concerns."

"Such as?" Wolf examined the extent of the damage.

"Suppose the device is now unstable. The collision, the change in pressure as the boat sank and the jar of its landing might have loosened a wire or a connection. Made the explosives unstable."

"Got you. Let's start at the back and work forward. We'll stay together."

They hooked their sonar detectors onto their belts and unsnapped their flashlights to illuminate their way back the passage to the back room, pushing floating objects out of their way as they searched for the explosive device. Closet doors were opened cautiously as were storage units.

A box of hand-rolled cigars caught Barclay's attention. "Why isn't this floating?" He glanced around at heavier items moving freely through the water. There were clear one-inch wide strips of plastic running lengthwise and across the width of the carton of Cohiba Cuban cigars, the ends of the strips screwed into the top of the counter in the boat's galley.

"Why ruin the Formica by screwing holes into it? Unless it was an item you wanted held secure and not jostled around over any rough water." He slipped his knife from his belt and carefully cut through the thick plastic. "Box is made of wood, heavier than a normal cigar box. Its edges are dovetailed."

Wolf stood by as Barclay slowly examined it. "I was suspecting something bigger. Weren't you, Ghost?"

"Depends on what type of explosive they used and how they

were going to make sure the target would be the one to open it. The top should have a paper seal holding it shut." He turned it over and peered at the edge. "But this one's glued. A man would need his pocket knife to open it."

Wolf squeezed Barclay's arm. "For now, I'd say our work here is done. If it's not the bomb, we'll come down again."

Molly called the number Cassie had jotted on the back of her business card. "Cassie, have you heard from Quinn?"

"Yes. Becca, Wendy Anne and Maria have too. The guys never call us unless they're going into a really dangerous situation, so it has us pretty worked up. We're all headed to the station. Do you know how to get there? I'm in Clearwater now or I'd come get you. Wait, is Milt there?"

"Yes." Dangerous? *Dear God, my Barclay is in a risky position?*

"Have Milt bring you. He knows where the station is. Park in the back near the Harleys."

Milt and her dad were just having coffee and going over the list Barclay had left for the day when she hobbled out of her bedroom and told them the news.

"I'll get us there, darlin'. Don't you worry." Milt stood and passed gas. "Go get dressed while Sam and I let out the dogs for a pee run before locking them back in Barclay's house. My boys are tough. Don't you fret now.

"She threw on jeans and a top, brushed her hair to a silky shine and, to save time, slipped on a pair of flip-flops over her broken toe, black and swollen. She was in no mood to deal with the cumbersome boot. Not that Barclay would notice. Frankly, she didn't care if he did. What was of paramount importance was his safety.

Ten minutes later, she was in the back of an orange bullet, once known as a classic seventy-six Cutlass Supreme, now resembling a hundred rolls of duct tape on wheels. As Milt leaned his skinny frame over the steering wheel, his bony shoulders hunched and his eyes as beady as Maggie Mae's, he drove well over the speed limit. "Them boys will be all right. Don't you worry, Baby Snooks."

Baby Snooks? Just what I need, another nickname.

Milt passed some gas and she nearly passed out.

Barclay had told her he loved her. Before he'd gone into a dangerous situation, he'd called *her* and told her how he felt. A frigid gust like the Colorado winter winds swept through her. No, it couldn't be. But the words he'd used and the tone of his voice told it all. She fought to make her freezing lungs work. Dear God, he'd been calling to say good-bye in case anything happened. He wanted her to know his honest emotions in case…

She covered her mouth as scalding tears filled and overflowed her eyes. How could something so hot come from such a cold, shivering body? She might lose him. She'd found a man she cared for, one who treated her as if she were his treasure and the call ended before she could gather her wits to tell him she shared the same emotions. And she did. She loved a man she'd known only a couple of days. He had to be safe. He had to survive this mission. He just had to. What were the men doing? What kind of hazardous situation were they in?

Milt yanked on the steering wheel to pull into the station's parking lot, the effort making him toot a little more.

All of the wives were talking to Boyd. Molly felt a little shy horning in when her relationship with Barclay was so new. Milt, on the other hand, evidently didn't give a shit. He bustled over, his arms swinging as if the extra movement would help him get there faster.

"Boyd, what's going on with my boys?" The senior citizen sounded like a concerned father.

The muscle-bound firefighter strode over and looped an arm around Milt's thin shoulders. "Gas Ass, calm down. It's okay."

As soon as she and her dad joined the two men, Boyd filled them in on the boats' collision. "Jace rescued three scared children with minor injuries. He gave medical attention to both parents, now airlifted to the hospital. Armando put out an engine fire and helped take care of the terrified kids. Wolf and Barclay found the bomb, hidden in a fake cigar box. The Coast Guard's bomb squad has it now. They're in the process of diffusing it. All the squad's men are fine. But anytime you're going into a situation with hidden explosives, things can go south in a hurry."

"So all your men are unharmed?" Molly could barely force the words from her dry throat. She knew them all, except for Armando. Everyone was a decent person and Barclay was someone she didn't know if she could live without.

Boyd turned his head from leaning toward Milt and smiled at her. "Thanks for asking, Molly. Yes, the whole Squad is fine."

She nodded and fought the tears of relief burning the back of her throat.

Within minutes, Station 32's Marine Rescue Unit's van rolled into the parking lot. The doors opened and the men hopped out. Each one headed for the open arms of his wife, except for Barclay who trod for the station. Molly's hands flew to her mouth. He really was okay.

Her movement evidently caught his eye. His head whipped around and that slow sexy grin she loved lit his face. He increased his pace and held out an arm. She hurried to him and stepped into his hold as he enveloped her in a tight embrace. Neither spoke words. They connected through their kisses and touches. A wellspring of feelings was shared through their precious silent, sensual communication. Molly had never felt closer to or more cherished by another person.

Finally, he cupped her cheeks. "I never dreamed you would come. When I saw you out of the corner of my eye, I thought I was hallucinating." His eyes twinkled. "But then I saw the wrapped ankle, the broken toe and the flip-flops...and no boot." He picked her up and swung her around before whispering in her ear. "Brat. How shall I punish you?"

She pressed her lips against his ear. "Pull my hair and demand

I tell you your name." That really had been a turn-on for her this morning.

He tossed his head back and laughed. "God, I love you, Sugar. I hate to cut this short, but I have to get back to work. We have equipment to clean. I'll have a report to file for the Coast Guard since I'm the one who identified the bomb." His hand swept down her hair. "I can't tell you what it means that you're here. It's been so long since someone cared for me. You're the most important person in my life, baby." Tenderness laced his voice and he kissed her one more time before entering the station house.

Molly's father hooked his arm with hers. "I'm thinking we should hire people to help us pack up and clean out the house, put it on the market and move down here. I'm tired of shoveling snow and scraping frost off windows. I'm ready for a change. How about you? Tell me the truth now, do you want to leave Florida before you find out what might happen between you and that fine young man?"

Oh, she knew what might happen. They'd end up in bed over and over with her becoming more and more under his control. She loved him, but she wasn't the type of woman to be bossed around. Although he did say his domination would only be in the bedroom. Still, how could she trust him on that?

"Part of me wants to say yes, but part of me is scared, Dad."

"Not all men are like Wade was. Did you ever see or hear me abuse your sainted momma?"

She smiled at the memory. "No, you doted on her."

He snorted. "Except in the bedroom, then she doted on me." He tossed her a wink.

"Dad! That was definitely TMI."

CHAPTER THIRTEEN

Things were relatively calm at the station. All the marine and diving equipment was cleaned and ready for its next use. Barclay had showered, dressed and grabbed the makings for a couple sandwiches from the large refrigerator. He and Jace exchanged a few words while Jace made three crockpots of chili.

Barclay took his plate of food and a can of soda to the dining table, glanced at the food and then at his cell. What will it be? Eat or Molly? In a split second, he chose to call Molly first.

As soon as she answered, he knew how bad he had it for her. Just the sound of her voice settled an old turmoil within him. "Do you have your boot on, Sugar?"

"No, and I'm not putting that damn thing back on, either." Something had her in a snit. He could imagine her lower lip pouched out.

So he softened his voice. "Sugar, I have a plate of food in front of me and I chose to call you first. Now, unless you want me to have a serious case of heartburn, you better tell me what's wrong. You know how I worry about you."

He was sure there were a few sniffles. "I worry about you too."

"I'm okay or I will be once you're honest with me and tell me what's got you upset." He picked up a sandwich and bit into it.

"I can't find Mom's ashes. I've gone over my bedroom like we did Dad's last night. I've checked the bathroom and living room. Nothing. I'm getting ready to start the kitchen next."

"On a scale of one to ten—"

"Don't you give me that scale shit. I need to find my mother's ashes." She was near hysterics. "And stop calling me Sugar."

Maybe if he changed the topic, she'd calm down a little. "What are the guys doing?"

"Bragging, farting and scratching their balls."

He choked on his next bite of sandwich. Christ, she was in a mood and comical as hell with it. "Are they doing any work?"

"Yeah, but you're not going to like it."

Oh Christ. "What in God's name are they doing?"

"Since it's such a gorgeous day, they decided to paint the outside of Milt's cottage. His is a strange shade of green. I mean, it looks nice and all, but it's not the lime color it used to be."

He snapped open his soda. "Yeah, well, Milt and I had a bit of a discussion about the exterior color if his cabin. I gave him a say since he's going to be living there as my manager. The cottage has always been lime green. But he moaned and groaned about living in a fruity-colored place. Geesh, he can bitch. So, we settled on a color similar to celery green."

"I loved the different colors of these cottages as a kid. I always thought they were so cool. Like living in a bowl of Fruit Loops."

"Yeah, me too. I spent a lot of time there as a youngster when I knew my sisters were safe, staying with our grandparents. If they were home, I felt I needed to be there to protect them from the old man and the effects of whatever bottle he was into at the time. He enjoyed striking out too much. If I was home, I could step between him and Mom or Kayla or Jasmine."

"Oh, Barclay."

He took a long swig of soda. "I don't want your pity, Sugar, just your understanding. I damn near beat the old man to a pulp the day he broke Jasmine's wrist. Child protective services stepped in and Grammy and Pawpaw hired a lawyer so they could get custody

126

of the girls." He finished off his soda and crushed the can in one hand. "Christ, what a hellofa mess. The old man ended up in jail for a few months. Mom was lost without her children and her husband, so as soon as he got out, she took him back. I joined the army. I was too full of rage to be in the same town as him. Now he's in jail for her murder."

"Did the army help with your rage?"

"It did. Gave me a healthy outlet for it. Taught me the value of brotherhood with the other guys. I already had it with my sisters. My third month home from my first deployment, I met Yvette. I was ready to start a family, but life wasn't ready to let me have one."

"Maybe someday, hon." It was the first time she'd used a term of endearment with him and it came as a surprise. The vision of her big with his baby also shocked him, which put an itch in the middle of his back where he couldn't reach. He wasn't able to go through having and loosing another child. His heart couldn't endure it.

"Family might not be in my cards. Both of my sisters are married and living in other states. Uncle Verne was always more of a dad to me than my biological father. Guess that's why that bundle of cabins mean so much to me. Sometimes, when the old man was on a terror, I'd sneak the girls out and take them there. If Uncle Verne had an empty cabin, he'd let us use it. If he didn't, we'd squeeze into his little place."

"So that's where you developed your Superman complex. Protecting your family from an abusive, alcoholic father. Now it's a core part of your personality."

He was uncomfortable about her analyzing his past. "I wish you'd wear the boot."

"I don't need it. I hate that cumbersome thing."

"Wear it until bedtime and all day tomorrow. If I had a voice in the matter, you'd wear it for a complete week."

"A whole freaking week? Boy, am I glad you have no say in the matter."

"Does the word brat ring a bell?"

"Only in the bedroom. That's what you said. I'm counting on your honesty."

Ah, he'd hit on another part of her mood—fear over his lifestyle and wanting to introduce her to it. "That's right, pet, only in the bedroom. That's a promise. Say, would you like me to call Cassie to come over after she gets off work to help you look? Would give you two a chance to get better acquainted. Check Milt's cabin, too, and the pink one. I'm not sure I've kept it locked. Oh, and check under the deck behind your place."

"I never thought of all those places. Yes, call Cassie for me, but don't put any pressure on her. I don't want to be a burden on anyone."

"You won't be a burden. How about a date my first night home? If you let me take you to dinner and a movie, you can go without the boot. We'll see how you do with just the bandage and crutches. How's that sound?"

"Dinner and a movie? What about Dad? And don't think I don't know what you're doing. 'If you let me take you to a dinner and a movie, you can go without the boot.'" She imitated his voice and he bent over laughing. God, she was something when she was wound up. "Listen, buster, I can go without the boot whenever I damn well please."

"Outside of the bedroom, I will show you affection and respect. I expect the same from you. We will not talk nasty to each other."

She sighed. "You have to know this scares me. I know nothing about domination and submission. I won't be in a relationship where I'm bossed around."

"Sugar, if I recommend a couple websites about the lifestyle, would you read them?" He glanced around to make sure most of the guys were busy elsewhere. "Do you have a pen and paper?" At least if she was reading things online, she'd be off her sprained ankle.

"Yes. I'm ready. Give them to me."

After he recited the sites to her, he knew he should lift her up some. "You looked very pretty today at the station. I was beyond happy to see you. Listen, love, I promise you if you haven't found the ashes by the time my shift is over, I'll help you hunt. Together we'll cover more territory. I'll do all I can for you, Sugar. I have to go. So, it's dinner and a movie in two days?"

"Yes. Oh and, hon, you looked quite fetching in that skintight wet suit today too."

He was laughing as he hung up. The woman had him well and truly hooked. She had her fears; so did he after all the people he'd lost.

He threw his trash away and went hunting Quinn. He found him polishing the chrome trim on the eMax 78-foot aerial ladder fire truck. The apparatus had a typhoon X cab and chassis. Since Quinn usually drove it, he kept it in gleaming condition. "What's up, Ghost. You look like you've got something on your mind. You ought to be relieved you found that bomb in the cigar box."

"Molly's dad lost her mother's ashes."

Quinn stopped polishing and glared at Barclay. "You gotta be shittin' me. How the hell?" He nodded once. "The dementia, right?"

"Yeah, and Molly's freaking out, looking through the cabins for them. She helped him pack the wooden holder into his suitcase, so she knows he brought them along to Florida. But where he placed them once they got here is a mystery."

"What a damn shame."

Barclay's cell rang and he checked the display and groaned. "My ex-wife. What do you wanna bet she needs money?"

"She still using?"

"As far as I know." He swiped his screen. "Hey Yvette. What's up?"

"I need help with my rent money. I'm short this month."

He rubbed his hand over his eyes. "I helped you with your rent a couple month's back. I told you then it was a one-time deal."

She exhaled heavily into the phone. "Look, they're going to evict me if I don't come up with some cash. You've got all those cabins out there by the beach I hear you're fixing up, how about letting me have one?"

"No way. Where's your boyfriend, Mr. Wonderful? Why isn't he helping you out?"

"He split last week. I need the cash, Barc." She sounded in need of a fix in a bad way.

"Get a job, Yvette. Get off the drugs. And quit bothering me. You're the one who left for greener pastures, so make the best of it. I'm not giving you any more money." He ended the call.

Quinn looked up from rubbing the chrome. "Does she need money for rent or more drugs?"

"With her, who knows? I refuse to be her ATM. I've helped her twice since she moved out over a year ago. She's not my problem." He paced the length of the apparatus a couple times to calm down and to convince himself he'd done the right thing. To help her would only enable her. *Hell, Yvette, what did you do to yourself?*

He stopped next to Quinn. "Listen, does Cassie have plans for after work? I thought maybe she could go over and help Molly. Maybe she could induce her to sit down and talk a little. Rest that sprained ankle. My stubborn woman refuses to wear the boot."

Quinn slipped the cell from his pocket. "No need to talk to me about stubborn women. They drive you freakin' nuts but, man, they're fun to love." He made the call and Cassie was evidently happy to go help. He shoved the phone back. "Things between you and Molly seem serious. Never known you to move this fast." He laughed and shook his head. "If you'd have seen the expression on Molly's face when I bungled things the other night, fuck me running, she snapped to your defense like you were already hers."

The alarm sounded once and the dispatcher's voice blared over the intercom, giving the address and building description of fire's location. Quinn jumped from the top of the cab portion, and both he and Barclay sprinted for the dressing room, where their uniforms and gear were stored.

The race was on. Quinn expected the men assigned to his

130

apparatus to be onboard once he was settled in the seat and revving the diesel engine. God help you if he had to blow the horn and holler your name, because he would ride your ass until the next slow-moving fireman rose to the top of his shit list. His truck *always* had to be the first one out of the station. Barclay was glad he'd been assigned to the newest piece of equipment at the station. He loved Quinn's tightly run unit.

The four-story wooden structure was in the older section of Clearwater. Half of it was fully engulfed in flames and the fire was quickly spreading. Noah, having ridden in one of the ambulances, was already there, getting information from residents and issuing orders to the firemen as they drove up. "Barclay! Boyd! The building's evacuated except for an old woman who lives on the second floor. She uses a walker. Needs help with steps on a good day. Everyone was too concerned with saving themselves to give her a thought. I need you two to bring her down."

"Got it." Barclay grabbed a hose and went inside while Boyd grabbed his hose and a fireproof blanket to wrap her in. The smoke was already dense on the first floor, where Barclay suspected the fire started. Visibility was fading fast. The walls and many of the supporting beams were gone; so were the first four steps. He hosed the remaining steps to sustain the fire.

"I'll keep the stairway saturated while you go up after her. Captain said her apartment is on the left. Name is Thelma Rosen."

Boyd was so long-legged, it was only a minor stretch for him to land on the fifth step which gave way under his weight. He held onto the old wide banister and moved forward, using his own hose, held over his shoulder, while Barclay kept water flowing on the steps from his end.

As other firemen entered the building, he directed them to remain on the first floor to find and distinguish the origin of the blaze. He dragged partially burned studs to cover where two of the steps were broken, enough to help Boyd as he exited the building, carrying the handicapped woman.

As Boyd maneuvered his way down the steps with the woman wrapped in the fire-retardant blanket, her hoarse, hysterical screams could be heard. She was blabbing about a cat.

Barclay pulled the blanket off her head. "Miss Thelma, do you have a cat?"

"Yes. Princess. She's all I have." Lord, he could understand how she felt. He had three girls who had kept him going most days for the past year or more.

"Where does she hide when she's scared?"

"Under the afghan on the sofa."

Barclay ran up the steps. The lamp on his helmet wasn't strong enough to help him see through the dark smoke. He used his flashlight. Flames ate at the floor outside her door, licking their way up the woodwork and walls on either side of her doorway. He hosed them out. Other flames seeped up through the floorboards. The fire would soon have control of this level.

He turned on his oxygen and flashed the beam of the flashlight around the room until he saw the shape of a sofa through the thick haze. Dragging his gloved hand along the seat, he finally felt the afghan and the lump beneath it—an unresponsive lump. He hosed down the knit blanket, held it to his chest and hosed off the exterior of the doorway before carrying the cat out...into a wall of flames.

Stepping back into Thelma's living room, he depressed the button on his speaker. "Second floor almost completely engulfed. Am exiting a window."

"Which one?"

"Second floor, left side." He kicked the window out with his booted foot, while Noah gave orders to the driver of the ladder truck, who wheeled the apparatus closer to the building so Barclay could grasp the extended ladder. He let go of the hose, held onto the cat and jumped from the window sill onto a wet rung of the ladder, grasping it with one gloved hand. He hurried down and yelled for oxygen. Laying the blanket on the ground, he unwrapped it and removed his helmet. He began giving the white and orange cat CPR.

Thelma crumbled on the ground behind him and ran her trembling, gnarly hands over her cat. "Princess. My darling Princess. Please don't die. Please, I need you."

Barclay kept working on the cat, hoping like crazy he could save her for the old woman beside him. He felt a faint pulse and heard a tiny wheeze. "Someone call a vet, STAT. I've got a pulse, weak, but getting stronger." Thelma draped her arms around Barclay's neck while he kept working on Princess, doing everything he knew to help a cat with smoke inhalation.

"Thank you. She's all I've got left."

"Miss Thelma, we're in a dangerous spot right here. I'm going to move Princess away from any falling debris and then come back for you so you can sit with her until a Vet comes to give her proper treatment. I also want the EMT's to examine you. Will you be a doll and let them check you out?"

"Young man, I'll do whatever you say." She coughed and wheezed from the smoke too.

"Good, I'll be right back for you." He removed the cat from the wet blanket and carried her to the side of an ambulance. "Need a blanket." Someone threw him one from the inside supply shelf. "I'm bringing the owner over next. Senior citizen. Partially incapacitated. She'll need her vitals checked."

He ran back and scooped frail Thelma in his arms. "I've got Princess wrapped in a dry blanket so she doesn't get chilled. She coughed a couple times which is good."

"I can't thank you enough."

"I've got three dogs that I love to death. I know how much your cat means to you." He placed her on the back of the ambulance and took her hand in his, brought it to his lips and kissed it. "You be strong, now, Miss Thelma."

He patted the EMT's shoulder. "Once you've checked this lady out, help her sit next to her cat. They need to be together."

"Will do."

Barclay took off running to grab another hose and climb the ladder to help extinguish the blazes rising from the roof. Some of the firemen were hosing down the building next door, not six feet away. The paint was blistered on its exterior. Noah directed a few of his squad to hose down the building on the other side, as well. They had a long day ahead of them.

More than six-hours later, the exhausted drivers backed their equipment into the firehouse. A couple suggested sleeping on the trucks. Becca stepped out of the living quarters. "I've got brownies and chocolate cake with peanut butter icing for some awesome firefighters, if you guys happen to know of any who fit that description."

A couple male heads popped up. "Is it your homemade chocolate cake and icing?"

"Yes. Would I serve my guys anything out of a damn box?"

Wolf jumped off the ladder truck and swept her into his arms. "See why I love this woman?"

"You guys go shower. I've got supper set up. Jace, you made some awesome smelling chili." She placed her hand on Wolf's face and whispered something to him. He kissed her palm and walked her toward her car.

The guys lumbered from the vehicles to the inside, hung up their equipment and headed for the showers, complaining about how tired they were. Once they ate, they had equipment to clean, examine and make ready for the next fire that could come tonight or next week.

Wolf strode in, glanced toward the kitchen and barked, "No one touches my wife's cake until they're clean. She went to a lot of damn work for you. Don't you mess it up with sooty hands. Oh, and watch channel six news tonight." He looked at Barclay and smirked. "We have a hero in our midst."

CHAPTER FOURTEEN

Cassie's cell dinged. She read a text and glanced at Molly. "It's from Becca. She wants to know if I have a way to reach you. We're to watch the channel-six news tonight. Okay if I give her your cell number?"

"Sure. Did she say why?" She poured them each a glass of iced tea and hobbled toward the living room to sit on the recliner. With Cassie's help they'd looked through all the kitchen cabinets and under the deck. The entire cabin had been searched with zero success. She needed a diversion so she wouldn't break down and bawl. *Will I ever see mom's ashes again?*

"I'm betting what Becca wants us to watch has to do with our guys." Cassie picked up the remote and turned to channel-six. "I'm going out to call in Milt and your dad." The men had cleaned up for supper and were out on the deck, talking like lifelong buddies. Your meatloaf and mac and cheese smells great, by the way." Cassie waggled her eyebrows. "Thanks for the invitation."

"We'll eat after the news. The food should be baked by then." Molly had to admit putting the boot back on had helped with the pain level on her ankle. Maybe she'd just wear it a few hours a day. God forbid she'd listen to Barclay's orders and wear it all the time.

The guys took their seats on the sofa and Cassie wiggled between them. "Look at me! Surrounded by two handsome men."

"You'd better watch her, Sam. She's always been a charmer. I wasn't so sure Quinn was the right man for my Sugar Plum, but he's proven me wrong."

"I just wish Tammy was here to watch the news with me. We watched it together every night for twenty-seven years. I didn't think I'd ever get married. Enjoyed being single too much, if you catch my drift." He glanced around as if looking for his deceased wife. "Where is she at? She told me she made a pie for dessert tonight. Apple, my favorite. She'll probably fix me a piece to have while we watch the news."

"Dad and Milt worked hard today. Dad's very tired." Molly hoped he didn't throw a fit when there was salad, macaroni and cheese and meatloaf, but no apple pie.

Cassie patted his knee. "Now you have new friends to watch the news with…Milt and me." She leaned into Molly's dad's side and pointed. "Look, it's starting now."

He smiled. "So, it is."

They watched the national news. Then the fresh face of a young, blonde announcer came on the screen. "A devastating fire took one of Clearwater's historic buildings on Mayflower Street today. While we consider all our policemen and firemen as heroes, a fireman from Station Thirty-two has emerged as a special kind of hero." Footage ran of a fireman, holding a small bundle in one hand and leaping from a window to the rung of a ladder on a fire truck to climb down. He ran to a clear spot, laid the bundle in the grass and removed his helmet before giving a cat CPR.

"It's Barclay!" Cassie exclaimed.

"Oh my God, it is!" Molly started to cry. First, the bomb and, then, rescuing a cat from a fire. He'd put in a rough day.

"That boy's all right in my book." Milt tooted a little to confirm his statement.

"Holy hell, wonder what it's like to kiss a cat? Think it has salmon breath?"

"Dad!" Molly went from crying to laughing. "You say the craziest things."

On the screen, an old woman hugged Barclay. The announcer spoke on, "As you can see, Thelma Rosen, the owner of the cat, known as Princess, was quite grateful to the fireman, identified as Barclay Gray, for saving her cat." Thelma came on the screen. "Princess is all I have left and that handsome young man saved her." She smiled and held a hand to her chest. "He called me Miss Thelma and kissed my hand after he carried me over to the ambulance."

The announcer gave a toothy grin. "Well now, wouldn't we all like to be rescued by a hero like that?"

Molly smiled as she sipped her tea. I *was* rescued by a hero like that. And boy, can he kiss. She pulled out her cell and sent him a text. *U didn't kiss my hand when u rescued me.*

Almost immediately, her cell chimed. *The mood you were in, u'd have ripped my lips off.*

She chuckled as she keyed in, *I have a new nickname for you... Princess.*

I'm going to bite your ass for that.

Her tummy fluttered and moisture pooled.

No response?

She might as well be honest. *Well, my panties just got wet.*

Jesus, ur killing me here.

This was a good place to stop the conversation. Let Barclay think on that for a spell. The oven buzzer went off. "Sounds like our supper's ready. Cassie, do you want to set the table?"

The men were leaning forward listening to the weather for tomorrow. They had the back side of Milt's cottage and the trim to paint and were hoping for another nice day like today to finish the job.

"If we can keep Dad focused on Barclay and the cat and the work scheduled for tomorrow, maybe he'll forget about Mom's apple pie." Molly set the pan of meat loaf and the round casserole of macaroni and cheese on the top of the stove to cool. She pulled the salad and a couple bottles of dressing from the refrigerator before pouring more iced tea.

Milt hugged Molly when he left. "That was one of the best meals I've had in a long time, Baby Snooks." He took Cassie's hand. "Come on, Sugar Plum, I'll walk you to your car." No sooner had Cassie and Milt left than her dad tugged his shirt tail out of his pants. "I'm heading for the shower." She went over to Barclay's place to let the dogs out for a while. To give them some exercise, she tossed a Frisbee for half an hour.

Wearing his pajamas, her dad stood at the door, watching. "Wouldn't you like to live here year round, Molly? You're making friends. This is a great little cottage. Good size for us." He opened the door and called for Maggie Mae. "You ready for bed, girl? Molly, might as well let the other two stay here with us too. Bring over some food and a couple toys. Any man decent enough to put his lips against a cat's deserves to know his dogs aren't left alone."

Molly was scanning the BDSM sites Barclay had told her about. She'd showered and left her ankle unwrapped. Her skin was starting to look funny from being tightly covered with an Ace bandage for days. Just that little difference of freedom inflated her mood. What she was reading both calmed her about the lifestyle and confused her. What parts was he into? All of it?

Her cell rang and the display read, Barclay. "Hey"

"Sugar. I'm about ready to crash for the night, but needed to hear your voice first. What are you doing, love?" He sounded so tired.

"Lola, Caroline and I are in bed, reading about BDSM."

"Are all my girls with you? That's nice. Is Maggie Mae with your dad?"

"Yeah. Hon, how much of this are you into? Should I read all of it?"

"Crap. No, I should have made that plain. Domination and submission."

"Okay, that relieves me a lot. And you will only practice

138

domination in the bedroom?"

"Yeah. I mean I might try to be domineering at other times, but that's when you have to call me on it." He snorted. " Course that's when I'll tote you into the bedroom to finish things."

"Well, you'll be happy to know I wore that gawd-awful boot until I took my shower."

He yawned. "You did? I'm proud of you, Sugar. Do you have unlimited calling?"

"Yes, why."

"Then don't hang up. Sleep with me like this, over the phone." There was another yawn. "I love you." And the snoring started.

She pulled the cell away from her ear and stared at it. Why waste the minutes? Why not just hang up? Because he'd asked her to sleep like this. Because he might become her Master. Maybe. *That* part she hadn't decided yet. She had more research to do first. But she *was* finding out more about her sexuality. Things he said and did turned her on more than she ever expected—or was it just her inexperience with only one lover in her past?

Her night was restless, full of dreams of abuse, beatings and unbearable pain. Although her mind had handled what she'd read on D/s relationships, during the dark hours of sleep, fears crept in, twisted and defiled it all. She woke in a cold sweat, gasping and begging Wade and Barclay to stop hurting her. Both dogs licked the tears from her cheeks, whining in concern. She hugged them to her and cried.

"Molly? Sugar? Sugar, what's wrong?"

She glanced around her shadowy room. How did Barclay get in here? "Where….where are you?" She scooted against the headboard and, in the process, felt her cell phone.

"I'm at the station. You must have been having a nightmare. Your crying and begging for mercy woke me up. What were you dreaming about?"

How could she tell him? After all, she'd had sex with him already with some minor Domination elements. It made no sense to have nightmares about it now. "I don't remember."

"We don't lie to each other. Were you having a nightmare about D/s?"

"Yes. You didn't tell me you loved me until after I crossed that line with you. After I allowed you to dominate me to a small degree, but what if I can't go any deeper into this lifestyle? It won't be fair to you. It'll break my heart to lose you. But will you still love me? Oh God, I'm not making any sense. Just hang up."

"No!" His voice was quiet, yet demanding. "I love you. Period. What happened between us, did any of it make you uncomfortable? Did I scare you?"

"No."

"If I promise you something, do you trust me enough to live up to it?"

"Yes."

"We'll keep things between us as they were the other morning, until you're ready to try something new. Honesty, trust and devotion are very important in this lifestyle. Now, go back to sleep. Keep the phone on in case you need me again. I love you, Sugar."

"I love you too." Before she and the dogs could get settled once more, Barclay's deep breaths filtered through her phone. Boy, that guy could drop off to sleep faster than anyone she knew.

After letting the dogs outside, she took a quick shower, got dressed, wrapped her ankle and put on her much hated boot. She made a pot of coffee and filled the dogs' bowls with kibble before calling them back inside.

"Who the hell are you?"

Molly whirled around at her dad's angry voice. He was looking straight at her. "Dad, it's me, Molly." Dear God, had he forgotten who she was? Her stomach did a double twist before it fell.

"My Molly just got on the bus for school." He pointed toward the door. "Now you get the hell out of my house!"

Her heart sank. He'd suffered a huge setback during the night.

How could she bring him back to the present? "Are you and Milt going to paint today? Or are you too tired?"

He stared at her for a minute as she pulled out the makings for pancakes. "Hell's bells, I'm not too tired to push a roller." He looked at his pajamas. "I better get my work clothes on."

"Dad?"

"Yeah?" Thank God, he'd answered her.

"I washed your painting clothes and put them on top of your chest of drawers. Do you see them?"

"Sure do. Thanks."

He'd answered her normally, but she still trembled from the look of strangeness on his face when he didn't recognize who she was and ordered her out of the cottage. The rumble of the metal gates sounded as they swung open and Milt's Cutlass coughed its way in. She walked onto the porch and waved. "I'm getting ready to make pancakes. Do you want some? Come on and join us." If the two men were going to work together, Milt needed to be aware of her dad's actions this morning.

While her dad's electric razor buzzed in the bathroom, she talked to Milt.

"He might need a change in his medicine. Look you're in the best place for this kind of disease." He waved his hands wide. "Hell, this is retirement home heaven down here. Experts in dementia and Alzheimer's abound. Let me talk to Charlie in my building. His wife had this same condition and he found her this great specialist. Can't cure the damn stuff, but we can slow its progression."

Milt was tucking into his second helping of pancakes when her dad stumbled in, rubbing his forehead. "Had the craziest dream. There was a stranger in this kitchen." His face lit up. "Oh, blueberry pancakes, my favorite."

While the men painted, Molly went shopping. She needed some clothes to replace what had been in her carry-on her dad had lost. A customer had paid her online, so she had some funds for shopping. Mainly, she needed a diversion. Her *own* dad hadn't recognized her this morning. She hadn't expected that degree of confusion for a couple years.

Could he have been dreaming? Sleep walking? Why would he suddenly not know her? One good thing, bringing him back to the present hadn't been hard.

On a whim, she bought three bra and thong sets in black, red and purple. At another store, she found a couple pair of jeans and a few tops. Then she hit the grocery store. By now, boot or no boot, her ankle was throbbing.

Her cell dinged. It was a text from Barclay. *How r u?*

Good. Shopping in my damn boot.

For?

She grinned. She'd never been able to tease with Wade. *Eggs and thongs.*

OMG woman! Will have that image all day. Ur ass in a thong. Tell me u didn't get red.

She didn't respond.

Well???

You told me not to tell u.

Every time I text u give me a hard on.

Stop texting. And it's a shame u don't like black lace. Crotchless black lace.

BRAT!!!

It was Barclay's day to cook and he was putting three chickens in the oven. Thongs, his Sugar bought and he had another twelve hours on his shift before he could see her again.

Wolf laughed as he poured a cup of coffee. "Molly's getting to you, isn't she? In a big way." He chuckled some more and shook his head. "Man, you have got it bad."

"What are you talking about?" He washed the remaining rub off his hands.

"You just put three half-gallons of ice cream in the oven."

Barclay snatched some paper towels to dry his hands. "The

hell I did."

Wolf motioned his cup toward the stove. "Check, Ghost."

He opened the door and swore in two languages as he yanked out three half-gallon blocks of chocolate marshmallow ice cream rubbed with curry powder, ginger, mustard and peach jam. He turned off the oven, looked in the refrigerator and pulled out three honest-to-god chickens. He sliced off the rub and rewrapped the ice cream in foil before tossing them back into the freezer.

"Something bothering you that you need to talk about?" Wolf pulled out three crockpots and plugged them in.

"No. She's having second thoughts about us moving too fast." He cut off the plastic wrap from the birds and ran cold water over and inside the chickens. "How soon did you know Becca was the one for you?"

"First time I laid eyes on her playing with Einstein in her back yard. The sight of her took my breath away."

Barclay plopped a clean chicken in each crockpot and added some chicken broth from a container he found in the refrigerator. "See? That's what I'm saying. A man sees what he wants, he goes after it." He reached for some spices and shook them over the birds like a man possessed.

"Alphas." Wolf gulped his coffee.

"Fuckin' A." He put the lids on and set the dials. Then he started peeling potatoes, cutting onions and scraping carrots to add to the chickens. He was in the process of cleaning up his mess when the siren rang once and the dispatcher's voice gave the location of the fire. He lowered the temperature on the cookers and sprinted for the equipment room to put on his gear.

Quinn was already yelling, "Scramble! Scramble! Scramble!" Damn his impatient ass.

An older ranch house had smoke rolling out the basement windows when they pulled up. As they clambered off the trucks, one of the firemen uttered, "Lay you odds it was a kid playing with matches or a gang cooking meth had their operation blow up."

They ran toward the house with their hoses when the bullets started to fly. As trained, they dropped to the ground and directed their water flow toward the windows the shooting came from. Noah was on the phone to the police. "Crawl backwards, fellas. I don't want to attend any of your sorry-assed funerals. We'll hose down the house as best we can, but from a safer distance. Let the cops clear the place out first."

"I'm going to need a medic." Jace's voice was strained.

Wolf and Barclay rolled toward him. "Where were you hit?" Wolf placed a hand on his younger brother's back.

"My thigh."

"I'm hit, too, and I'm gonna kick some ass," Ivy Jo warned. "Someone get me a gun! Bastard shot my butt and the first one of you guys who laughs gets his ass kicked next. Oh God, I can feel it swelling...and don't y'all look, either."

Noah cursed before he issued the order to blast the house with the strongest water pressure they had to give Wolf and Barclay cover to carry Jace and Ivy Jo to the ambulance.

"Wolf, call Wendy Anne after the ambulance leaves. Tell her it's just minor."

"I'm going with you. Do you think I'm deserting my brother?" The medic cut away Jace's pants leg, revealing lots of blood and an entry wound. Big, bad, ex-SEAL Wolf took one look at his younger brother's blood and crumbled in a dead faint.

Quinn grinned from ear to ear. "Oh, am I glad I got to see this. Ghost, you ride in the ambulance with Jace. I wanna be here when this candy-assed brother comes to."

"Hey, go easy on him. Family can create some strong connections. Wait until Cassie has a baby. When that baby hurts, you'll hurt." Barclay shook off the anger and deep-seated pain of the loss of his own baby and jumped in the ambulance. Someone shut the door and the vehicle sped off, siren blaring.

"Where's Wolf?" Jace raised his head from the gurney.

"As soon as he saw your blood, he passed out."

Jace's expression of shock was priceless. "Wolf?"

Barclay patted Jace's shoulder. "You know how much he loves you, his whole family."

"Call Wendy Anne for me. Tell her what happened, but that it's just minor."

He reached inside his protective gear for his cell. "I'll call her, but I won't lie to your wife." He pressed a speed dial number. "Wendy Anne?"

"Barclay? What a surprise. You never call me. Jace, yes. Me, no." She gasped. "What's happened to him?"

"I'm in the ambulance with Jace. Evidently a meth lab blew up and started a house fire. When we got there, the cookers started shooting. Both Jace and Ivy Jo got hit. Jace in the thigh and Ivy Jo in her behind." He looked at Jace. "He's conscious, but in pain. He's losing blood and they've started a transfusion."

"Why are you with him and not Wolf?"

"Well, sweetie, when the medic cut Jace's pants and Wolf saw his brother's blood, he fainted."

"Get out of town. *The* Wolf passed out?"

"Yes. Can I tell Jace you'll meet him at the hospital? He'll need surgery. It'll help if he knows you're waiting."

"Hold the phone to his ear."

Barclay didn't know what Wendy Anne told Jace, but strength slipped into his expression. "I love you, baby. I need you. Bye." He swiped the screen to end the call.

CHAPTER FIFTEEN

Molly searched in Barclay's cabin and found the keys hanging on his wooden dog key holder for the fuchsia cottage. It was the next place to start searching for her mother's ashes. As soon as she stepped inside, she got an uneasy feeling. Odd, since the place was empty and only partially refurbished. New studding was put in to widen the bathroom to accommodate the washer and dryer. All of the kitchen cabinets were removed and new tile was on the floor.

Yet, there was food and beer in the refrigerator. A towel and washcloth hung in the partially usable bathroom. In the back bedroom was a sleeping bag, a lantern and a duffle bag. On the floor was Wade's tan blood-splattered t-shirt from the fight he and Barclay had. So, this is where he'd been staying.

She dialed Barclay.

"Yeah."

He sounded wrong. Tense. "Hon, are you okay?"

"Rough day. Jace and Ivy Jo got shot. I'm at the hospital with them, waiting on Wendy Anne and Ryder, the man Ivy Jo dates. Both are in surgery."

"My God, what happened?"

"A meth lab blew up, started a fire and when we arrived on the scene the bad guys started shooting at us. I rode in the ambulance with the two who were hit."

"You're okay?"

"My nerves took a beating, but I'm fine, baby."

"I'm calling to ask your permission to do something."

He exhaled what sounded like an annoyed breath. "Are we in the bedroom?"

Her temper raised a notch. Her day hadn't been roses and chocolate either. "No."

"Then do what you want. I am not your boss. That's not how this works. Gotta go, here comes Wendy Anne."

He hung up and in frustration she charged out of the cottage. "Okay, buster, you don't want to hear me out? Fine. All I wanted to do was offer you the courtesy of asking your permission to bring the police onto your property. But don't you worry, I'll handle this myself." She stormed into her cottage and opened one of the kitchen drawers to remove Deputy Darius Tomlin's card.

She told him what she'd found and he assured her he'd be right over. Since it was almost lunch, she made meatloaf sandwiches for the men and called them to come eat. She filled them in on what she'd discovered.

Milt tooted extra-long in his excitement. "That rascal! He could see by the sign, these cottages were closed for repairs so he found one to hide out in. He probably looked in the windows to see which units were getting worked on. Saw it was mine and yours. Made a nice, cheap arrangement for him."

"Wonder where he put that SUV of his?" Her dad slapped his sandwich on his plate. "Egg sandwiches! Molly, you know how I hate egg sandwiches."

"They're meatloaf, Dad."

"No, you gave Milt the meatloaf sandwiches and I got stuck with stinkin' egg sandwiches." His anger surfaced. "You think I don't know the difference?"

She yanked the small amount of left-over meatloaf from the refrigerator and made the sandwiches in front of him. "Here you are, Dad." The gate squeaked open and she glanced out the window.

"The policeman's here." Recalling how fresh he'd gotten with her the other night, she turned to Milt. "Milt, could you come along? Since you're manager and all?"

His pigeon chest puffed out. "Yes, I think I better."

"I know what meatloaf sandwiches are!"

She hurried behind her dad and wrapped her arms around him before she smacked a loud kiss on his bald head. "I know you do. I was only trying to be silly. Don't be angry with me."

He patted her hand. "I'm not mad. You go do what you gotta do. I'll wash the dishes while you're gone."

Darius knocked at her door and stepped back when she and Milt walked out. "Officer, you remember Milt. He's the manager of the cottages." She pointed to the green unit. "He'll be living there in about a week." She led the way to the pink cottage. "Like I told you, I've been trying to find where my dad misplaced my mother's ashes. We had them sealed in a wooden heart-shaped container.

"I've searched every nook and cranny of our cabin, so I decided to give this place a going over this afternoon. When I came in, the refrigerator was running, which I thought was odd. Why waste the electricity?"

The officer snapped on latex gloves and opened the door. "Takeout and beer. Bachelor food."

"If you'll look in the bathroom, you'll find a towel and washcloth."

Milt followed the officer into the small space and pointed. "There's a shaving kit."

"Don't touch that, please. I'll want it dusted for fingerprints."

Molly led them into the back bedroom. "Here's where I learned who everything belonged to." She indicated Wade's bloodied t-shirt. This is what he was wearing the night he attacked me and Barclay beat him off."

"Do you recognize the duffle bag?" Darius stooped and opened the gear.

"Yes, it's his." Molly looked around, raised her hands and let them drop at her sides. "But none of this explains who shot Wade or for what reason? I mean, why would someone want to kill him? Sure he was a bossy jerk, but there are a lot of those in the world and they don't all get shot. His killing is just so surreal. Have you found anything out about that strange key?"

"No, not yet, but George is working hard on it. He's been on the phone a lot with the police and businesses in Breckenridge."

"I wonder how he got in here?" Milt looked at the closed windows.

Darius strode to the sliding glass doors and opened them. Molly and Milt followed like lost sheep. "Forced entry. Come look, Milt. Once he pried the lock on these doors, he taped the lock so it wouldn't latch again."

Milt scratched his neck. "I will be damned."

"I'm going out to the squad car for evidence bags and gather up his things. We'll examine it all at the station. Looks like we'll start searching this area for Wade's vehicle." He took a couple steps and stopped. "Miss Molly, I was unduly fresh with you the other night. I wanted to see how angry Barclay would get. He's a suspect too."

Milt eyed her. "That's why you asked me to come along, isn't it, Baby Snooks? You needed my protection. You never need to fear with ol' Milt around. He hiked up his khakis with the inside of his arms. Why, I've got experience in the protection department."

She squeezed his hand. "Thanks for taking care of me." She leaned in. "He makes me nervous, apology or no."

Darius came back in and Milt patted her shoulder. "You better go check on your dad. I'll be here if the deputy needs someone to hold the door open for him when he carries the bags out."

Her dad and Maggie Mae were asleep on the recliner. The other two dogs came over for some attention. Lola carried a ball and she tossed it through the cottage a couple times. Her dad had done a good job cleaning up the kitchen. Odd, the dish towel was dry. So was the sink. She opened the refrigerator and found the dirty dishes stacked in there. *Oh, Dad.*

She had the dishes about washed when the gates opened and the creepy officer left. The door opened and Milt came in. He took one look at her dad sleeping and tip-toed over to the sink. "We're done painting outside for the day. I'm going to wash out the brushes and rollers and head for home. Sam and I could use an afternoon to rest. Maybe working him so hard is part of his problem." He handed her a slip of paper. "You need me, here's my number."

"Thanks, Milt, I'm glad you were here to help me with that fresh policeman. He touched me a few times in front of Barclay."

Milt's mouth gaped. "Huh. Fool has a death wish, that's all I can say." He tip-toed to the door and quietly closed it behind him.

Molly was showered and in her pajamas, reading a romance centered in a BDSM club when her phone rang. She was still half-ticked with Barclay and almost didn't answer. But that would be childish, better to tell him how she felt.

"Molly speaking."

There was a pause. "This doesn't sound like my Sugar. This sounds more like vinegar."

"How are Jace and Ivy Joe?" She'd had them on her mind all afternoon and evening.

"Resting. Both came through the surgery okay. The cookers of the meth were arrested. How was your day?"

"I don't think you really want to know."

"I asked, didn't I?" His irritation was evident.

"Well, my dad didn't recognize me this morning. Yelled at me to get out of his house. When I made lunch for him and Milt, he accused me of making him egg sandwiches, which he hates, and giving all the meatloaf sandwiches to Milt. Of course, I hadn't. They both had the same thing."

"Jesus, baby."

"When I went into the pink cottage to look for mom's ashes, I found evidence that Wade had been staying there. I called you for your permission to call the police onto your property, but you told me I didn't need your permission for anything except in the bedroom.

"So I called Officer Darius Tomlin. You recall he'd given me his card. He came over and examined the place. He found where Wade had jimmied the lock on the sliding glass doors and gathered all Wade's belongings in evidence bags. Dad promised he'd do the dishes from lunch. Instead, he put the dirty things in the refrigerator. Milt and Dad got the outside of the green cottage painted completely, trim and all, so they knocked off early for the day. No big deal. I handled it all without asking for your permission on anything."

"You had Darius Tomlin on my property? You and he were alone in one of the cottages?"

She bolted upright in the bed. "Excuse me, haven't I heard these words from you about the lifestyle? That truth, trust and devotion are very important? So, you don't trust me with Darius? Well, for your information, I asked Milt to go along since he's manager of the property and I was uneasy being alone with the officer. You can call him for verification. And don't call me Sugar." She ended the call and turned off her phone.

She was mad enough to chew lead pipe and spit out nails.

They'd both had a rough day. It was better to not talk to each other for a while, before they'd said things in the heat of the moment they really didn't mean.

Forty after six in the morning, the gates squeaked open and a Harley rumbled onto the property. A minute after the engine was turned off, someone knocked on her door. She crawled out of the bed and the dogs were exuberant with happiness, sniffing at the crack of the door. Maggie Mae whined from her dad's room. She hurried back to let the Chihuahua out before the dog's commotion woke dad.

When she unchained and opened the front door, Barclay was

hunkered, his arms open, braced for three canines who had missed their master. He petted and kissed and talked to each one before they raced off to answer the call of full bladders. When he stood, his gaze drank her in as if he were dying of thirst.

Damn, he looked great in his leathers. "Sleep well today. We'll do our best to be quiet over here." She started to close the door and a large hand slapped against it.

"Don't I get a hug?"

Before she could answer, he had her in his arms and his face buried in her hair, inhaling its smell. His hand swept down her back. "You turned your phone off last night, didn't you?" He bit her neck before soothing it with a gentle kiss.

Something hard poked her under his leather jacket. "What is this?" She felt the solid shape.

"What you've been looking for, love." He unzipped his jacket enough to reach in and pull out a wooden heart…her mother's ashes.

She held the container to her heart and her eyes flooded with tears. "How? Where? Frankly, I don't care. Thank you." She wrapped her arm around his neck. "Thank you!" That was all she could say before the dam of emotion broke and her sobbing started. She'd worried so much over her mother's ashes. It was hard to believe this nightmare was over.

He opened the door and whistled for the girls, who ran back inside, before he slipped out of his jacket and filled their bowls with kibble. He scooped Molly into his arms and sat on the recliner. "I had a lot to think about last night after one angry and hurt female turned off her phone. We didn't recheck your dad's packing when we left the condo. Nor did we make the beds. So, I stopped at the condos on the way home, talked to Zelda, asked her if she found anything strange when she cleaned the condominium. She pulled the heart from under the counter. When I told her what was in it, she all but tossed it at me. Some people have superstitions about stuff like that. She said it was buried in the sheets as if he'd been sleeping with it."

"I'm not surprised. We're both having trouble letting go of Mom, especially him."

He kissed her softly, his hand cupping her face. "I know I'd have trouble letting go of you. A suggestion. Hide this from him until you two are ready to spread her ashes. The loss or misplacement of them has been a bigger strain on you than him." He held both hands up. "Just a suggestion. Not an order. I trust you to do the right thing."

"Trust." She stared into his sea green eyes. He was referring to their brief conversation last night.

"We have a lot of things to air out. First off, before we start, Zelda had some mail she was holding for your dad." He reached behind him for his jacket and removed two envelopes.

She felt them. "They're the replacement of his charge cards. I'm not so sure he should have free access to them. There's a card for me, too, from each bank." She tapped the edges of the envelopes against her palm. "I'll hide them with mom's ashes and think about it. Lord only knows what he'd buy or where he'd lose the cards next."

"Sounds wise, Sugar. Can we talk about us now? I'm not fond of bad feelings between us. Will you give me a chance to explain? When I lost Mom and Uncle Vern in the hospital, I came to hate the smells and sounds of them. They make my skin crawl. I was there for Jace and Ivy Jo, but I wasn't happy about it. I'm sorry I was rude to you when you called. Had I given you half a chance, you would have told me about finding Wade's things in the pink bungalow. God, I cannot believe he'd been hiding out there. How did you know it was him and not some other bum?"

She told him what she found. The creepy feeling she had. How she'd called Darius and then asked Milt to go along with them when the officer arrived.

Barclay brought her hand to his mouth and pressed a kiss to the palm of her hand which made all her female parts do the happy

153

dance. "I trust you. It's other men I don't trust. I am one jealous, possessive son of a bitch and it wouldn't matter if I was pure vanilla sexually, I'd still be this way with you. I'm complete when we're together." He kissed her again, sweetly, slowly, so sensually her toes curled and her nipples peaked into needy points.

"I want to touch you, Sugar. Taste you. I'd like nothing better than to take you home and make love to you over and over, spoon against you and sleep." He kissed below her ear and slowly worked his way down her neck. "I've never desired anyone the way I do you, but you need to know I want you in my life for more than sex. For talking. For emotional comfort. For laughter. For quiet moments of being close. You need to learn to trust me."

He palmed a yawn. "And I need to go home and grab a few good hours of sleep. Is our date still on for tonight?"

"What about Dad?"

"Already talked to Milt about it. He's taking him to his place for one of his Rambo movie marathons. They'll order in pizza. Gorge on bar-b-que chips and pork rinds." The corners of Barclay's mouth quirked as he eased her off his lap so she could stand.

A dinner and a movie did sound nice. "I'm not wearing that boot."

"Your choice, Sugar." He stood and reached for his jacket.

She had to make a few things clear so he had no sexual expectations. "Let's lay some ground rules first because I'm still struggling with, still fearing parts of this lifestyle."

He laid his jacket back on the chair, his eyes narrowed and he crossed his arms. "What kind of ground rules?" It was plain he wasn't used to being told what he could and couldn't do. *Well, too bad.*

"No touching me from the waist down unless I say so." His gaze zeroed in on her boobs. "And no touching from my armpits to my navel either."

Minutes ticked by as he stared at her face. She squirmed under his close scrutiny. What was going through his devious mind?

"But I can touch your head, neck and your arms? That's all you're leaving me, Sugar? You really think you can tell a Dom what he can and cannot touch?"

"In our case, yes. You said you'd give me time." *Really, what damage can he do with having that little bit to touch?*

He slipped his hands in the back pockets of his leathers. "I'll abide by your rules if you abide by mine." His one eyebrow arched and he waited. His lips a firm line of resolve.

For Pete's sake, what kind of rules could he possibly have? After all, she hadn't pulled his hair and ordered him to tell her what her name was. "Okay. What are yours?"

Mr. Arrogance stared at the ceiling for a bit. "No touching my shoulders or my abs. And no staring at my hard-on." He had the audacity to shake his finger at her. "And for damn sure, you can't touch it to feel how big it really is, because it has various degrees of lengths."

She laughed. "That's the silliest thing I've ever heard of. Why I would never…"

"Those are my rules, take them or leave them. We can hold hands, but no touching of thighs. I think we should make that clear too."

"Well, yes, I suppose…" Why was she the one suddenly being hemmed in by guidelines?

He grinned and headed for the door. "Good, I'll pick you up at six. Oh, and wear your hair down, so I can touch it all I want. It's supposed to be cool, so wear a sweatshirt and a pair of jeans." He spun toward her door.

"You're a damned bossy guy, Barclay Gray. Do this…wear that."

He stopped and slowly glanced over his shoulder. "You've met your alpha male. What we seek is one woman we can trust to be faithful, to belong to us in every way and to do what we tell them in the bedroom. We love taking care of our woman—protecting her, indulging her and satisfying her any way we can." He cupped her face and looked into the depths of her eyes. "I'll abide by

155

your silly-assed rules tonight, because I owe you for my rudeness yesterday. But tomorrow, all rules are off."

CHAPTER SIXTEEN

Molly kissed the wooden heart holding her mom's ashes before putting it and her dad's new credit cards in her underwear drawer. She dressed, brushed her hair into a ponytail and put on the hated boot. A fresh cup of coffee in hand and two slices of toast, she opened her work programs on her laptop sitting on the kitchen table. The last few days had her behind on her web design schedule. Today, she hoped to put a big dent in her backlist.

Shortly after eleven, her dad stormed out of his bedroom and into the bathroom. She got up to pour him a cup of coffee. "Girl, why didn't you wake me earlier? I'm late for work."

"Milt called. He was tired and said he wasn't coming over until later. I think he said twelve o'clock, or so." Her dad was too agitated at the moment for her to bring up going to Milt's for the evening. "I poured you a cup of coffee. It's on the counter behind me. I've got some good news for you this morning."

"What the hell is this shit? It's not coffee. Are you trying to poison me?"

Scalding coffee struck her back. She gasped and screamed almost in the same breath, instinctively closing her laptop. Piping hot liquid soaked through her shirt, burning her skin. "Dad, why? Why would you do that to me?"

Pounding sounded at the door. "Molly! Molly, are you okay? I thought I heard you scream. Open the door for me, baby."

She backed away from her dad—the man she trusted above all others—and opened the door. "Help me get this shirt off! It feels stuck to my skin." She shook her hands, anxiety clawing its way from her chest to her stomach. "Dad threw a scalding cup of coffee on my back. Dear God, it hurts! Do you have any ointment to stop the pain?"

"It wasn't me! It wasn't me. I would never hurt my little girl." Her dad's mental clarity was returning.

Barclay's face was a mask of anger. "Turn around, love, so I can see what I'm doing. Let me examine the burns." He pulled the neck of her shirt away and peered down. "Your skin's not sticking." His hands swept over her sides as he removed the coffee-soaked top. He handed it to her so she could hold her wet and scrunched up t-shirt in front of her bra. She jerked away as his fingers lightly trailed over her burns. Even his slight touch led her one step closer to tears.

"Holy Hell! You did this to her?"

"Don't, Barclay, he was confused. He thought I was poisoning him with the coffee."

"We're going into the bathroom so I can wash you off. Then I'll go get my first aid kit." He wrapped his arm around her waist and escorted her into the bathroom. He blotted the burned areas of her back with the warm washcloth, then ran cool water over the cloth and gently touched the areas again. "God, Sugar, I'm afraid to leave you alone with him."

"Milt mentioned a neighbor of his who took his wife to a specialist in Tampa who helped her with a change of medicine. He said the couple thought highly of the doctor."

He draped a towel over her back. "I'll call Milt while I'm getting my first aid supplies." A few minutes later, Barclay strode back into the bathroom with his plastic supply box and the cell to his ear. "Any day or time. The sooner, the better. Two weeks? No, we need him seen sooner...aren't there any other openings? Can we have him there in an hour and a half? Where's your office located?" He tapped information into his cell and a screen came up. "Hold on, let me ask his daughter." He held the phone to his chest. "They have a cancellation in an hour and a half. Otherwise, it'll be a two-week wait."

"We'll take it. If I can just get him dressed and in the car."

"I'll help with that." The gate on the complex opened and Milt's eight-cylinder rumbled in. "Hold on, I'll ask Milt to drive us." Barclay rushed out.

Her dad came to the door, tears streaming down his face. "I'm sorry. My little girl, you have to know how sorry I am. I get confused and befuddled more and more."

She blinked away the tears. Her dad had always been the gentlest of men. "Are you sorry enough to see a new doctor? One who will change your medicines. They might help clear your mind a little?"

He walked in and dropped to his knees and pressed his face to her thighs and wept. "I'll do anything to keep from hurting you again. Anything, Molly girl."

"Stand up, Dad, and we'll go pick out clothes for you to wear. We were able to get you an appointment today. Milt says his friends really like this doctor."

Her dad tilted his head to the side. "Well, if Milt says, then it must be so."

She followed him into his bedroom and pulled a navy pair of pants and a yellow shirt from his closet. "Get dressed now. We'll have to leave soon."

By then, Barclay and Milt were in the cottage. "Where's your dad?" Barclay practically vibrated with anger.

"He's in his room, dressing. Would it be easier if I lay across my bed while you apply the ointment?"

"I'll do whatever causes you the least amount of discomfort. Have a seat, Milt. Give me a second to get my case out of the bathroom." Barclay squeezed tubes of burn ointment over the affected sections of her back and with gentle motions, he rubbed it in. Then he applied large bandages over the areas.

"How about a desk in here, Sugar, so you could work in a safer environment? I'll buy you one. Maybe I can find a corner unit with a small amount of work space on either side. Would you like that? Or do you want a plain, straight version?"

She looked over her shoulder at him. "You don't have to do that. That's an expensive investment when we aren't sure how long we'll be staying."

He lay on the bed beside her, his elbow pressed into the mattress and his head propped on his upturned hand. "Sugar." He wrapped his other hand around her pony tail and slid it along its length. "Don't you get it? I would go to any lengths for you. Any. I want you to stay and give us time to grow closer, to work on a solid relationship. And, while I know you don't want to hear this, you have to start thinking about the future when you can't care for your dad anymore."

"I'll hire help." She swiped at tears. "I have to hope this new doctor can slow the progression of his dementia." Her dad had always been her hero. The one person she could count on to be on her side, no matter what. She could not comprehend the person he was mentally turning into. Someone who didn't recognize her, who got easily confused and, now, showed the beginnings of violent tendencies. How many times did one's heart have to break? First, losing Mom. Then Wade's betrayal and beatings. Now this.

She glanced at Barclay. How many times had his heart broken? He'd lost so many people he loved. The fact he could even reach out to her and her dad showed a depth of character, a generosity of heart.

Barclay kissed her gently and reverently. She turned into his arms and sobbed. He cupped her head and made comforting sounds. "When I heard you scream earlier, my heart nearly stopped. I must know the woman I love is safe. Do you need help putting on a clean top?"

Love, he said. Was there truly such a lasting emotion? "No, I have a blouse I can just button up. I guess we better soon hit the road to make Dad's appointment on time. I never even got to tell him you found Mom's ashes. I'll always be grateful to you for that."

"It's not your gratitude I want. It's your love and for you to be as devoted to me as I'll be to you." His eyes warmed when they locked on hers. "We both have to remember your dad can't help the change in his personality. I yelled at him earlier." His fingers swept his blond hair back. "That was a reaction to seeing you hurt. I was wrong to bitch at him. I'll get the guys loaded in the car while you put on your shirt."

By the time she hurried out, Milt was revving the engine on his old Cutlass. Her ass had no sooner hit the back seat than he took off, tires kicking up gravel. She reached to close the door before it got knocked off as they zoomed past a palm tree.

Milt leaned over the steering wheel, his knuckles white with his fierce grasp. He glanced over his bony shoulder at her for a second, his eyes wild and the waxed eight hairs, still remaining on the top of his head, standing on end. "Don't you worry, Baby Snooks, I'll get us there on time."

She glanced at Barclay. "Why does that scare the hell out of me?"

He slid his arm around her shoulders. "Don't worry, Milt's a top-notch driver. He only looks demented."

Just then, Mr. Top-Notch swerved around a delivery truck into the oncoming lane of a man driving a convertible. The wide-eyed man yelled an obscenity at Milt about duct tape. Milt gave him the finger as he veered back into the proper lane. "Blow it out the other end and get yourself a car with some character to it. My car can take your pristine piece of shit any day."

Molly covered her eyes. *Dear God, I'm being driven by a maniac!*

Barclay laughed. "I'm thinking of having Milt give me driving lessons." She backhanded his chest, causing him to laugh even more.

Milt waved an open hand at the white van in front of them. "Would you look at this moron? Who the hell drives seventy anymore?" He passed the vehicle and when he read out loud the "Camel's Speedy Plumbers" painted on the side, he passed gas and yelled, "Plumb that, you slow-moving camel."

Within minutes, he rocketed around a black SUV with its back end smashed in. "Hey, the ass end of your car is almost as flat as your head."

The driver raised a revolver and pointed it at Milt.

Milt laughed. "He thinks a little pea shooter like that is gonna scare the daylights outta me? Hell, I've been on secret missions."

Molly's Dad clasped Milt's shoulder. "I want you to stop yelling at everyone. There are nuts out on these highways. The last thing we need is a bullet in someone's head. Bad enough I hurt my daughter this morning. Besides, sometimes she gets car sick."

Milt pulled his car in front of the SUV. "Okay. Okay. But fuck 'em and all the fish nuts they eat, if they can't take a little joke."

"Time to pack that shit away, Milt. Molly and Sam have both had a rough morning." Barclay tucked her closer. "How's your back feeling?"

"Still stings, but thanks to you, I'll be fine."

He lifted her and twisted he around on his lap so one hand rested on her bottom and the other arm draped around her neck so nothing touched her burned skin. "Close your eyes, Sugar. Sleep for a few minutes." He pressed a kiss to her forehead. "Want me to sing to you?"

The car lurched, brakes squealed and, in true fashion, Milt leaned his head out of the open window. "Where did you learn to drive? Idiots-R-Us?"

By the time Milt zipped into a parking spot at the medical center, Molly didn't know whether to laugh or pound Milt's head with her purse. Honest to God, the man had grumbled and cussed every driver on the highway and bridges between Indian Rocks Springs and Tampa, while he'd broken at least twelve driving violations.

As they hurried across the parking lot, her dad asked the same question she was thinking. "Milt, have you always driven like that?"

"Oh, hell no. I've slowed down a lot. My nerves just can't take the daredevil moves like it once did. We change as we age. Right?" He elbowed her dad.

"Jesus, God help us." Barclay took her hand and winked.

"I'm asking the doctor for anxiety pills for our driver while we're in there with him. He's one of the sweetest men alive until he gets behind the wheel, then he turns into the chainsaw killer. It's barely one o'clock and already I've had the high of getting my mom's ashes back, the sensual sweetness of having you hold me, the shock and pain of dad throwing scalding coffee on me and the horror of riding with Madman Milt. Honest to God, what else can go wrong?" Her hand flew to her mouth. "Our date tonight."

"Yeah, but we set up rules. Remember?"

Dr. Stafford was a question asking doctor. More importantly, he listened to and wrote down her dad's answers. Then he'd ask her if she had anything to add. Was she seeing things the same way? There were things she talked about, her dad didn't recall. Like not recognizing her yesterday and ordering her out of the cottage and the fuss he made about meatloaf sandwiches when that's what he was eating. He'd already forgotten throwing the cup of scalding coffee on her back this morning. He knew he'd done something bad; he couldn't recall what. She turned, unbuttoned her blouse and showed them both the patches over the worst of the burns.

Her dad burst into tears.

The doctor asked her if she wanted him placed in a special home for patients with dementia and Alzheimer's.

She grabbed her dad's hand. "My father and I belong together. We're here for help. Is there a way you can reduce his confusion that only seems to happen in the early hours of the day and slow up the progression of this disease?"

The three of them talked some more and in the end, Dr. Stafford took her dad off the medicine he was on and placed him on two newer types. He also ordered some tests, including an MRI. Dr.

Stafford slid his wheeled office chair in front of her dad and took his hand. "Lots of people your age are going through this mental confusion."

"They are?"

"Yes. I have hundreds of patients who have the same symptoms as you and I'm only one doctor. There are over twenty doctors like me, who only treat patients with dementia. This—what you have—is nothing to be ashamed of, but you need to trust me." He patted her dad's hand before releasing it. "You need to follow my orders to slow up this disease. We can't make it go away, but we can keep it from getting worse for a while. Will you let me help you, Mr. Devon?"

Her dad looked at him for a while as if taking his measure. "Yes, son, I think I will."

"Good." He shook her dad's hand. "I like you, Mr. Devon. I think we'll make a good team."

A beam of pride lit her dad's face. "Well, hell's bells, I like you too."

When they walked into the waiting room, their hands full of pamphlets on dementia, prescriptions and orders for lab tests, Barclay and Milt both stood, concern on their faces.

Barclay clasped her dad's shoulder. "What did you think of him, Sam?"

"Sharp fella." He nodded. "I liked him. He told me I shouldn't be ashamed, and we're going to work as a team to ease some of this confusion. I'm glad we came. Real glad."

Molly patted Milt's back. "Could we trouble you to take us to a drug store? Dr. Stafford put him on two new medicines."

Now, Baby Snooks, you know I'd do anything for you or your dad."

While the drug store filled the prescriptions, they went to a fast food joint for something to eat. Molly told her dad about Barclay recovering the lost heart with her mother's ashes. His whole demeanor seemed to lighten. "So we have my Tammy back? You know it's a beautiful afternoon. The sun is shining and the sky is the shade of blue she always loved. Maybe we should spread her ashes when we get back. You know that's what she wanted."

"She wanted them spread at sunset."

Barclay reached for her hand. Somehow he knew she wasn't ready to let go of her Mom. "Hold on. Let me check the weather for tomorrow. You know some of the guys will want to be there to support you, Hell's Bells. Friends do that for each other. Right?"

Her dad nodded. "True. I've been to many a funeral to show respect to a co-worker or neighbor when he lost his wife."

"So have I, Sam." Barclay slipped his cell out of its scabbard and tapped a few screens. "Weather's to be slightly warmer tomorrow. Sunny. How do you feel about tomorrow at sunset? We could have a little meal afterward, if you want."

"Well now, son that would be right nice. Tammy always did love having company over, didn't she, Molly?"

Barclay tapped a screen on his phone. "Sunset is at six-twenty tomorrow. What if everyone gets to your place at six? Does that sound okay for you two? Or we could wait for another day. This is a decision you two should make." Barclay looked from Sam to Molly.

"No matter when we do it, it'll be hard. But not as hard as the day we lost her." Molly glanced at Barclay with woeful eyes. "Having some of our new friends there will help get us through it. Are you okay with all this, Dad?"

"This is how she wanted things. We need to honor them. I'm just relieved Barclay thought to check back at the condo where we were staying."

On the way home, her dad took the first pill of one of his new medicines. Milt asked him about coming over to watch some movies. Before long, they were engrossed in which Rambo flick was the best.

While the guys painted the inside of Milt's bungalow and office, she laid on the bed, holding the wooden heart and saying her own goodbyes. She fell asleep and didn't wake until her dad came inside to clean up to go to Milt's. She quickly hid the ashes and went out to the living area. "How did the painting go?"

Milt opened a bottle of water. "Place is shaping up nice. We painted the office a pale gray with white shelves and desk." He took a couple long gulps. "The living room and kitchen is an off white and the bedroom's a sage green. Barclay's painting the bathroom yellow like you've got in these rooms. Listen, I told your dad to pack an overnight bag. We might fall asleep in front of the TV and be too tired to make the drive back here. If you put his medicine in a baggie and label it with the time, I'll see he takes it. Best you give it to me, though, so it doesn't get misplaced."

She glanced toward her dad's bedroom door. "You know he's been worse with his disorientation in the mornings. I'd feel awful if he hurt you."

Milt hiked his pants up. "I know how to handle him. Don't you worry. If things get too bad, I'll call Barclay. I figure you two will be snuggled in together anyways."

She wasn't so sure how she felt about that. For darn sure, she wasn't going to ask what he meant. His smirk explained it all and she was rather embarrassed. "I'll get Dad's meds ready."

CHAPTER SEVENTEEN

After Milt and her dad headed off for an evening of Rambo and junk food, Molly wiped off the kitchen table and chair where her dad had thrown coffee. She also mopped the sticky mess off the floor. After opening her laptop, she was relieved to find no effects of spilled liquid on it. She turned it off. Another day of no work. She'd soon have to fire herself. After placing her computer on the counter, she went into her bedroom, undressed and slipped into her robe, planning to take a long bubble bath, trying her best not to get her bandages wet.

Soaking in the warm water, she fretted over the evening that lay ahead. She was going on a date with a sexy, attentive man. A Dominant. Yes, she'd laid out rules, but would he adhere to them? Dominants expected submission. While she didn't mind obedience, to a degree, she wanted it to be her choice, not her duty.

Since Barclay said it would turn cool this evening, she chose one of her new pair of jeans and one of the Florida sweatshirts she'd bought in pale lavender with a row of sea shells across the bust line. The ugly, cumbersome blue boot went into the closet; she'd not wear it tonight. Since her foot was still swollen, she removed the shoestrings from the sneaker to accommodate her fat food and then obsessed over whether or not she should remove them from the other shoe.

This is my problem, I obsess over simple shit and let my hormones blindly lead me into potentially dangerous situations. Domination and submission for god's sake. I sampled it once. Liked it. Now walk away before he drags me deeper into the lifestyle and I get hurt.

At Barclay's request, she brushed her hair until it shone and sprayed it with rose and orchid spray just as she sprayed it on her body earlier.

She was so nervous, her stomach was going on a rollercoaster ride, up and down, twisting and turning. She was going to drink her dinner. Wine…both red *and* white. With a margarita chaser.

Six sharp, someone knocked at the door. She hobbled on her crutches to open it and Barclay stepped inside, his gaze sweeping over her as if he was a starving man and she was a sirloin steak with all the trimmings. He backed her against the wall beside the door.

"You look beautiful."

"Thank you." He had a way of making a woman feel special.

"The color of your sweat shirt was a good choice. It brings out the lavender in your eyes." He cupped her face, allowing his fingers to sift back through her hair. "I don't think I've ever felt hair this silky."

He leaned in, minty breath feathering across her face and her heart rate kicked up. Lime and ginger cologne invaded her nose. The plain black pullover he wore, with the sleeves pushed partway to his elbows, showcased his muscles and tight faded jeans hugged his thighs like a pair of lover's hands. He looked like sex in sneakers, whatever color they were. Her gaze really hadn't made it that far yet.

What it did grasp was the way his sea green eyes grew more intense as his head lowered and his lips covered hers. He drank from her lips as if he were savoring a fine wine, sipping, licking and sucking. On a male groan of need, his mouth took command of hers, scorched her feminine synapses in her brain so all she could think was *yeah baby*. She'd have to call this kiss "The Scorcher." Her crutches clattered to the tiled floor as her arms drifted over his shoulders and he pulled back.

His eyebrows rose. "Rule number one. No touching my shoulders."

So, this was how he was going to play it, the big jerk. Fine. She bit his lower lip and he fisted her hair, pulling her lips to his again. My God, the man could damn near kiss a woman senseless. She couldn't recall a rule about touching his back, so she placed her hands there and pulled him toward her.

He broke the kiss again and slowly shook his head. "Rule number two. No touching my abs. With you pulling me against your fantastic body, you're rubbing against them so you can feel me up. I see how you work, young lady."

"Oh, for heaven's sake."

"In fact, you're damn near about to break rule number four by jerking me against you like that. You were trying to feel how big my hard-on is. And I'll have you know I'm going commando tonight, so don't take advantage."

"I...I most definitely was not!" Gee, *does* he have a hard-on? And, my God, *no* underwear? Her gaze dropped, ever so slightly.

He tsked several times as he waved his finger back and forth. "Now you're breaking rule number three. Looking to see if I have an erection." He bent and picked her crutches off the floor. "Take these and get that pretty behind of yours out to the truck before we break all the rules we laid out for tonight."

She jerked them from his hands and spared him a scowl. Damn, if she wasn't pissed. He'd purposely set her up. And she'd fallen for it. *What a dope I am.*

Quite pleased with himself by the smirk on his face, he had her by the elbow, escorting her to his pick-up. "Never took you for a rule breaker, Sugar."

"How many times do I have to tell you, don't call me Sugar?" She raised her crutch to make another stride and jammed it onto the top of his foot before she made her next step.

"Awl. You did that on purpose!" He limped for a couple paces.

"You're lucky I don't smack your backside with this crutch. You and your damn rules."

He grabbed her biceps and lifted her so they were eyeball to eyeball. "You just do that, Sugar, and all rules are off. I'll carry you back inside and kiss you from your scalp to the soles of your feet. Believe me, I won't miss one inch of your delectable body. So, go right ahead. Smack my ass with one of those crutches, you can't seem to hang on to, and I will love you like you've never been loved. And I'm going to start with this sexy beauty spot that worries the hell out of me." The tip of his tongue circled it.

Her legs wrapped around his waist and she didn't give a damn if that broke a rule of his, or not. "You can't be serious." Her hormones and all the trembling parts of her body told her to shut up for once in her life. To stop being so damn reasonable. They'd like to see if he really could make love better than Wade, who'd been her only sexual partner. "I won't deny I find you attractive and very caring, but we've only met a few days ago."

"Yes, and we clicked right away. I've gotten on your nerves and you've gotten under my skin. I can't recall ever wanting a woman the way I want you." He ran his teeth along her jaw and then bit her neck.

She quivered in his arms as common sense fell to the ground on top of her crutches. "Take me inside. Show me if a fireman knows how to start a fire. *God, I can't believe I said that.*

He spun toward the cottage, his hands holding her ass while he bit and sucked her lower lip repeatedly. "Oh, Sugar, it's not the starting of the fire you need to worry about. It's how I plan on putting it out."

"Did you make reservations at Guppy's like you mentioned? Can we have sex and still get there on time?"

He stopped and stared at her as if she'd grown three noses. "Hell no, we can't make love and still have time to go out to eat and see a movie. I plan on taking hours with you. *Hours,* baby. The hell with sea bass at Guppy's, although they do make the best in the area, and we won't make it to the Bond movie either."

170

She planted her palms on his cheeks. "You were going to take me to see the newest James Bond flick? I *adore* double-oh-seven."

His eyes narrowed and a muscle in his jaw jumped. "There was something about the way you breathed 'oh' that I don't much care for."

Oh, so the man had a little streak of jealousy in him. Not just with police officers, but with movie stars too. She tapped her index finger against her cheek. "Gee, I don't recall there being a rule against the way I said double-ooohhh-seven."

"Make your choice. Bond tonight and me tomorrow or me tonight and that wuss, double-ooohhh agent, tomorrow."

She reached between them and wrapped her fingers around his erection and, in her best Bond impersonation, quipped, "Well, a bird in the hand…"

Barclay stepped over her crutches and laughed the whole way to the front door. "God, woman, you know how to make me happy."

He stopped kissing her long enough to ask for her keys to unlock the door and held her while she dug them from her small purse. She squeezed her legs tighter around him and he didn't think he could get them inside quick enough. As soon as they stepped over the threshold, he locked the door behind them. He spun around to brace her against the wall because he had to taste her mouth again. Her eyes were wide and violet, focused completely on him. The pulse at the base of her neck was beating like a frightened rabbit's.

She wasn't ready for this. He was pushing her.

"Sugar, if you're not one-hundred percent with me on this. I can stop. Because once we step into the bedroom, I'll go all Dom on you. The bedroom is where I'm in charge. I'll also show you Doms care about their submissives. I might push you, but I won't hurt you. I promise."

"I know, but I'll still be scared."

"Oh, baby, you're not ready. Look, we'll go to dinner and the movie just like we'd planned." He planted kisses to both of her cheeks. "It'll be an enjoyable evening, I promise. I won't push you to do something you're not prepared for."

Her thousand-watt smile that lit him from the inside out blazed into him. "Oh, I'm ready. I might be more than a little nervous. I'm not as experienced or as small as the kind of women you're probably used to, but I want this. Do you have condoms?"

He carried her into her bedroom. "I only brought two. So we'll have to make each time count." After he sat her on the bed, he knelt between her legs and slipped off her sneakers. "I promise not to hurt your burns, pet. You have to promise me, no matter what position I put you in, if it hurts, even a little, you'll tell me right away. Do you follow me?"

Her forehead scrunched. "Oh, Master, I'm dumber when it comes to sex than I thought. Positions, as in pleural?"

He ran his hands under the front of her shirt to feel her satiny soft skin. "How many lovers have you had?"

"Wade and I dated off and on since high school. Once we got engaged two years ago, we started having sex, but he only ever did it one way...Master." Bless her sweet subbie heart, she was trying to remember the rules.

Barclay rested his head against her thigh and slowly raised his gaze to meet hers. He smiled. "My pet, you are every man's dream. I know you were mine the other morning. Making love to you was the sweetest experience."

"Then why did he cheat on me? I still don't get it."

"Let's undress while we talk about this." Maybe if he kept her engaged in conversation, he could have her naked before she froze with fright. Her fingers were fidgeting with nerves even though this wasn't their first time making love. That bastard Wade had done a number on her. He grabbed the hem of his shirt and she did the same with hers. "Now, a man can tell a lot about how a woman will be in bed by the way she kisses." He yanked his shirt partway off. "By how much of herself she puts into the kiss."

He dropped his shirt to the floor and reached in his back pocket of his jeans to slip out two foil packets to place on the nightstand. "The way you kiss empties my mind of life's troubles. All I can think of is you. All I want is more of you."

Her sweatshirt was off and she'd just removed her bra, showcasing full, firm breasts and the prettiest pink nipples he'd ever seen. He remembered how good they felt and tasted. His mouth went dry and his dick swelled. She aimed her beautiful eyes on him. "Your kisses completely drain my brain, too, Master. All I can think of is wanting more. You're an aggressive kisser, yet you provide me with a sense of protection." She shook her head as she stood to unzip her jeans. "I guess I'm not making any sense."

His engorged cock fell out as soon as he unbuttoned his jeans. What a relief. Things were getting mighty tight in those worn Levi's. He stepped out of them and waited for her to finish undressing.

Molly's jeans and bikinis were halfway to her knees when her gaze landed on his pecker. Her fingers wrapped around him. "Back home, I heard two neighbor women exchanging jokes. One said 'men's peckers came in five sizes: small, medium, large, extra-large and holy moly.' I think I've just seen my first holy moly...Master."

God, she was a delight when she wasn't in a scrapping mood. Barclay leaned his head back and laughed. "And you, my beautiful woman are my treasure after so much bad shit happening in my life." He stepped around her and pulled back the quilt and covers. Warm fingers trailed across his back.

"What are these names tattooed here? I saw writing tattooed on your back the other morning, but you were on the move too much for me to find out what it all meant."

"They're the people I've lost. The ones I couldn't save in a fire or in the water." They were failures he never wanted to forget.

"So the F after a name signifies fire and the D...drowning?"

"That's right, six people I let down, so I'll carry them with me forever and hope like hell I'll never have to add any more names to the list." He lay in the bed and opened his arms for her. "Come here. Lay on top of me and drape that beautiful hair around my

173

head like a curtain of black satin while we kiss. I think the time for talking has run its course and the time for feeling and enjoying has begun."

She chewed on her bottom lip. "See, the thing is I worry about how heavy I am on top of you, Master."

"Stop chewing on that lip. No one gets to touch it, but me. As for you being heavy, whoever put that idea into your head was a moron. In my eyes, you're perfect, beautiful and damn desirable. Besides, I thought we'd cleared this issue up the first time we made love, pet. Don't let me down by mentioning it again. Come here. Press your incredible body against mine."

She did as a faint blush kissed her cheeks.

"Is your back hurting like that?" He swept his hands down her sides and over her ass.

"No."

"No...who?"

"No, Master."

"Good. Remember what I told you. The minute it hurts, you *will* tell me. Now, kiss me, until I memorize the feel of your lips and the touch of your long hair over me." His fingers sifted into her long tresses as he brought her face to his. "I haven't been able to get you out of my mind since the moment I laid eyes on you."

His tongue touched her beauty spot and then outlined the shape of her lips before he sucked the bottom one into his mouth. He big it at the same time he squeezed her ass cheeks, then ran his tongue over her lip to soothe it as he gently rubbed her bottom. "I'm going to kiss every inch of you except for what's covered with the bandages. Some places I'm going to suck and some I'll bite, but tasting every bit of you will be a sensual treat for me. And I hope for you, too, because I'm going to give you at least two climaxes on my kissing journey."

"Two, Master?"

He bit her earlobe and then sucked it. "Not enough, pet? Want three? We can do three, but once I go inside you, watching you climax three times will have me so worked up, I might not be able to hold back very long."

She leaned her head back as he bit and kissed his way down her neck. "I'm lucky if I can climax once, yet you made me come twice the other morning."

Cupping the back of her head, he brought her face closer until their noses practically touched. His eyes narrowed. "You fell apart in my arms that morning. Those climaxes were mine, pet. No one else will ever get another chance to touch you. Is that clear? From now on, every climax you have will belong to me. Just like you'll belong to me."

He was talking through his Dom passion, of course. Molly didn't argue with him. How could she when he was making her tremble under his touch. Once he'd been satisfied, his tune would change just like it did so often for Wade. Barclay would forget what he proclaimed and so would she. For now, she'd concentrate on all the glorious things he was doing to her body. Still, his tune hadn't changed after they'd made love a few days ago. In fact, he'd become more affectionate, more caring, more possessive...and she loved it.

Her arms were his current main focus as he planted gentle kisses on every surface while his other hand fondled her breast and his thumb and index finger tweaked her nipple. The combination of gentleness and roughness was a heady one.

"Open your hand for me, pet, so I can kiss your palm." His tongue touched the sensitive area in the center, followed by a gentle kiss that made her abdomen do so many twitchy things, she could barely catch her breath. There was no way he could make her react any stronger. Not with the languid way he paid homage to her arms. She was used to being rushed.

His other hand left her breast and he rolled her over before he separated her folds. "Are you okay lying on your back? Any discomfort?"

It did sting, but she could handle it if she laid real still. Her eyes widened and she inhaled a deep breath, for she'd experienced already the various talents he possessed. His fingers circled her bud until she was writhing on the bed, damn near oblivious to any pain. First one finger and then two entered her. "My stunning woman." He pumped the fingers in and out of her at the same pace he sucked her nipple.

The muscles in her abdomen coiled and tightened to a point she was gasping for breath. His thumb grazed her clit a time or two, and she moaned his name over and over.

"Come for me, pet." He put more pressure on her clit and her release made her shudder all over, almost to the point of tears. "Watching you come is so beautiful, so fucking beautiful." He wrapped his arms around her neck, laid his face between her breasts and held her close. "I love breathing the rose and orchid fragrance of your hair and the odor of your climax. Damn what a sexy combination."

While her breathing and shuddering slowed, Barclay kept one hand on her bottom and his other hand tangled in her hair.

She raised up on her elbow and slipped her hand between them, wrapping it around his cock, making a few strokes. On impulse, she licked his nipple and bit it. He sucked air and fisted her hair harder, easing her head back.

Though she did it easy, she scraped her fingernails across his balls and along his length until she circled the head. She was sure his eyes crossed. "I've never done this before. What if I do it wrong, Master?"

"Sugar, you haven't done a thing wrong yet." He rolled her over onto her back, his forehead against hers. "Don't think I'm not onto you, though. Even if you get me to come a couple quick times—and that's a big *even*—we are not going to see Bond tonight."

"But he looks so good in a tux. I think you're jealous."

"Of a screen star? Who you want to go salivate over? And get all hot and bothered about? Fuckin' A." He ran his tongue over her nipple. "But I'm telling you right now, that idea is a total bust." He drew her nipple into his mouth and sucked it hard. Then he kissed his way around the mounds of her breasts before he feasted on her nipples some more. His fingers and lips trailed a path down her abdomen.

"Spread your legs for me, pet, let me taste some of this sweetness." His tongue delved between her folds and circled her clit. Then he entered her with his tongue as if it were his pecker. She'd never known a guy would do that. She gasped.

"Am I hurting your back?"

"No, I've just never had a guy…I mean I didn't know…you're putting your tongue in there."

"Oh Sugar, wait until I make you come this way." He started tonguing her again while his thumb slowly circled her bud, closer and closer, yet never touching. Her abdominal muscles tightened again and her thighs quivered. The pressure building was beyond intense. *Dear God!*

"Come for me, pet."

She was clasping the sheet and blanket. "No. It'll be too strong. I'm afraid of the power of it." Even as the words all but clawed from her throat, her climax built to a tight coil.

Barclay wrapped one arm around her hips. "I've got you. Now, give me that climax and tell me who it belongs to." He entered her again with his tongue and made two more circles around her clit with his thumb before he pressed on it.

Her breathing stopped. Her muscles cramped. And then the sexual storm burst. She screamed his name.

"Is this climax mine?"

Hell, she couldn't talk. She nodded.

He slithered up her body until his eyes, hooded with desire, stared into hers. "I asked you a question, pet. Is this climax mine?" His chin jutted as if he were determined to have an answer.

"Yes, Master," she exhaled on a pant.

One of his sexy-as-hell smiles spread. "You're damn right it is. As long as you're in Florida, they'll all belong to me." He rolled to his side and pulled her close, sifting his fingers through her long hair.

She could barely breathe. Holding a conversation was beyond her at this point.

His wide hand covered her bottom and nudged her against his erection. Frankly, more sex at this point was the last thing she wanted. A nap seemed in order and if he didn't quite stroking her head, calming her as her trembling subsided, she'd be out for the count.

Kisses feathered across her forehead and along the side of her face. He bit her earlobe and eased the sting with a gentle sucking. "You are so special, pet." Lips trailed down her neck, a nip here and there to make her gasp. "You taste just like your name."

"Molly? What does a Molly taste like?"

He smacked her bottom once. "Smart ass brat." Another crack landed on her butt cheeks.

She wiggled against him. Darn, if she didn't like it, which was the strangest thing.

Barclay's voice deepened. "I think if I spread you across my legs and smacked you until your bottom turned a pretty pink, you'd get turned on as hell."

She leaned her head back and narrowed her eyes. "Pink? Oh, I don't think so. Is this part of that power exchange you were talking about before? Because I don't see where I hold any power in a situation where I'm getting my ass beat."

"A power exchange starts with open communication. Both parties list what they like, what they might like to try a time or two and what they definitely don't want to do. We call those 'hard limits.' I'm different from a lot of Doms. For me, a hard limit is taking my partner to a BDSM club. I don't want other men looking at her. She's for my eyes only. My enjoyment only. I'm possessive as fucking hell or I would be if I had a woman as perfect as you.

"As far as spanking, initially, you may only want enough swats to turn your skin a pretty pale pink or a bright pink. I don't leave bruises. It reminds me too much of my dad. So, I'm very careful

178

in that regard. I prefer toys like clit stimulators or butt plugs."

"But where is my power, Master?"

"You give me the power to do those things to you. Things that heighten my sexual pleasure. If you say no, I never cross that power line. In return I watch your reaction to things to judge what might bring you a stronger orgasm. I'm looking for a private Dominate/submissive relationship in the bedroom only. I might try to order you about when we're outside of the bedroom, but I'll enjoy your pushing me back. I do love to tease. Sometimes that can be a great turn-on."

Memories of Wade's abuse flooded back. "But you wouldn't put bruises on me?"

His hand was gentle against her cheek. "God, no, Sugar. Never. You'll have a safeword. As soon as you reach a point you want me to stop, say it. Let's make yours hummingbird. You use it and I'll cease whatever I'm doing right away."

"Hummingbird?"

"It should be easy for you to remember. In fact, if it makes you feel better, the first few times I smack you, you'll tell me how many times and you'll count them out. Since I'm your Dom, you'd follow the count with Sir or Master, as a sign of respect."

"This is a lot to take in. You better give it to me in small increments." She bit his collarbone. "Like five."

"Five?"

"Yes, I think I trust you enough to give me five smacks, Master."

Oh God, the look of surprise on his face is priceless.

CHAPTER EIGHTEEN

Sweet Mother of God. She'd given him permission to smack her. By doing so, she'd shown her willingness to be his sub, if only for tonight.

He slid his hands around her sweet face. "You honor me by giving me this power, pet." His lips covered hers in a gentle, caring manner and he poured all the emotions he had for this woman who'd suddenly become the healer to his raggedy heart.

After the kiss, he pressed his forehead against hers and sighed. "I won't be smacking you in the same spot every time. I might rub my hand in a circular motion over where I've slapped you to ease the sting or I might lay my palm over the spot to hold in the heat. Sometimes I might check your pussy to see how wet it's getting. Remember, with your safeword, you hold the power to make me stop. You are to follow each count with Master. Tell me your safeword."

"Hummingbird, Master."

"If you're still willing to give this a try, then lay across my lap."

Had he scared her off? He had to be honest with her, especially after her abuse with Wade. She crawled off the bed and stood, her hands clasped in front of her crotch. "I...I'm ready."

He detected a tremor in her voice. Damn, but he was pleased with his sweet sub. She was facing her fears...with him as her

Dom, who'd promised to protect her. And protect her, he would.

He sat on the edge of the bed and pointed to his thighs. "Lay so your cunt touches the inside of this thigh." He used his lower Dom voice. She quietly and somewhat awkwardly assumed the position.

Her breathing was more rapid than usual. To help her relax, he ran his palm slowly down her sides, avoiding her patches. "You're being very brave. You please me greatly." His hand leisurely circled her firm, large ass. "You're a courageous woman." He paused, so his statements would sink in. "One to be admired. You honor me by allowing me to be your Dom tonight." He began trailing his way down her spine again. "I will honor you by watching every movement, every twitch of your body for any stress. You have chosen five. That's the most I shall administer."

He was trembling almost as much as she. He raised his hand and thought of all Wade had done to her. *Please God, don't let me hurt her. I have to keep the force of my smacks firm, yet gentle.*

The first smack was on her left cheek. "Count." He rubbed over the spot to erase the sting.

"One, Master."

His next swat landed on her other cheek. "Count, please."

"Two, Master. You're being awfully gentle with these."

"If we were in a relationship, I'd add another swat to the count because you were a bit of a smartass with that remark. To answer you, my aim is to make your first experience one of arousal, not pain. God, baby, a good Dom never wants to hurt his subbie. Push her limits, sure, but hurt her intentionally...never." He added another smack.

"Three, Master. Am I allowed to ask for harder hits...Master?"

He smiled. She was a quick learner. He delivered a firmer slap and she sucked air. "Does that please my pet?"

"Oh yes, Master. Four, Master." She squirmed her delicious bottom in silent invitation.

Damn, she likes this. He held his palm over the pink handprint to hold in the heat. Slap number five was a tad harder and she moaned. "Are you okay, pet of mine?" He slid two fingers between her folds and found them wet with arousal. "Your bottom is a beautiful pink." He leaned and pressed a trail of kisses over her back as his hand softly tended to her pretty pink ass.

"Stand up, Sugar, and lay on the bed while I put on a rubber. Do you think your ankle can handle being on all fours?"

Her eyes widened. "You mean like getting on my hands and knees, Master?"

"Only if it doesn't hurt your foot, pet." He tore the end of the foil packet and sheathed himself in latex. The past hour had him so turned on he didn't know if he could last more than a few strokes, but he wanted to teach her another position besides missionary.

Two hours, many climaxes and a shower later, they slipped into theater seats with a large bucket of buttered popcorn and sodas. Barclay grumbled the entire time about her rushing him through sex so she could see the eleven o'clock showing of double-ohhhhhhhh-seven.

"You're kinda cute when you're peeved about something." Molly settled in her seat and set her Coke in the holder. "I'm quite pleased with the five climaxes I had." She'd rarely gotten one with Wade and they'd been mere tremors compared to the earthquakes Barclay had put her through. "Besides, you used all the rubbers."

The two elderly women in the row in front of them whirled around, slack-jawed and wide-eyed.

"I won't run out again for a day or so. I bought four boxes at the drug store."

The gray-haired woman choked on her soda, while her friend with the dyed, bright red hair pounded her back. "Four boxes of rubbers, Vivian," the gray-haired woman wheezed. "I don't think Ellis used that many in our entire marriage."

Vivian reached for the turquoise glasses hanging from a beaded necklace and perched them on the end of her nose. She made no pretense of checking out Barclay's body. "I'm thinking Mr. Atlas,

182

here, could deliver. My God, Weeza, he's got bigger boobs than you."

The gray-haired woman—Weeza—waved an open hand. "Hell, everyone's got bigger boobs than me. Ellis used to call me Cheerio tits."

Barclay pointed to his pecs with a fistful of popcorn and placed his lips to Molly's ear. "Do I look like I have man boobs? These are hardened pecs from lugging fire equipment and working on the cabins."

She patted his thigh. "Pay her no mind. She's probably never seen a man built like you, up close." Her teeth gently bit his earlobe. "Personally, I like you just the way you are."

He trailed his pinky finger between the juncture of her legs sending little sparks of remembrance through her system...and what a *joyous* recollection it was. He leaned his lips to her ear again. "I think I showed you earlier how damn perfect I think you are. Now, let's put on a bit of a show for these two nosy broads."

He grabbed another fistful of popcorn. "I should have gotten us each a bucket. I'm starved. No dinner. Just four hours of continual sex."

Vivian spewed soda and whatever she'd been chewing.

Weeza whirled around and scowled. "Must you keep talking about your sex life?"

"Oh, I'm sorry. Were you eavesdropping?" Barclay gave her one of his charming, sexy smiles before he leaned against Molly. "Sugar, I'm going for another barrel of popcorn and a couple slices of pizza before the previews start." He handed her the half-eaten tub and hurried off. Golly, the way he'd waded through the popcorn already, he'd better buy it by the wheelbarrow size.

What was she going to do about him? Having casual affairs was not her thing, yet here she was having one. She and her dad would fly home in a little over six weeks. As attached as she'd gotten to Barclay in almost a week, how close would they be by then? Their time in bed this evening hadn't been all sex. There'd been snuggling and sharing of ideas and secrets. He was helping her heal after losing her mom and she hoped she was helping him reconcile to all he'd lost, as well.

Talking to him was very easy. When she spoke, he gazed at her as if he were drinking in every word she said. As if her thoughts and opinions really mattered. Six weeks and it would all be over. She'd be back in cold Colorado and no doubt hearing the wrath of Wade's family. If he'd stayed in Breckenridge instead of following her here to the shore, he'd still be alive. They'd no doubt blame her for leading him to his demise.

If only I could talk Dad into moving here. Could we afford the year-round rent of a beachside cottage? Maybe. If we sell the house back home and my web-design business grows.

How much sense would it make to do all that just so she could be closer to a guy who might not want more than a short fling? How foolish would it be to give up everything and move here to be with a man, only to get dumped? A man as handsome as he would have women lined up at his aqua cabin's door and she'd have to watch the feminine spectacle. No, better to make the best of the life she had.

Barclay squeezed his way in front of other theater goers to reach his seat. She had to grin. He had two buckets of popcorn, two slices of pizza and two soft pretzels slathered with mustard. How he'd carried it all, she hadn't a clue. But it was food and he was a guy; there seemed to be a natural connection there.

"Are you really this hungry?"

He placed the cardboard containers holding the food on her lap and set the popcorn between their legs. "Hell yes, I'm hungry!" He leaned a little closer to Weeza and Vivian. "Once you put on your six-shooters and cowgirl hat. Then rode me like I was a wild mustang on an imaginary ride from here to San Antonio, you depleted my system in more ways than one."

Weeza patted her forehead with a tissue.

Vivian opened a bottle of aspirin and popped two in her mouth before giving a couple to Weeza. She shot him a narrow-eyed scowl.

"Young man, you need your ass beat."

Barclay's head bobbed. "Oh, she did that too. Used a leather flogger. Pink."

Both elderly women choked and sputtered on their drinks, trying to swallow their pills.

Molly could barely contain her laughter. "Would you just shut up and eat, before your food gets cold? Besides the previews are starting."

"I think you forgot to take out my anal plug. Every so often it starts to whirl and I want to squeal like a pig." He winked at Molly and shoved half a slice of pizza into his mouth.

Vivian and Weeza got up and moved to other seats farther up front.

"Gee, Sugar, was it something I said?"

"I think Vivian was right. You do need your ass beat, egging them on like that."

"Imagine the conversation at their next bridge club meeting or their aquatics session?" They glanced at each other and giggled. Barclay reached for another handful of popcorn. "I could never figure out why people are so anti-sex. You talk about it and their panties wad into a twist."

Previews of a futuristic flick played and he elbowed her. "Do you wanna come see that?"

"Sure. Looks like it has some great visual effects."

Once James Bond started, she cupped Barclay's manhood. He choked on his drink. "Sugar, what are you doing?"

"I'm holding *my* ooooh seven." She bit his earlobe. "Go ahead and eat your popcorn, hon, pay no attention to me."

CHAPTER NINETEEN

Barclay was having a bonfire tonight after a few more rounds of sex and his pet was sound asleep. He was burning every damn DVD he'd collected of all the James Bond movies. She was practically in a sexual frenzy. One hand on his cock and the other hand shoveling in popcorn so fast, it was like a blur of movement out of the peripheral of his vision.

When Bond came on screen in a tuxedo, Molly's grasp on Barclay loosened and she breathed, "Ohhhhh myyyy."

Yep, he was setting fire to all his double-oh-seven movies and buying a damn tuxedo. Not that he was a jealous sort. And later in the movie, when the sombitch strutted out of the ocean in a pair of white swimming trunks and *his* Sugar moaned and pointed with a fistful of popcorn—pointed, mind you—non-jealous Barclay added a white swimming suit to his shopping list.

At that point, he coiled his fingers around her wrist and whispered, "You've got butter on your fingers. You might get some on your pretty top." Then one by one, he sucked on a finger, slowly swirling his tongue around it. When he ran his tongue between each digit, she exhaled a deep breath and her eyes crossed. HeFuckin' A, he knew how to get his pet's attention away from "shaken, not stirred."

On the way home after the movie, she sat next to him with

her hand on his thigh. Being with her was both comfortable, yet stimulating. He stopped for a red light and cupped her face, leaning to cover her lips for a quick, sweet kiss. As he turned the truck right onto Gulf Boulevard, she laid her head on his shoulder.

"Tired, Sugar?"

"No. Just enjoying the closeness."

"Yeah, baby, so am I. Why don't you pack what you'll need for tomorrow morning, while I let the dogs out, and come spend the night with us? I'm not ready to be apart from you yet." Damn if he ever would be. She was a keeper. Not the kind of woman for a short-term, heated affair or a long-term live-in relationship. There was a purity about her. Beneath her sass and sexuality and her burgeoning submissive nature, there was a sweet, endearing purity.

He loved all those qualities.

He loved her.

His emotions had grown too fast, too strong. Maybe it was just lust and not love at all. Hell, he needed to change his train of thought before he proposed marriage to her in his Uncle Verne's antique truck.

He took her hand and entwined their fingers. "I called everyone I thought who'd want to come to the celebration of your mother's life tomorrow when you spread her ashes. Becca suggested pot luck, with everyone bringing a dish. We'll provide the drinks and some crabs."

She stiffened from his reminding her of the rough day that lay ahead. "Thank you. That was very thoughtful. I know Dad will appreciate it too."

"You'll get through it. I'll do whatever I can to help you." Hell, it seemed as if she'd barely had a moment of happiness since she came here. One thing after another had gone wrong. For a Dom who wanted to protect his sub, he so often felt out of control. It was his job to take care of her.

She exhaled an audible sigh. "I know I can rely on you, Barclay. Not every man has the kind of inner strength you do."

He stopped at the iron gates to the property and keyed in the security code. "Seems like we see things in each other that no one else does." He eased his truck in front of his aqua bungalow. "I'll give you time to get inside your place before I open the door to my cottage. Otherwise, the dogs will charge out to jump on you and lick you to death. Hold on while I come around to help you out of the truck."

He shoved her against the side of the door and braced both of his forearms against the truck. "I'm in over my head with you, Sugar. I love you and six more weeks isn't going to be enough time to spend with you." He leaned in and took control of her lips. "No, not nearly long enough. I keep dwelling on the day I'll have to say goodbye and you'll walk out of my life forever." He grabbed her in a fierce hug and burrowed his face in the crook of her neck. He'd lost so many people already. The thought of losing her tore at something deeper in his soul for he felt she was his other half. Just like Wolf said he felt it the moment he first saw Becca.

She sifted her fingers though his hair. "We never know how long we'll have someone in our lives. That's why it's best to love them all we can, show them how precious they are to us and absorb every moment of enjoyment we have with them. I don't want to leave you either, but we have a house in Colorado with a garage and a couple outbuildings all filled with stuff. It would take us a year to clean that mess out to move here. By then, you'll have found someone else." She swiped at tears. "When I think of the reality of it, I see how hopeless it all is."

He held her close again. Hopeless was a word he couldn't handle. "Go get your things. I want you against me every night from now on. And before you mention it, I'll talk to your dad about our arrangement."

She shook her head. "He won't remember it."

"Then I'll keep reminding him, because as long as you're in Indian Rocks Beach, you're mine."

Molly stood her crutches in a corner of her bedroom. As far as she was concerned, she was finished using both them and the boot. She sat on the edge of the bed and tried to calm the pounding of her heart from all Barclay had said. He'd sounded sincere. She had no reason to doubt him. Still, while moving from the cold winters of Colorado to the year-round temperate climate of Florida sounded grand, the job of clearing out their property would be a Herculean task. One she'd end up doing the majority of herself. It was all so disheartening.

So, while she was here, she might as well make some memories. Sweet recollections to keep her warm during the cold, windblown nights of the rest of her life. Because once she left Barclay, there'd never be another man who could measure up to him.

She changed out of her clothes, put on her black-lace, front-hook bra and matching crotchless thong and rubbed on more of the rose and orchid lotion Barclay was so fond of. Just for the element of surprise, she slipped on her robe. In a small bag, she put her toiletry items and clean clothes for tomorrow.

Barclay was tossing a couple of balls with the dogs when she came out of her cabin. "I was beginning to think you'd fallen asleep in there."

"No. I just put on my night clothes." She nonchalantly headed for his front door.

He tossed a ball again and Caroline jumped, snagging it mid-air in her jaws. "You won't need them. We sleep naked."

Knowing they were the only ones in the cottages, after she deposited her overnight bag on his sofa, she stepped onto his porch and slipped off her robe, draping it over her arm and struck a pose. "You mean, you don't like this?"

He did a double-take. "Holy Mother of God. Are they the crotchless ones?"

She laughed. "Are you going to take my word on that or would you rather find out for yourself?" She turned and sashayed inside.

"I'm bringing the dogs in and by the time we get there, you

damn well better be in that bedroom."

She glanced over her shoulder. "So, tell me, what's *your* safeword?" By his stiff-jawed reaction, she was winding him up so tight, he'd be like a raging bull when he closed and locked the bedroom door.

Good. She would see how much control he had over his Domination. How far would he take things? Would he listen to her safeword, if she used it? Could she handle it if he went too wild with her?

Barclay ordered the dogs to lie down before he opened the bedroom door and stepped inside the room where he maintained he was in charge. He stood with his arms folded and his stance wider than usual. "We need to get a few things clear. No one tops me from the bottom. Ever."

Damn, he looked and sounded pissed. She raised her opened hands and let them fall to her sides. "I have no clue what that means."

"A Dom does not have or need a safeword."

"Oh, for heaven's sake, I was only teasing you. Are you saying a submissive cannot have a sense of humor, Master?"

"You do not try to seduce me. That is topping from the bottom. That is you laying down the rules. I am the Dom." His voice was growing louder. "I run the show in this room. You wear what I tell you."

If he was going into the macho verbally-abuse-her mode, she'd just as soon be covered up. She jerked her robe off the bed and put it on. "Clearly we have two different ideas of how a loving and caring relationship works. I bought this uncomfortable thong set for you. I bought three, in fact. So when am I to wear them? When I'm fully clothed and you can't see how they look?"

"Yes," he replied as if she were a simpleton. "It will tease me, knowing you have something like that on under your clothes and no one is aware of it, but me."

"This...this lifestyle is all about you, isn't it? What you want.

What you need. What pleases you. Think about this for a minute, if you can get beyond thinking about yourself, I'm a heavy woman. It took a lot of nerve for me to put these on and parade over here as if I were some slim, sexy super model. I was nervous, embarrassed but, silly woman that I am, I thought it would be a turn-on for you. Well, believe you me, it won't take any nerve to walk over to my place and cut these thongs and the others to shreds."

She trembled with humiliation, disappointment and anger. To top it off, she felt a first class crying jag coming on and damn if she'd let him see it.

"I know you're just learning the lifestyle. I'll overlook it this time. I didn't mean to hurt your feelings." He shifted to block the door.

"You'll overlook it? Well, how big of you. I was so crazy about you, I'd have gone to almost any lengths to be with you including this lifestyle crap. Oh, you talk a good game. The Dom cares about his sub's feelings and never wants to hurt her." She poked her finger in his hardened chest. "Well, I think maybe you need a refresher course. Now, move the hell out of my way."

The flood of tears had started, which only made her angrier. She didn't want him to see the wounds he'd inflicted on her, the disappointment of how he saw her femininity—what little she had of it.

He forked his fingers in her hair. "I'm not letting you go. We need to talk. Give me a chance to explain."

"My nerves are shot, Barclay. This has literally been the trip from hell. Dad lost his wallet, my carryon and laptop. I worked at two jobs to keep us afloat since I had to buy a new laptop to keep my business going. I was beaten by Wade and suffered a sprained ankle. A guy, who wanted me for his BDSM partner, came on to me and, hell, I barely knew what BDSM meant. I found Wade with a bullet hole in his forehead. I searched for my mother's ashes for almost four days. My dad doesn't recognize me half the time. He threw hot coffee on me and burned my back. Now you yell at my first attempt at being sexy as if it disgusts you."

She inhaled a deep, shuddering breath and stared at the floor as she slowly exhaled. On one hand, the weak side of her personality wanted him to apologize and hold her while she cried. The stronger part of her, however, wanted to give him a fist in the eye and storm out. Maybe a middle of the road reaction would be more prudent. "Please move out of my way or I will break a window and crawl out. I desperately need to be alone." She was doing her best to hide how close she was to tears. Hell, a bottle of wine and she could cry herself into a major breakdown.

"Stay here. I can see how upset you are. Let's talk this out."

"If you have any shred of decency in you, you'll step aside. I can't be what you want or need." She glanced into his magnetic eyes and reached out to touch his face one more time. "We're through, Barclay."

"I'll let you go, but I won't accept it."

She was too emotionally drained to respond. As she walked past the dogs, she scratched each one behind the ears, kissed Lola on the head and made her way to her own cabin. By the time she'd made it to her bedroom, she'd removed the black bra and thong. She pulled pajamas out of her drawer, and then changed her mind, reaching for the clothes she'd worn to the movies.

Her anger grew. Whether her wrath was against Barclay, herself or the entirety of her life, she couldn't say at this moment. She took a pair of scissors to the sexy bras and thongs she'd foolishly bought for *the* Dom and shoved them into a trash bag. She stepped outside and down the driveway to the trash bin and tossed the bag in. Purchasing them had been such a foolish idea.

Barclay stood on his front porch like a sentinel. No doubt pretending he cared. She couldn't talk to him anymore tonight.

All she wanted was some quiet, a bottle of wine and a box of tissues…maybe a pound or two of chocolate. She unlocked her rental car and drove onto Gulf Boulevard in search of what she needed. Fifteen minutes or so later, she punched the code to open the gate for the driveway to the cottages. In her rearview mirror, she thought she saw a shadow or person walk by. Someone walking home late at night. She drove in, parked her car and strode for the beach with her tissues and cheap wine. Hell, she'd already devoured the two candy bars she'd bought.

It was after two am, so the shoreline was pretty quiet. A few parties were going on further up the beach, complete with bonfires. Other tourists sat on their decks or balconies, talking and laughing. Meanwhile, the more wine she drank, the faster her crying jag blew into her system like gale-force winds. It seemed as if the weight of the world were on her shoulders, which was silly, of course. Many people had bigger and scarier problems than she. No doubt, those poor souls were stronger too.

She sat on the sand, drew her knees up to her chest and laid her forehead against them to sob away much of the insecurity she felt. So she liked a little roughness in her sex and having her bottom smacked. That did not make her a submissive. It just made her weirder than she figured she already was. Ironic, wasn't it? She was too kinky for a normal guy and not submissive enough for a man with BDSM tastes. Time to face it, she was old maid material. Go home, get her business rolling again, buy a couple cats and spend her life taking care of her dad. Lord knows, he'd do the same for her if she had an illness.

The waves were an excellent backdrop to a good cry. Their continual rolling forward and receding was oddly loud, yet quiet. She needed to memorize this sound for she'd never hear it again. Maybe from the Pacific shoreline, but not the Gulf of Mexico. She could never come back to this beach. Craziness. All this worry about her mother's lost ashes and they were spreading them here where under no circumstances would they ever come again.

"Why would we do this? Why would we spread her ashes in Indian Rocks Beach where I'll never be able to return? Barclay will have his obedient submissive and I won't be able to bear seeing them together. I'll be stuck in Colorado and Mother's spirit will be here, alone. This is madness."

"Is it madness to grant your mom's wishes? Besides, you can talk to her every day. Just stay here with me, where you belong."

She whirled around. Barclay stood not four feet behind her. "How do you do that? I never heard you walk up on me."

He shrugged in the moonlight. "That's why they call me Ghost."

"Go away. I can't cry with you watching." She tipped the bottle to her mouth and gulped more wine.

"Don't you think you've cried enough? If all you want is vanilla sex, I'll learn to curb my deeper desires. We'll make it work. Don't leave me."

"From what I've read, men who don't get their kink at home, seek it elsewhere with hookers or in private clubs. I won't share you with anyone."

"But you do like a little kink." He stepped in front of her and reached for her hand. "Come home with me. No sex tonight, Sugar. Just let me hold you close."

"There's no way we can lie next to each other and not end up having sex." She took his hand and stood. "I'll go back inside because I'm cold, not because of you. And don't call me Sugar."

"That's my girl." He reached for her hand.

CHAPTER TWENTY

Barclay was emotionally gutted. Listening to Molly sob and try to express her pain to the sea and the bottle of wine she'd practically emptied nearly did him in. And to know he was the biggest cause of her unhappiness made him wonder if he *didn't* need a refresher course in Domination. Maybe the fault was with him, not her. Hell, she was perfect...and she was his. Somehow he had to convince her she belonged with him.

She was submissive. Over time, maybe he could introduce her to some sex toys. If she didn't like them, he'd be happy with the kink she could already handle and enjoy. It had to be more about her and less about him. If being a tease in the bedroom made her feel good about herself, then why the hell not allow her to do it? God, he was an ass.

Since she wouldn't hold his hand when he reached for it, he casually slung his arm across her shoulders. "I guess you feel I was out of line to follow you, but I didn't know how far you'd walk. There were some bonfires farther up the beach, no doubt with some drinking going on. I didn't know if they'd bother you or not." He didn't want a bunch of drunk men to grab at her, or worse.

"No. No one would bother me. I'm usually invisible to most people. Besides I wanted to be alone. I wouldn't have gone close to a group."

The dejection in her voice was something new and it really bothered him. "Spend the night with me, love. We'll take a shower so we don't get sand in the bed. There's no reason why we can't snuggle and not have sex. Let me hold you close and tell you how sorry I am."

She shook her head. "I'll need pajamas. If I go inside my cottage to get some, I might as well shower and sleep there."

"You could put on your red thong outfit. Red against your pretty pearl-like skin would look great." He knew how to make a woman feel good about herself. If Molly only gave him the chance.

"A little late for that. I cut them all to pieces and threw them away. I'd bought them to tease you and since that idea blew up in my face, there was no reason to keep them." She chuffed a laugh. "The cashier kind of laughed at me when I bought them. I guess even she knew what a fool I was being." She brought the bottle of wine to her lips and took another couple of sips.

There was little emotion in her voice, just a soul-deep sadness that he understood. He'd been in that cold, dark place himself until he stormed into Walgreens in a panic, asking what aisle douches were in. One look at her blue-violet eyes and full lips and he was a goner. He'd never been that strongly attracted to a woman so quickly and completely. Now, he'd damn near destroyed her.

The thought of her spending the night alone worried him. Somehow, he had to try to bring her out of the depths of her depression. In a few hours, they'd be spreading her mom's ashes and the mood she was in, he wasn't sure she could emotionally handle it. How could he keep her with him tonight?

"Don't you think it would be a wise idea for me to take the bandages off your burns so I can see how they're healing? They probably need a fresh dose of antibiotic cream. The tape will come off easier if it's wet." He steered her toward his cabin.

She dug in her heels. "I can shower at my place. If you insist, I'll call when I'm done and you can come over and smear on some cream. But it's so late, I'd sooner you just went to bed and got some sleep. I'll be fine on my own."

He coiled his arm around her waist and drew her closer. "We'll both be asleep faster if we do it at my house. I've got a large shower. Room for both of us. I can tend to you better in there." He unlocked the door and led her back to the bathroom. Take your clothes off."

He handed her a towel for her hair and she laid it across the vanity. "I'm not taking my clothes off in front of you." She emptied the bottle of wine and shook her head. Her head must have spun a little for she plopped on the commode lid.

"I don't feel secure enough anymore to let you see me naked. If I'm staying the night with you, I'll need an old t-shirt and shorts." A sadness blanketed her features as she bit her bottom lip. "The biggest ones you've got."

Damn him to hell and back. He'd done this to her. She'd opened herself to him and with a dose of his Dominant nature tonight, he'd made her feel insecure again. Was this how a man treated a woman he loved? Were the D/s rules so damned important if they hurt his Sugar?

"Look, we both have some insecurities to get over. I had to listen to you moan and groan over James Bond in a freakin' tuxedo and when he walked out of the ocean in those white swimming trunks, I thought you were going to crawl over every seat to get to him on the screen."

She laughed for a couple seconds and then caught herself. "I did not."

He pulled her up by the elbows, backed her against the wall and cupped her sweet face. "And I didn't mean to make you feel inferior earlier. Having you in my life is more important than anything." He kissed her softly, gently, as sweetly as he knew how. "Let's both be brave and take our clothes off. I'll never be a double-oooohhh, but you'll always be perfect in my eyes."

He reached back with one hand and tugged off his shirt. And waited. Finally, she heaved a sigh, crossed her arms and pulled the hemline of her top up. He toed off his sneakers and she stepped out of her flip-flops.

He stepped out of his jeans. "You know, for all the damn good it did me, going commando tonight didn't seem to bother you much. Hell, I bet you know what brand of underwear double-ooohhh wore in the flick."

She shimmied out of her jeans and panties, which was such a delight to watch. "I think they were Brutes." She had the nerve to wink at him before she turned to wrap her hair in the towel. Oh yeah, she could be real cheeky, but at least she was opening up a little.

Once he had the dual-head shower temperature to their liking, they both stepped under the spray. He handed her the bar of soap. "Would you wash my back for me, please?" Firm hands swept up and down his spine and paid extra attention to his trapezius muscles. "You've got strong hands."

"Housework." To his surprise she stooped and soaped his ass and legs. "Turn around. I'll soap your arms and chest." When she squatted to wash the front of his legs and feet, she purposely ignored his cock and balls. She handed the soap back to him. "All done."

He pointed. "You missed a spot."

She rolled her eyes. "I'm here so you can take care of my burns. Right? Wash your own damn cock because we are not having sex."

He leaned his face on her shoulder. "But I think it's got sand on it. I can feel it scratching and everything." He knew she secretly liked his poor soul act.

"And I can feel your nose growing from that lie you just told me." Her soapy hand wrapped around his cock and began slithering up and down, while he slowly slid into Nirvana.

"Turn around, love. Let me wash your back and start easing away the tape." Eventually he soaped her ass and she stepped away. "I can wash that myself, Barclay. I feel really uncomfortable—"

He spun her around. "Stop this! I have touched this beautiful ass, kissed it, smacked it and ridden it. In my eyes, it's beautiful. Big, solid and round…just the way I like it."

She looked away, blinking her eyes rapidly as if to fight off the tears. "It…it's like you're one person everywhere else and a different, scarier man in the bedroom. I don't know the rules. I don't know what to expect. Hell, I don't…I'd rather you were more stern all the time so I could get used to it. But that doesn't really matter does it? Dad and I are leaving soon. My time with you will be a memory I'll cherish forever. It's time for me to start backing away emotionally and physically." She turned her back to him once more. "Pull the tape off and examine the burns. How do they look?"

Pull away from him? Like hell. He laid his face against her shoulder. "Sometimes people make mistakes. They do things the incorrect way. I treated you wrong tonight. Please forgive me for acting like a domineering ass."

"There's nothing to forgive. Things are the way they are. How do my burns look?"

She was going to be all business about this. He pulled the tape away and very gently washed the burned area with his soapy hand. "On a scale of one to ten. How does that feel?"

"Four."

"We'll dry off and I'll put more ointment on it. No bandage tonight." He stepped out of the shower and handed her a towel. "We'll let some air get to it. And we *will* sleep together, naked and curled against each other." His phone rang and he pulled it from his jeans on the floor. "Oh God, the ex. Hello, Yvette. What? I can't make out your gibberish. What long hair? Look, whatever it is you called for, the answer is no. In fact, make that hell no." He hung up and put his phone on vibrate, turning on the silent mode.

"Bad blood?" Molly unwrapped the towel from her hair and shook her tresses out.

"Drugs."

"Oh no. What a waste. That must be hard for you to see."

199

He shrugged at her remark as he gently applied more ointment to her skin. "I'm thinking two more days of using this cream and you should be fine. I don't know if your skin will completely peel, or not, but it will in the most burnt places."

"Are the dogs sleeping with us?"

He led her out of the bathroom. "Normally, I'd say yes, but I'm afraid Lola will lick at your burns. You know how she is about you and your injuries." He snapped his fingers and pointed to the dog beds in the living room. Caroline and Maggie Mae slowly prodded out of the bedroom, their heads hanging. Lola hid behind Molly, her black eyes peeking around Molly's legs. "Oh baby girl, don't give me that sad-eyed look."

Lola whined and licked the back of Molly's knee as if asking for her to speak up in her defense.

"We could tuck the sheet around me so she couldn't reach my burns."

His hands rose and dropped to his sides. "I give up. I can't argue with four girls. Sugar, you get in bed first or you won't stand a chance." He helped tuck her edge of the sheet under her. He rounded the foot of the big bed, crawled in and then clapped once. "Bedtime, everyone. Come on, girls."

By the shocked expression on Molly's face, she hadn't expected all the foot stomping and sniffing and face licking and snorting and turning around three and four times before each one laid down. "You…you go through this every night?"

He slipped his arm under her neck. "Lay your head on my shoulder, Sugar, and be prepared for more stomping and sniffing."

"You're kidding?"

"I'm telling you, these dogs are like canine birth control. There's no way we could have sex with them in this bed with us."

She snuggled against Barclay's warm chest. Lola snorted and moved closer to Molly's back. Caroline moaned and slid between Molly and Barclay's legs, her chin resting on her owner's thigh. Maggie Mae scowled at Molly and barked.

"Maggie Mae, you better settle down or you're outta here." Barclay glanced at Molly. "You're on her shoulder."

The Chihuahua lay on his other shoulder and growled once at Molly as if to get in the last bark. Barclay tapped the dog's nose. "Bad." Maggie Mae bared her teeth at Molly in silence. "I saw that. One more smartass display and you're banished from the bedroom, young lady." He gave Molly a look of chagrin. "We call this tough doggie love." The dog sighed and closed her eyes.

Several minutes later, Molly whispered half-asleep, "Is that your hand on my ass, Barclay, or is Lola kneading me with hers?"

This woman he adored sounded so endearing, Barclay started to chuckle and laughed so hard, the bed shook. The dogs, figuring it was playtime, barked and bounced on the bed, creating canine mayhem. Molly bolted upright in the bed. "This is like a freaking zoo! Lola bounces like a twenty-gallon drum on springs. Caroline wiggles her ass like she's in heat. And Maggie Mae looks like she's practicing for the high jump." Molly's mentioning their names wound them up even more as they barked in total abandon.

Barclay crawled out of bed, snapped his fingers and pointed to the living room. "Out." He closed the door behind the girls. He stumbled back to bed, slipped under the covers and wrapped his arm around Molly's waist, tucking her ass back to his groin. God, what a perfect fit. "I'm sorry they woke you, baby. Go back to sleep."

He pressed a gentle trail of kisses across her shoulders and was almost asleep again when her hand reached back and stroked his cock. Holy Mother of God. He slipped a hand over her breast and felt the beaded nipple against his palm. He rubbed it with his thumb and index finger and Molly moaned. His hand slid down her stomach and his fingers found the folds of her labia were wet.

She twisted her head so she could kiss his lips. Their tongues met and mated. Was he dreaming this or was she really coming on to him?

With a quick roll, her hands pushed him onto his back and she straddled him. "I was dreaming about what you told those two old women in the theater."

He was so sleep-hazed, he couldn't recall what he'd said at the movies. His cock was trying to send him a message by Morse code, but damn if he could understand the thumping and twitching going on in that part of his anatomy. It seemed to be the only thing awake at this hour, except for her hands roaming over him and her wet folds trying to capture his cock.

"You know, I might not have a six-shooter or a cowgirl hat..." she slipped his cock inside her and sunk balls deep, which woke him quicker than the alarm at the station. "...but I bet I can ride the hell out of you." And damn if she didn't!

Once they'd both climaxed, she collapsed over his chest in a dead sleep, her raven hair spread over his shoulders. He should be asleep, too, but two things kept going through his mind.

One: he'd just had one of the most mind-blowing orgasms of his life with the female in charge.

Two: he hadn't worn a condom.

CHAPTER TWENTY-ONE

The cell's vibrating on the nightstand woke Molly. Why was she spread out over Barclay? His arm encircled her bottom as he reached for the phone with his other hand. He blinked at the display as if trying to bring it into focus. "Yeah, Milt. You guys up?" He glanced at his watch. "How soon?"

Molly raised her head to rest her chin on her hands clasped over his very fine pecs and the room spun. She moaned and tried to roll off Barclay, but his hold on her tightened. That's when she realized he was inside her. What the hell? Was he having sex with her while she slept? She narrowed her eyes. *Oh, he has a black eye coming. What kind of freak did that?*

"Yeah, we'll meet you there. I'm starving this morning." He tossed the phone on the stand. "Milt and your dad are going to the Silver Sands in about an hour for breakfast. We're supposed to meet them. It's a good thing you left your bag of clothes and stuff here last night when you stormed out. You can take a quick shower while I let the dogs outside and then feed them."

Well, wasn't he all Mr. Cool, Calm and Collected with his cock secretly slipped inside her? "Would you mind explaining to me why I'm on top of you with your cock stuck in me while I was sleeping?"

"You passed out after you had your way with me and since you never moved an inch, junior had no way to get out." He spared her a sheepish grin. "When he woke up a little bit ago and realized where he was, he hardened out of sheer happiness."

"After I had my way…" She rolled off him, the wetness trickling out. She jerked back the sheet and gawked. "Where's the rubber?"

"Well see, Sugar, that's the thing. You never gave me a chance to put one on."

"What do you mean, I never gave you—" *The lying, horny bastard had two black eyes coming.*

"In a half-sleep state, kinda like sleep-walking, you straddled me and rode me like I was a wild horse. Then collapsed over me when you were done and slept like the dead. Probably that bottle of wine you had while crying out on the beach."

"Kinda like sleep-walking?" He nodded with that silly-assed grin showcasing his dimples. "Are you trying to tell me I sleep-fucked you?"

"Yup. That's pretty much the size of it."

She sat cross-legged on the bed and glared at him. "You lie!"

He rubbed the sleep from his eyes. "No, not about this. Because when you leaned over me, pulled a hank of my hair and yelled, 'Say my name, bitch!' I nearly came on the spot. Damn, it was the best sex I've ever had. I think my eyes rolled back in my head twice when I climaxed."

"Is that a fact?" She straddled his stomach and placed her hands on his cheeks, although his throat looked a more likely spot for the interrogation. "And just what name did you say?"

"Sugar."

"When was the last time you were tested for diseases and stuff?" He went to BDSM clubs, who knew what kind of wild sex he engaged in there and with whom.

"Three months ago. I'm clean. What few times I've had sex since then, I've always used a condom. What about you? Are you on the pill?"

She rolled off him and sat on the edge of the bed, her hands pushing back her hair. "No. And until you tricked me last night, I've never had sex without protection."

"How do you figure I tricked you?" He rolled toward her and kissed her back. "You stroked me until I got hard, spanned on my crotch, grabbed my cock and sat on it. Sugar, you went balls deep on junior. It was so fabulous, you took my breath away."

She stood and shook her finger at him. "This is all a sick lie. I've never behaved like that. I'm taking a shower and you better stay out of my way or you're going to breakfast with a black eye." She opened the door and stormed out to the living room for her bag of clothes.

"I guess asking for a good morning kiss is out."

She wanted to scream, to slap that smirk off his face or beat him over the head with her bag of clothes. The last thing she needed was to go home to Breckenridge pregnant with some guy's baby…and that handsome man lying on the bed was one total whack job. *Pull my hair, bitch. Yeah, I bet. What I'd really like to do is pull his short hairs and totally put him in some serious pain.*

While Barclay showered, she went to her cabin to use her hair dryer. He mentioned taking the Harley and she didn't think a helmet would go over a head of waist-length hair. Maybe she'd have Cassie give her a trim before she went back home. She'd talk to her about it if she came to the spreading of her mother's ashes.

Riding on a Harley was a new experience for her too. Barclay ran his palm up her thigh and told her to relax and press her thighs against him. She had a strong feeling that was a bunch of malarkey too, but she listened. And worried. What if she'd gotten pregnant? Taking care of a baby and her dad while trying to run a home business would wear her out. But other women did it with several children…and so could she. Besides, what were the chances she could get pregnant from having unprotected sex once?

No sooner had they ordered breakfast than Barclay's cell rang. It was a brief, no nonsense conversation. When he hung up, he glanced at her as he smeared jam on his toast. "That was Officer

George Pauley. He's got some new information he wants to share with us as soon as possible. Us being you, Sugar. I told him I'd bring you over as soon as we're done eating. He was fine with that."

"Well, maybe I ought to go along with my daughter." Sam's face was wrinkled with concern. "She might need my council."

Molly reached under the table and grabbed Barclay's thigh and squeezed as a sign.

"The officer didn't mention needing to talk to you."

Her dad stuck his jaw out in that mulish way he had. "I'm going with her. Murder is some serious shit. If she needs a lawyer…"

Molly ate the last piece of her French toast and drank her orange juice. She hoped her hung-over stomach would keep everything down.

Milt took charge. "You two head off on the Harley. Sam and I will follow in the car. We'll be in the waiting room. If Molly needs help, her dad will be right there."

Sam nodded. "Sounds good to me. That be okay with you?" He patted her hand.

"Yes, dad. It'll help ease my nerves if I know you're waiting in the outer room."

Barclay swallowed the last of his bacon and snatched the bill. "Then let's head off and get this over with."

George was ensconced behind several piles of folders on his desk in a small windowless office next to the restrooms. Darius was sprawled on a red plastic chair, but quickly stood to offer Molly his seat when she and Barclay entered.

The younger officer stooped in front of her and stared into her face for a few awkward minutes. "Your eyes are swollen. Have you been crying?"

"Too much wine and remembering the past last night. We're scattering my mother's ashes this afternoon."

He took her hand between his. "So, you found them then?"

She glanced over her shoulder at her lover, ex-lover, non-rubber wearing ex-lover…whatever. The rage in his eyes was almost feral.

Although he casually leaned one shoulder against the wall, he resembled a tiger, tightly coiled and ready to pounce.

"Barclay found them. Or thought of a place where we might have left them—the condo where we stayed when we first came here."

"Well, now, wasn't that smart of him?" Darius kept his hands around hers and grinned at Barclay like a Cheshire cat. The tension between those two was so thick, it almost rolled shimmering waves.

"Well, I appreciate your kindness, but you can let go of my hand now. We're here to talk to Officer George." She withdrew her hand from his and, evidently smart enough to understand her dismissal, Darius stood. She turned her attention to the older officer and smiled. "How's your gout doing, sir?"

"Getting better, thank God, and thanks for asking. Molly, I've been in touch with a lot of people from your hometown. Exactly when did you break up with Wade? I think I asked you that already, but I can't seem to find it in my notes."

Well, no wonder with the mess he had on his desk. "January twenty-fifth. That's when he attacked me."

George laid his forearms on what little bare spot there was on his workspace. "Did you go to the emergency room or your doctor for treatment and to have pictures taken?"

She shook her head. "No. I was too embarrassed. I didn't want everyone to know, so I hid indoors until we left for here six days later. But Dad did take a couple Polaroid's." She started digging in her purse for her wallet. "He told me to keep them as a reminder when I chose my next husband which, of course, won't be happening." She handed them to George, who swore when he saw them.

"I was afraid Dad was going to go after him with a gun."

Darius jumped on her remark right away. "Did he threaten to?"

"No more than any irate father who sees his daughter looking like that. We all say things in the heat of anger."

Barclay asked to see the photos. George passed them to him and his face turned red with wrath. "That mother fucking bastard could have killed you." She suspected some of his anger resulted from memories of his home life and the beatings his mother had taken.

The officer took the photos back and shook his gray head. "That's the problem with women and high school girls too. They feel the shame for the beating rests with them, so they don't seek treatment. Later, when something serious happens, we don't have the proof we need." He shook the photos at her. "But here we do. Mind if I keep these?"

"No. I don't want them. He had a few bruises, too, officer. I socked him in the eye and raked my fingernails over his face while he was choking me. When all I could see were black spots, I just gave up, figuring I was going to die."

"Jesus," Barclay muttered.

George pulled a thick folder off the top of one stack and quickly reached with both hands to keep the rest from toppling over.

He flipped the file open. "Wade's mother claims he lost his car keys in a barroom brawl, two or three days after you two broke up. She claims he was so broken-hearted over losing you, he'd taken to drinking heavily."

"Yeah, right." Molly picked a dog hair off her jeans.

"She said he had another set of car keys and she gave him an extra one she had for her house, so he would have had everything he needed, except for the strange key on your keychain. I called the manager of the bank where Wade had his accounts and described the key to him, the printing, markings and all. He said it sounded like one of theirs. So I called the police chief of Breckenridge, hell of a nice guy, explained the mess we had here and asked if he could lend a hand. I over-nighted the key to him direct. He had to get a warrant from a local judge, but once he explained this was a murder investigation, the judge granted the search warrant immediately."

Molly's heart rate picked up. Maybe she'd finally find out why Wade had changed these past months. "Were they able to open the lock box? What was in it?"

"Five bags of heroin."

"Her…heroin? Why would he have drugs? I've never seen him use anything. That would have been a deal breaker right there."

"You don't use recreational drugs, Molly?" Darius touched her shoulder.

"Touch my woman again, Officer, and you and I are going to step outside to get a few things straight."

She thought of stepping between the two fools, but was too shocked by the contents of Wade's lock box at the bank. She spared Darius an annoyed glare. "I've never used drugs." Her focus returned to George. "Any idea why he would have those bags? Was he selling them? Or was that his personal supply? How much would something like that cost?"

"Cost? More than all of us in this room makes in ten years. Let's just say a couple million on the street. To get his hands on that much, he'd have had to be working on creating a strong level of trust between the head dealers and himself for a long time."

"Wade could talk a good game, if he wanted to."

George shifted in his chair. "Had his personal appearance changed? Had he lost weight?"

"Yes, some. Twenty pounds, maybe." She couldn't wrap her mind around this. Wade using heroine? No, the police had to have made a mistake.

"What about his attitude? George started taking notes. "Did his behavior change? Like, did he stop caring about his appearance? Did he seem lazier? Was he hostile toward his loved ones? Did he stop making eye contact?"

Her hand rose to cover her mouth. "Dear God. All of it. I kept thinking it was me. That I was just getting on his nerves between grieving over Mom or going on about wedding plans. I wanted a smaller affair with Mom gone, but his family wanted a big, showy wedding. But it wasn't any of that. It was his heroin use. Where would he get that much in drugs? How would he pay for it? This is some illegal shit."

George stared at her. "So's murder, Molly."

Well, didn't she feel like the fool. "Yes, I *know* that. Is there any way you can track who the drugs came from?"

Darius snorted. "And what? Return them?"

"You insult my lady again and I'll drag your ass outta here before I beat the smart out of it." Barclay spun toward George. "Listening to all this, I have a couple questions for you. Did whoever shot him know about the lock-box? Did he tell them he didn't have the key anymore that Molly was the only other person who did? And, is she in danger?"

George's gaze locked on his for a few beats. "Those are all questions we don't know the answer too. We do know from one of Breckenridge's informants that word on the street is a seller stole ten bags of heroin and then left town."

"Ten?" She leaned forward. "But you said there were five bags in his bank box. They must be talking about another guy."

"We found his SUV. Had drug sniffing dogs brought over from Tampa. The canines smelled drug residue in Wade's small Igloo cooler. Tests showed he'd hauled heroin in it."

"So, you're thinking he brought some along to sell? Business must have been bad if he had to hideout in an abandoned cabin. For all we know, the thugs on the street may have been referring to someone else. Do they know where this thief went when he left?"

George tapped his stubby fingers. "Florida."

Fear seized Molly's lungs before common sense took hold. "But they wouldn't know what I look like."

Darius pushed off from the wall. "Remember the duffle bag I took from the cottage next to yours? It had an empty five by seven picture frame in it. We have to assume it held a photo of you and whoever killed him got it."

Her gaze rose to Barclay's as she fought the trembling starting at her knees and quickly spreading to her hands. He advanced on her and lifted her from the chair, his strong arms around her. "I got you, baby. I'll protect you and keep you as safe as I can. Give me a chance to think all this through, I'll make sure you're okay."

Barclay held her close and looked at George. "Is it okay if we leave now? She has a rough day ahead of her."

Darius opened the door for them. "Molly, darlin', you call me if you need me."

Her dad stood when she and Barclay stepped into the outer office. "Everything go okay?" This whole business was taking a toll on him; his face looked haggard.

In hopes of making him feel more important, she wrapped her arms around his neck. "I'm glad you were here, Daddy. Remember that strange key we couldn't figure out where it came from?"

"Yes."

"Well, it turned out to be a key to his bank lockbox."

"Didn't I tell you it looked like ours?"

Molly leaned in and whispered in his ear. "There were drugs in it. That's why he was acting so strange. Evidently his duplicate key was stolen at a bar along with his car and house key."

"Well, I'll be."

"Will you be okay with Milt for a while? I need to get my haircut and Barclay needs to get some things, so we're going to head off."

Milt shoulder bumped her dad. "We can go pick up that paint I need and a couple new ceiling lights."

CHAPTER TWENTY-TWO

Milt's Cutlass roared to life and he and her dad took off in a cloud of smoke.

"I'm going to need a bit of disguise, aren't I?" Molly glanced at Barclay as they approached his bike. His appearance surprised her. His jaw was clenched. His face red and his fingers curled into fists.

"Don't talk to me right now. I am so fucking mad at that touchy-feely Darius, I need to walk off some steam. I want to yell. I'm warning you, I want to tear something apart. But it's not you I'm mad at, so you need to know my rage is not aimed at you." He fisted her hair and jerked her head back. "Whose woman are you? Who do you belong to? Tell me, dammit!"

With the mood he was in, this was no time for arguments or to remind him how he'd made her feel last night. It was the time to tell him what was in her heart. "I'm yours. I belong to you."

He backed her against a palm tree and kissed her with such passion, she thought she'd melt to liquid goo and reform into one of those pink plastic pelicans. Her panties were already wet. He could do that to her, make her melt. He stepped back when he finally released her lips. "Damn straight you're mine, but that asshole in there doesn't seem to get the message.

"I told you…" he shook his index finger at her as he stomped around his Harley, "…I told you I'm one possessive son of a bitch where you're concerned. He *openly* put the make on you. Kept touching you. Called you darlin'! I wanted to ram my fist in his mouth so hard, he'll be shitting his teeth for the next week."

Barclay's macho rant was kind of a turn on. He sounded as if he cared for her.

"Why are you so upset? Why, when I'm not the kind of woman you need?"

He grabbed her shoulders and pierced her eyes with his bluish green orbs. "You are everything I want. Everything I desire. You complete me and I have a need to take care of you, to spoil you. I know I acted like an ass last night when you wore that sexy as hell lingerie. I need to reevaluate my need to dominate. Maybe I'm just a man who likes kink from either party during sex, because when you took charge this morning, it was phenomenal."

The way he kissed her this time was pure gentleness. "I love you, Sugar. I love that you're no pushover. And I love the generosity of your heart."

She laid her head on his shoulder. "I love you too, for many reasons." She winked at him. "Maybe I'll make you up a list sometime."

He laughed. "You do that."

"Meanwhile I need to call Cassie to see if she can cut my hair and give me a new look before mom's ceremony this afternoon. A disguise." She slipped her new purple phone from her purse and dialed Cassie's shop.

"You know how I love your long hair, but I love you alive more."

After Molly briefly explained her situation and that she needed a make-over, Cassie told her to come right over. In her usual exuberance, Cassie said she'd have a new design all worked out for her by the time they got there. "I don't want my hair too short. Barclay likes it long. Maybe just a few inches?"

"Don't you worry. I know just the thing."

"I'm worried." She looked at Barclay as she slipped her cell phone into her purse. "She told me not to worry. She knows *just* the thing."

He slipped on his helmet. "I've been worried since I first laid eyes on you, Sugar. Whatever she does to your hair will be fine."

After Barclay dropped Molly off at Cassie's shop, he drove to an optical supply company and bought her two pair of brown contacts so her pretty violet eyes wouldn't be noticeable.

Cassie had told him to get lost for two hours. . When he walked into Cassie's Place, he really didn't know what he'd find. His raven-haired beauty with hair nearly to her waist now had caramel brown hair that fell in loose curls to below her shoulders. She had bangs that resembled fringes and, damn, but she was just as gorgeous this way as she was before. It was the beautiful light that shone within her soul that lit her up. She had loveliness that glowed from the inside out. There was nothing fake about his Sugar.

She hadn't noticed him yet. She was too busy staring into the large mirror and chewing on her bottom lip.

He had to alleviate her nervousness. Her eyes widened when he sauntered toward her and, with his fingers, swept her hair from her neck so he could plant a kiss on it. "I didn't think it possible you could look sexy with shorter hair but, Sugar, you look great. How do you like it? Oh, and you better stop chewing on that lip. No one gets to do that, but me."

He pivoted toward Cassie. "You did a super job. I loved how she looked before and I love how she looks now. I think I just love her, no matter what."

Cassie slid her arm around Barclay's waist. "Molly, you are a miracle worker. You truly are. I didn't think I'd ever get my old friend back, but a short time around you and the Ice Man is gone." Cassie did a quick glance over both of her shoulders. "I'm so excited. I started my last period this morning. I am off the pill and I'm going to screw that husband of mine morning, noon and night until I get pregnant."

Barclay groaned. "Cassie, honey, that's just TMI." He glanced at Molly, whose face was red with a blush. Her gaze darted to his and then to her clasped hands on her lap. He could almost read her mind. Had they created a child a few hours ago when she'd ridden him like a wild woman?

"Sugar, I've got one more thing here. The most predominate eye color is brown. I bought you two pair of brown, clear vision contacts and solution to hide those fabulous eyes of yours. Do you want to try putting a pair in?"

"Okay, but I'm so clumsy."

Cassie hip-bumped him out of the way. "Let me show you, Molly. I've been wearing contacts for years. I'll give you a quick tutorial."

After some instructions and nervous tries, Molly blinked them in place. She looked at Barclay. "Well?"

"I've got to be honest. I prefer your real eyes. But for a few weeks, we need to do whatever works to keep you safe. Thanks, Cassie, for fitting her in so quickly. How much do I owe you?"

"I can pay for this." Molly reached for her purse.

He fisted his hand in her hair and pulled her head back so she had to stare into his eyes. "Whose brown-eyed woman are you?"

She blinked twice and his heart stuttered a beat. "Yours."

He never took his gaze from Molly's. What the hell was that delay about? "Cassie, ring up my bill."

As they walked out of beauty shop into the parking lot, Barclay kept fingering her hair. "Do you wanna tell me what's wrong?"

"Cassie's so excited about making a baby with her husband. What if we made one and I barely remember having sex? Going home to a dead ex-fiancé's family and an unexplained pregnancy is not something I'm looking forward to."

He unlocked her helmet. "Then don't go home. Call a cleaning company to come in and empty your house of stuff that won't sell. Contact an auction company to sell your dad's tools, appliances, furniture and dishes. Then list the house with a realtor." He passed the helmet to her. "Stay here with me." He rubbed his thumb over her plump lower lip. "Let me love you and take care of you...pregnant or not...just stay and build a life with me."

She didn't say a word, just put on her helmet. That put a twinge of fear in his gut. She couldn't walk out of his life. He couldn't lose her.

Once they got back to the cottages, she and her dad went for a walk on the beach. She'd said she wanted to talk to her dad about the reason for her disguise. He'd barely recognized her with her new hairstyle and contacts, which put Barclay somewhat at ease. Hopefully the drug dudes couldn't identify her either.

He grabbed two bottles of water out of the refrigerator for him and Milt after he let the dogs out. "How much more needs done at your place before we can move your stuff in? I'm going to need you and Killer's sharp eye for a while."

Milt perked up. "You know I've got experience in the security business." He hiked his pants up with the insides of his elbows and put-putted during their walk down the driveway.

Barclay slung his arm over Milt's bony shoulders. "I need to take you into my confidence."

Milt nodded. "Uh-huh. You know me. My lips are sealed. What do you need?"

Barclay told him about his and Molly's earlier visit at the police station. He didn't mean to, but he spilled his guts on how Darius acted toward his woman.

"I get where you're coming from. I think he's a slimy bastard and if I had a daughter, I wouldn't let him within ten feet of her. Man makes you jealous, doesn't he?" Milt opened the water and took a sip.

"Christ, Milt, you have no idea. I get so freakin' mad I want to beat him from here to next week. I don't want her and Sam to leave. I want...I need to keep her here with me."

"Show her respect, son. She's not had much of that from a man. Respect, admiration," he elbowed Barclay, "plenty of hot sex. But I'm thinking the worst thing you can do is tell her how to live her life. She's a bit of a spitfire."

He smiled. "Yeah, don't you just love it? Now, show me what needs done. I need you here on duty as soon as possible."

As the lower tip of the sun, orange-red in its brightness, touched the water's horizon, orange and purple hues shimmered across the edge of the water. Molly and her Dad walked onto the beach, followed by Barclay, Milt and all the new friends they'd made so quickly from Station Thirty-two, the firemen and their wives. Boyd brought along his four-year-old son, Matthew, who he called Matty. Boyd sat him at the table with a coloring book and a huge box of crayons and stickers to occupy him during the brief service.

Molly began by reading her mom's favorite versus of scripture. Her dad told how he'd met his Tammy Fay and had loved and missed her every day. Molly wrapped her arm around him as he sobbed in sorrow. All this eroded Molly's composure when she began to read a poem she'd written in her mother's honor. A large, warm hand settled at the small of her back; Barclay silently providing his typical comfort and strength. Then as everyone sang Tammy and Sam's favorite song, "Endless Love," from lyrics sheets Molly had run off earlier, she and her dad sprinkled her mom's ashes as the ball of the sun sank below the horizon. Their chore of love was finally done, just as her mother wanted.

Everyone went up on the deck to lay out the food, while she and her dad hugged each other and murmured words of love for each other and the special lady they'd lost. Her dad wiped his eyes with a pristine handkerchief. "We did right by her. Now it's time to do right by us. I like the warmth and the people down here. I also like that young man whose plum crazy for you. I say we think hard about selling what we've got in Colorado and moving here permanent. Now, let's go eat with our new friends."

CHAPTER TWENTY-THREE

The evening soon turned light-hearted. Loads of food, contagious laughter, gentle teasing amid the relaxing backdrop of gentle waves. Mattie got cranky and demanding, so Boyd packed their things to take his boy home to bed. Before they left, he made his son go to each female and thank her for the food and high-five every man present. Molly smiled watching them, wondering if she'd ever have the chance to teach manners to a child of her own.

After Boyd and Mattie rounded the corner of the peach-colored cabin, Wolf's wife, Becca, leaned across the table. "He's so good with that little boy. So attentive. I hope he wins custody. It's bad enough to go through a divorce."

Molly held a brownie mid-way to her mouth. "Why is he seeking custody?"

"Boyd's ex is a vindictive bitch who uses the child as a pawn to hurt Boyd because he couldn't stand living with her anymore."

Cassie poured more iced tea. "I think he suspects abuse."

"Against that sweet little boy?" Molly glanced over her shoulder in the direction where father and son had walked. "Oh, that's awful." Her heart sank. She'd been so loved and adored by her parents, she couldn't understand how the minds of abusive parents worked.

"Could I convince any of you beautiful women to go inside for two six-packs of beer? The cooler's empty."

Molly stood and glanced at Becca. "Your husband's a real charmer, you do know that. Right? I'll go in." She opened the sliding door and noticed the door to her bedroom was open. She had clothes scattered everywhere in there and was sure she'd closed it to hide the disarray. So she hurried over to save herself the embarrassment of having her guests see her sloppiness. Two of her drawers were partially open. So was her closet door.

"Molly?"

She turned. "Yeah?"

Two men, in black, stood with guns drawn. A third grabbed her from behind and covered her mouth with his gloved hand. "You've got a bag of heroin that belongs to us." She shook her head in the negative. He rammed his fist into her cheekbone and she saw stars.

Why did men always aim for the face?

She elbowed him. "I never heard about the drugs until this morning. I had no idea Wade was using. Where he got the money to buy your drugs, I have no clue."

"What kind of shit damn nonsense is this bitch talking, Snakeshit?"

"At least we can understand her which is more than the strung-out loser we shot last night."

The man holding her from behind, jerked her elbows back until they almost touched. "Jako, shoot her in the shoulder. Then we'll ask her again. If she doesn't give us the answer we want, shoot her in the stomach."

The "fwwpp" from the silencer propelled burning pain through her shoulder. With a gloved hand over her mouth, she couldn't scream. But dear Lord, it hurt.

"So now, we come to question number two, Molly." The man the other two called Snakeshit whispered in her ear, "Actually, it's the same question. Where is our horse, our heroin?"

He moved his hand slightly away from her mouth for her to reply. "Shoot me again. I have no freakin' clue."

The second "frwpp" sounded again and she doubled over in pain like she'd never experienced before.

"Molly? You okay?" The back door opened. "It was Wolf."

She ignored the intense pain and kicked back into Shit-for-brains shin. His hold on her mouth lessened. "Shooters! Three!"

"Woman down. Three shooters."

Doors and glass broke. Knives whizzed and guns fired. And Molly passed into dark oblivion.

Becca called 9-1-1, while Milt and Quinn searched the perimeter of the cabins. Inside the pink one, they found Yvette's body. Barclay and Wolf took out the three intruders. Two would probably live. The one who held the gun would never shoot another innocent victim. An irate Barclay had shot him with his own gun he'd hid in the back of his slacks. Wolf tied the wrists and ankles of the other two men with the rope Milt had handed him.

Meanwhile Barclay leaned over the woman he loved more than anything in his life. "Molly, Sugar, don't leave me. Don't leave me. I can't live without you." He looked over his shoulder at her dad who stood frozen to the spot...shocked, confused and scared for his child. "Sam. Sam! Come hold your little girl's hand. Molly needs you."

Sam's mind lifted from its fog and he hurried over to her side and kneeled. "Molly, Molly girl, now you listen to your daddy. Don't you die on me and Barclay. We both need you." Tears flooded his wrinkled cheeks.

Barclay kept kissing her hand, her palm, her forehead as he and Quinn gave her as much first aid treatment as they could. They were able to slow the bleeding, but didn't have the equipment to remove the bullets or repair the damage they caused. Barclay hooked her up to an IV of saline solution to keep fluids in her. "For God's sake, don't you leave me, love."

The ambulances and police cars rolled in. A few minutes later, Molly and her dad were speeding off in the ambulance. Barclay had to stay behind to answer some dumbass questions for police, especially after they found Yvette's dead body next door.

"She called me this morning about two, talking gibberish I couldn't make out. Let me think." He replayed her words in his mind. "She talked about her next door neighbor with the long hair. She asked me where she was. Hell, I thought she was talking about some woman in her apartment building. I didn't know she'd snuck into one of the cabins and was asking about Molly. She had called me a couple days ago for more money to pay her rent or she'd be evicted. I figured it was just a ploy to get some drug money."

"Did you help her, Barclay?" George stopped taking notes and peered at him.

"No. I did a few times before and found out she used it to buy coke. I haven't helped her since. Her habit had really gotten bad. She must have really gotten evicted this time and came to one of my vacant cabins for shelter. These sunsabitches tortured her and I guess she told them Molly was living here."

George nodded. "Makes sense. I'll do some more investigation. Question these two. Barclay, you have a woman to go see. I don't want you driving, son."

Milt shook his keys. "I'm taking my boy to see my girl. We're all family."

Barclay slung his arm around Milt. "Thank God for you. You're right. We're all family.

Milt glanced at Barclay as he stomped the brake for a traffic light. "You gonna stop wasting time and ask that fine girl to marry you? I know you're afraid of losing someone you love. You've been through that enough. But, hell, son. The tide changes sometimes."

"I can't think about that now. All I can think about is her surviving. The shoulder wound probably nicked her collarbone. The bullet to her abdomen is what has me worried." She lost a lot of blood." He wiped his eyes with the swipe of his hand. "I love her so damn much."

Milt zipped his car into the emergency parking area of the hospital. "Wonder how Sam is holding up or if he's roaming the hospital, lost and confused."

Both of the men hurried into the emergency room. Barclay asked about Molly and was told she was in examination room three. Sam waddled toward them from the waiting room. "They won't let me see my baby. I decided to stay here until you got here, that you'd sneak me in.

Barclay stared at Hell's Bells. Well, what the fuck? "Go in that restroom and stay until I find you a gown and hat." He grabbed the old man's shoulders. "Repeat what I just said." Sam did and stepped into the restroom. "Milt, you stand guard."

"You got it."

Barclay jogged up the corridor, noting the signs on each door. One read supplies and he slipped into it, hoping he wasn't on some hidden camera. He pulled down two blue gowns and matching caps. With his procured items tucked under his arms, he strode back up the hall and into the restroom. Minutes later, they both stepped out, looking as official as shit, except for lack of bandages. But all they wanted was one quick look.

"Don't say a word, Sam. Things might look bloody and gruesome, but mum's the word."

Sam nodded. "I just need to see her."

"Go in and count to ten and then quietly slip out." Barclay watched him in the opening of the curtain where he'd snuck in. He also paid attention to the numbers on her monitors. She was stable, thank God. A surgeon was discussing surgery and Barclay absorbed every word. They'd have to remove her spleen and repair some other damage.

Sam walked out of the examining room backwards and took off his gown and hat. "I don't ever want to see a sight like that again," he whispered.

Barclay helped him to a chair. He got on his knees in front of her father. "I know it looks bad, but her vital signs on the monitors are good. She'll need surgery to remove the bullets. I'm thinking she'll be fine. I have to think that, sir, because I love your daughter."

"I know you do."

"Do I have your permission to propose to her? Will the two of you move down here with me?"

"Well hell's bells, I thought you'd never ask."

A week later, the nurse helped Molly into a wheelchair to take her down to the exit so she could be released. She was so glad to be going home to her little apricot cottage. Barclay sauntered into her room with that sexy as hell grin.

Oh God, what's he up to?

"You know, I get tired of Quinn and his story of handcuffing Cassie to the bed to propose to her." He pulled out two pair of purple fuzzy handcuffs and clicked them on both of her wrists and then to the front of the armrests of the wheelchair.

Handcuffs? What the hell?

Her dad, Milt and Cassie tiptoed in. Cassie held a camera. She was all smiles. "Oh, this is so going to get me off the hook. Now, Barclay can claim bragging rights.

Bragging right to what? He isn't...he wouldn't...

He got down on one knee and locked gazes with Molly. "I think I fell in love with you the first moment I laid eyes on you. Stay in Indian Rocks Beach and marry me. I promise I will love you more every day for you are the healer of my heart, the strength of my spirit, the love of my life." He opened the ring box he held and a square diamond surrounded with round amethysts sparkled like the love in his eyes.

"Marry me, Sugar." He slipped the ring from the box and waited for her to reply.

"Yes, I'll marry you, love of my life."

And he slipped the engagement ring on her finger while Cassie snapped pictures and Sam and Milt wiped tears from their eyes.

EPILOGUE

NINE MONTHS LATER

"Didn't expect to find you here." Barclay clasped Quinn's shoulder. "Which one is she?"

Quinn scowled at him for a minute. "What the hell do you mean? The prettiest one." His chest puffed out with paternal pride as he pointed. "We named her Gabriella Sue. Six pounds and fourteen ounces of sheer gorgeousness."

"She's got a pretty head of dark hair. Cute little bow-shaped mouth," Barclay remarked.

"Yeah, she's perfect, man. Didn't expect to get all goony over a baby, but I can't make myself walk away from this window." Quinn rubbed his eyes. "I think I'm allergic to the smells of this hospital."

Poor sap couldn't admit he was crying with joy over a tiny human being.

"Molly doing okay?"

"Yeah, they didn't think she could deliver him natural, but you know how scrappy my wife can be." The nurse pushed in a bassinette and said, "Gray." He raised his hand. She pushed the bed closer to the window. "Look at him. Eight pounds, three ounces of sheer male. Molly already says he's got my looks and we both know my wife is never wrong."

Footprints hurried down the hall. Someone passed gas. Barclay

224

and Quinn laughed.

"One thing I don't understand is how we both ended up here the same night, especially when Molly got shot twice and was in the hospital for a week. What the fuck did you do? Slip one in early on us?"

Barclay laughed. "I was taken advantage of by a wild woman." He turned to the two old men hustling toward them. He moved so he could stand between Sam and Milt. You guys got yourselves a big, healthy grandson. Isn't he something? Look at him."

Sam wiped his eyes. "Damned if he ain't. Molly doing okay?"

"Yeah, she's resting. She did really well."

"I knew my girl would do fine. What did you name him?"

"Samuel Milton Grey, after both his grandfathers. We'll call him Sammy."

Both men shook their heads, unable to speak.

"I'm heading back to my wife now. I'm sleeping in her room tonight. Milt, will you check on the girls for me?" Just to fire Quinn up, he patted him on the back. "Imagine, our kids going to the prom together. First kiss. Skinny dipping."

"Don't you start that shit with me. That's my little angel in there."

Barclay laughed as he strode back to his wife's room. Her eyes opened when he slid the chair over by her bed. "How's Sammy?"

"He's the handsomest kid in the nursery."

"He takes after his daddy. You talked me through nine hours of labor. I love you."

"I love you, too, Sugar. You are so damn perfect." He leaned over and kissed her, feeling the silk of her hair slip through his fingers. Life with her was better than he'd ever had.

"You're pretty damn perfect yourself, double-oooohhh-mine."